Sleep Tight

JUDITH BOHANNON

CROSSBOOKS

CrossBooks™
A Division of LifeWay
1663 Liberty Drive
Bloomington, IN 47403
www.crossbooks.com
Phone: 1-866-879-0502

First published by CrossBooks 9/11/2012

ISBN: 978-1-4627-2027-9 (hc)
ISBN: 978-1-4627-2028-6 (sc)
ISBN: 978-1-4627-2029-3 (e)

Library of Congress Control Number: 2012913599

Printed in the United States of America

This book is printed on acid-free paper.

*Any people depicted in stock imagery provided by Thinkstock are models,
and such images are being used for illustrative purposes only.*

Certain stock imagery © Thinkstock.

DEDICATION

To Dr. Robert A. (Bob) Bohannon, who faced the invasion of Alzheimer's disease with his characteristic dignity and poise. An honorable man—an honorable life.

ACKNOWLEDGMENTS

To JoAnne James who was so willing to read each chapter—over and over—and to offer suggestions for better phrasing and for eradicating those pesky grammatical errors that always eluded me. You have my gratitude forever for making this story so much better!

To my son, John Dorton, always the light of my life, my daughter-in-law, Suzanne, whose devotion to "Bobo" holds such a special place in my heart, and my grandsons, Ben and Gardner. Thank you for being amazing, fine young men—and so much fun!

To Maria Verti Hopes and her husband, James. Maria, you epitomize your grandfather's oft spoken words, "To the stars through difficulty." And to Scott Verti—forever in my prayers.

To my brother, Bill Rollins, who left this earth much too soon, and to his sons, Mark and Chris, and their fine families. He would be so very proud of you!

To all those who served as angels during my husband's struggle with Alzheimer's—especially Dave and Jayne Geissler, Joyce McLean Hardy, and to those special caregivers at both the Memory Care Cottage at Cypress Glen in Greenville, NC and those at Little Creek in Knoxville, TN who showed patience and kindness and who understood the disease.

To my very special Marabou friends. To my sisters in the Emmaus reunion group, The Morning Glories. And the wonderful, fun Potato Group. You all know who you are. What a blessing you've been in my life.

And finally, to all those along my path who have made me a better person either by example, encouragement, or exhortation—family, friends, teachers, students, neighbors, Bible study groups, ministers, and the list goes on. God's grace on each and every one!

CHAPTER 1

Today was Maggie Bales's thirty-sixth wedding anniversary. As the gray light of dawn snuffed out her dreams, she instinctively slid farther under the covers to hide from the sadness that lurked just beyond the next thought. However, as always, it did not work—the sadness pounced on her with crushing force. It held Maggie captive and reminded her that this anniversary was the second one she would spend alone.

Two years, five months, and sixteen days—or eight hundred and ninety-nine times—she had awakened without Carson beside her. She missed him most in the mornings. When she forgot—as she often did—and reached across to *his* side of the bed, the un-warmed sheets sent a cold reminder through her fingertips and into her heart that he no longer shared her bed.

Carson had stood beside Maggie thirty-six years ago on this day and promised to love, honor, and cherish her. Through the years, he had fulfilled that promise and so much more. He had laughed with her, cried with her, protected her, and applauded her. But today, on this anniversary, it was doubtful he knew her name.

The blankets could not insulate Maggie from the chill of loneliness, and she shivered as she thought of Carson waking up at Carolina Manor. Were his first thoughts of her, or was she now only a vague wisp that occasionally floated by in the shadows of his memory? She feared it was the latter.

Maggie sighed and swung her feet to the cool oak floor. She needed the warmth of coffee. Padding into the kitchen, she noticed the sunlight beginning to cast subtle shadows on the floor. She poked the switch on the already-prepared coffee maker and walked over to the large window that looked out over the back yard.

The huge maple at the edge of their lawn had been the sentinel that heralded each season for her since they moved into this house some thirty-four years ago. Today she drank in its autumn majesty as the brilliant gold leaves caught the early rays of the sun. The shimmering effect held her gaze.

Finally, the aroma of fresh coffee pried her from the window, and she poured her first cup of the day. She held the steaming mug in her hands, soaking up its warmth in her palms, and turned once again to stare at the maple. It was like an old friend. Carson had loved it, too. She would tell him about it tonight. However, she suspected the tree, like so many other memories, had surely been lost in the deep abyss of Alzheimer's disease.

This morning, thoughts of their early life together flooded over Maggie. She had been a graduate student at North Carolina State University when she had unknowingly locked her keys in her car and gone in for a night class. It was an art class, and she had a project due the next week, so she stayed at the drawing table long after class was over. Other students had finished one by one and drifted from the room before she put down her charcoals and looked at her portrait of an aging woman with the years etched across a defeated face. She gathered her supplies into her portfolio and found her coat. Weariness accompanied her down the hallway.

When she returned to her car and fished for her keys to unlock the door, her heart sank as she realized they were still in the ignition. It was late. A small sense of panic swept over her. She looked around the parking lot. There were only two other cars. She ran back to the side door of the building, jerked it open, and started down the long, shadowy hallway. The hollow sound of her loafers on the tile floor emphasized the emptiness of the building as she searched for a lighted office. Finally, she saw a sliver of illumination seeping from under a door at the end of the hall. She jogged toward it and knocked.

A male voice called out, "Just a minute." The nameplate on the door read Dr. Carson Bales.

She could tell he was on the phone by the muffled sounds of only his voice. She waited nervously, wondering if he would be annoyed by her intrusion. Almost as soon as she heard the receiver give the familiar thud, a man Maggie guessed to be in his midthirties opened the door. Even in her semi-panic, she noticed his warm brown eyes.

"May I help you?" he asked pleasantly.

"Yes!" she gushed. "I mean . . . I hope so. I can't believe I did this stupid thing, but I've locked my keys in the car. I'm so sorry to interrupt you this way." She was almost whimpering. She made an attempt to pull herself a little taller.

"Oh, don't worry about the interruption. Just glad I was still here. It's getting late, and it's cold outside. Not a good night for walking to find help. What kind of car do you have?" he asked.

"It's an ancient Plymouth—nothing fancy."

"Well, that may make our job easier. Now if I can only find a coat hanger around here. Step inside, if you'd like," and he motioned to her.

He turned and walked to a file cabinet, which somehow struck Maggie as an odd place for a coat hanger. While he rummaged in the drawers, she took note of his slender build. He had wavy, brown hair that looked like it last saw a comb early that morning. A solid brown tie was knotted at the collar of a nondescript plaid shirt, and it all blended with his khaki pants. A conservative sort, she thought.

"Eureka!" he exclaimed as he pulled a distorted hanger from the last drawer. "I usually keep a hanger around for my own sake. I've had to use it a few times, if that makes you feel any better." Maggie relaxed a little as she recognized his effort to put her at ease.

"Now, if I can work it in between your window and door frame and grab the lock, we can have you on the road shortly," he said with a smile. That smile sent a surge of warmth into her weary bones. He walked quickly down the hallway toward the door, and Maggie had to pick up her tempo to keep pace as the portfolio bumped against her hip.

She stood shivering while he probed at her car window with the bent hanger until he found an opening and patiently maneuvered a small loop around the lock. Three tugs brought the blessed sound that told both of them the door was open.

"Oh, thanks . . . thank you!" she cried. As relief swept over her, her exhilaration brought an unfamiliar boldness.

"Could I buy you a cup of coffee as a small payback for your rescuing efforts?" Immediately, she was chagrined. Why would he have any interest in having coffee with a student, particularly at this time of night?

She was ready to mumble a retraction when he smiled at her and said, "I don't believe I know your name, and I've never had coffee before with someone I didn't know."

"Maggie . . . Maggie Gray." The words rushed out of her mouth.

"Nice to meet you, Maggie Gray. And I'm Carson Bales. Say, I might just take you up on that offer. It's been a long day. I'll get my coat and meet you wherever you suggest," he said. His words were accompanied with frosty puffs of air.

Maggie quickly tried to think of a place close by, wondering how much time he wanted to spend on this impulse of hers.

"I'm buying," she said, "so why don't you choose?"

"How about the Wolf Den just off campus? They're open late and their coffee only keeps you awake until three o'clock," he chuckled.

Maggie was glad she had been there before and wouldn't have to ask him for directions. "Sounds good. I'll see you there."

Driving off, she still couldn't believe she had been so bold as to invite a professor she didn't know for coffee. Maggie was always mindful of a professional distance with faculty members. She normally wouldn't have asked even her advisor to have coffee.

She arrived first and selected a booth near the front so he could easily spot her. There were several other people there either studying, judging by the books and papers spread about, or chatting with friends. She looked around but didn't recognize any of the other late-nighters.

She saw him through the window as he pulled into the parking lot. Wow, and she thought her car was old! He was driving a real clunker, and to add to its well-used appearance, it was a dull brown. Mr. Excitement, she thought facetiously. Judging by his car and his clothes, his money was not spent to impress people. Maggie liked that.

"Feels great in here," he said, sliding into the booth. "And that coffee is just the ticket for tonight." Maggie signaled the waitress. He ordered his black. Maggie had never liked the taste of coffee as much as she liked its warmth, so she asked for lots of cream.

"Tell me, Maggie Gray, what class brought you out on such a raw night?"

"I had a sketching class on third floor, and I have a project due next week, so I stayed later to finish it. When I found my keys were locked in my car, I was afraid no one was still in the building. You must work late," she said hesitantly.

"Tonight I did. I was grading an exam I gave earlier this week. I leave tomorrow afternoon for a conference, and I wanted to get students' grades posted before I take off."

Maggie was impressed. She had professors who didn't give scores back until near the end of the semester from tests taken in the first two weeks of class. She saw them as lazy and unconcerned. Apparently, Dr. Bales was neither, and she admired that.

The coffee came, and they each tested it gingerly before taking a chill-ending swallow. He seemed relaxed and in no particular hurry to make inane conversation. She, on the other hand, was quickly searching her mental index, looking for appropriate comments. He rescued her by asking, "So you must be an art major?"

"Well, not exactly. I've been interested in drawing since I was young. However, when I first entered college, I didn't think I had the talent to be an artist, so I majored in elementary education. After teaching for a year, I decided to work on my master's degree in elementary ed. and get a second certification in art, also. You know—if you can't do something, teach it." She instantly regretted that remark. What if he thought she was trivializing his profession? Instead, he smiled and nodded as if telling her to continue.

"I've only taken four classes, so I still have a long way to go. I have to take night classes because of my teaching job during the day. That's what pays my tuition." Maggie decided she was beginning to sound too chatty, so she abruptly stopped talking.

He looked at her for a moment and simply said, "I admire your work ethic. Many of my grad students aren't especially motivated because their parents are still forking out the dollars."

Maggie realized she didn't know what he taught, and that seemed like a safe question. "What is your field?"

"Chemistry," he replied.

"Oh. Chemistry was my hardest undergrad class," she admitted, "so I'm impressed."

"That's okay. I can't draw a stick man who doesn't look as if he has arthritic joints. We don't all get the same talents, and we're a better society for it," he said, as he swallowed the last sip from his cup.

A big part of her was relieved she had fulfilled her obligation to do something nice for him, but a small part wished they could stay and talk. She liked his easy smile and warm, brown eyes. She did notice there was no wedding band. Dating was the last thing on her mind, but she wondered if he needed to hurry home to a wife. Anyway, he was getting his jacket off the bench, so she knew he was taking leave.

He extended his hand across the table and said, "Nice you meet you, Maggie Gray, and good luck with your studies. Thanks for the coffee. Now I need to go home and pack."

"I'm the one who owes you the thanks," she said. "I have no idea what I would have done if you hadn't been in your office. And," she added from out of nowhere, "had that handy-dandy coat hanger stashed in a file cabinet." She turned beet red.

He laughed. "Chalk that up to my tenure in the Boy Scouts. Good night."

He gave a half wave as he walked out the door. She watched him get into his car, and she wondered if it would start. But it fired immediately, and he pulled out into the street. A plume of exhaust punctured the cold night air. He was gone. Her knight had ridden off on anything but a white horse.

Maggie quickly paid the bill and put on her coat. It was late, and she had to be up by six o'clock. She hoped the coffee she was completely unaccustomed to at this hour would not keep her awake, but that was a vain hope. Lying in bed at 2:45 a.m., she was still begging for sleep to come. She trusted what Dr. Bales had said about the coffee only keeping you awake until three o'clock would be true. He must have been right because the next thing Maggie knew, her alarm clock was prying her reluctantly from her dreams.

Suddenly, Maggie was startled from her reminiscence by the ringing of the phone. She dropped her gaze from the golden maple and picked up the receiver. It was the car dealership reminding her of the appointment to get her car serviced today. On Saturdays, the dealership liked to get customers in and out before noon when the technicians made a beeline for the door.

She poured her second cup of coffee and reached for the cream.

CHAPTER 2

Maggie was so glad she had trusted her instincts that cold evening when she had quickly decided a very nice man lived behind those brown eyes. Now, shutters had closed behind those same eyes, and Maggie could no longer gaze into them and glimpse his memories of their life together. The thicket of tangles and snarls created by Alzheimer's disease pushed ever harder on those shutters, squeezing them tight except for occasional shafts of light that defied the disease and demanded to glimpse the world once again, if only for a few moments.

Maggie set her mug on the counter as she remembered items she needed to take to Carson tonight. Tearing a sheet off the memo pad on the refrigerator door, she jotted down baby shampoo, cotton swabs, deodorant, and shaving cream. She took inventory each week of the supplies Carolina Manor did not provide and picked those up on Saturdays. Maggie hated the feeling of failure that somehow crept in when she found a note from the staff reminding her of something he needed.

Maggie folded the list and thought of the months following her first encounter with Carson. She had only passed him once in the hallway that semester. He recognized her, spoke pleasantly, inquired about her class, and moved on. She thought he looked tired in some benign way.

In the spring, she took a class in art therapy. She could use the elective in teaching her fifth-graders. At the end of the fourth week, the professor asked her to stay after class. With trepidation, Maggie waited until the other students had gone.

Dr. Warden said, "I'm very impressed with your work, Maggie. Each semester I'm asked to select a student to intern at Magnolia Hospital. The student gets extra credit hours for this internship, and it looks great on a job application. Do you know what Magnolia is?"

"I've heard the name, but that's about it," Maggie replied.

"It's a private hospital for the profoundly retarded. Patients there have a very limited range of abilities. They can't articulate their thoughts except through guttural sounds that take some getting used to. Some people find this very distracting. That's why I hand select the students I send.

"You would develop very simple projects for them to complete while you are there. I have no say over who your students will be. Magnolia chooses them." She stopped and waited for Maggie's response.

Maggie had never given much thought to people with handicaps. "I guess I'm really not certain how I would react until I see them," she replied thoughtfully.

"I would expect you to be skeptical, but I really believe you will move past any initial hesitancy once you get there and see the good you can do. Are you willing to give it a try?"

Maggie nodded.

Dr. Warden spent the next hour showing Maggie examples of posters that were appropriate and explaining some of the teaching techniques she could use. The simplicity of the projects was Maggie's biggest surprise.

As they finished, Dr. Warden said apologetically, "I hope the extra hours of credit will be an incentive for you to spend a big part of your Saturdays at Magnolia. I know weekends are precious to students, but that's the only time that works for the patients and staff. I expect you to be there about two hours for each class. Okay?"

Ouch. Including travel time, that would mean all of her Saturday afternoons, but Maggie decided not to resist. This assignment meant she wouldn't have to pay for those credit hours. And she quickly calculated it would only be ten weeks.

She tried to make up for the first moments of silence by attempting an enthusiastic, "Oh sure, that's fine. But where is Magnolia?"

"About thirty miles from campus. Will that be a problem?"

"Oh, no," Maggie said, realizing it would be a miracle if her old car made it through the semester.

"Fine. Here's a voucher for supplies, a map for getting there, and you will ask for Miss Austin when you arrive. I look forward to hearing about your experiences next week after class. We'll discuss any questions you have at that time." With that pronouncement, Dr. Warden picked up her brief case and left the room. Maggie gathered her books and walked out into the night with far more questions than answers.

Immediately after an early lunch on Saturday, Maggie loaded her supplies into the car. Driving to Magnolia Hospital, her stomach grew tense along with her shoulders. She wondered what she had gotten herself into. What if her students had handicaps she found uncomfortable to be around, or what if she couldn't communicate with them? Well, too late now. She had said she would do it, and, by golly, she would.

As she waited in the lobby, Maggie watched a short, plump brunette walking toward her. "Hi, you must be Maggie. I'm Rachel Austin." The brunette smiled as she extended her hand.

"Hi, Miss Austin."

"Oh, goodness, call me Rachel." Well, it's not Jane, Maggie thought with fleeting amusement.

"We have several regulations here that are meant to protect both our residents and our teachers, Maggie. I need to go over all of this with you before we go to the activities room." They sat at a table in Rachel's office for nearly an hour while she explained the long list of dos and don'ts.

"Just a little advice for handling the students if they don't want to cooperate—remember, they are like very small children, toddlers even, in their ability to comprehend what you're telling them. You have to repeat things over and over. They get distracted easily, so you will have to deal with that. Also, Harlan will be one of your students, and he has what we call echolalia. He will start repeating a word you say to him—though you may have difficulty recognizing it—and he goes on and on. It sounds like an echo. He may say this for thirty minutes. Just ignore it, if you can. Any questions?"

Maggie replied, "I just hope I can remember all you've said, but I think I'm ready." What she really wanted to do was pick up her things and run out the door, but instead she tried to walk with confidence beside Rachel down the long, institutional hallway to meet her three new pupils.

Harlan was a tall, stout man who appeared to be in his thirties; Sally was a very thin woman who was probably older than Harlan; and Beth was maybe ten, with a mop of pale, blonde ringlets. Later, Maggie would notice the ringlets covered a sloping forehead and malformed ears.

Rachel soon left the room, and Maggie felt a sinking sensation in the pit of her stomach. Where would she start? She decided to ask them to repeat "Maggie" as she said it. It took several tries, but finally each one got the hang of "Mah-guh." The difficulty of this assignment was beginning to settle in.

As Maggie laid out brightly colored shapes cut from construction paper, she noticed Beth's eyes suddenly light up. Maggie smiled at her. Beth's lop-sided smile in return was such a poignant response that tears came to Maggie's eyes. How could such a sweet little girl have such a terrible affliction, she wondered.

Maggie spent the next two hours helping them pick out a variety of shapes and colors to put on their posters. As they worked, she had them repeat the names of colors. Finally, Maggie attached a ribbon hanger to the tops of each piece of artwork. She praised all of them for their efforts, but it was clear that Beth was the most capable of the group. Her spontaneous enthusiasm tugged at Maggie's heart.

Rachel appeared in the doorway promptly at five o'clock. Maggie couldn't believe the time had passed so quickly. "Hey, how did it go?" Rachel asked.

"Well, actually quite well. Let's show Miss Austin our posters," Maggie said to her unlikely threesome. Harlan and Sally sat passively, but when prompted, Beth enthusiastically held hers up for inspection.

"Oh, Beth, I love it!" Rachel sang out. She praised the others and then indicated it was time to wash up before dinner.

"After I get them settled, I will hang these posters in their rooms. Every room has a large area of corkboard where we put seasonal pictures or just anything to brighten their walls. That was my idea when I came here," Rachel informed Maggie, with a note of pride in her voice.

As they were leaving the room, Maggie noticed all three students had unusual gaits. Beth rather swayed from side to side as if her legs were different lengths. All at once, Beth turned and swayed back to Maggie and hugged her hard around the waist. Maggie would remember that hug for a long time.

Each Saturday that spring, Maggie dutifully loaded the car and drove the thirty miles to Magnolia. Good thing she didn't have any social life, she thought.

It was her fifth Saturday, and she was busy unloading the car in the Magnolia parking lot when she noticed a girl swinging in the playground nearby. She recognized the pale ringlets. A man with his back to Maggie was pushing Beth, and both were laughing. Beth looked back at the man and spied Maggie, who was struggling with all her supplies. Beth dragged her feet to stop the swing. The man seemed puzzled but helped her off, and she swayed to the gate and tugged it open.

Maggie suspected she was coming over to give her that weekly hug, so she bent down to put her bags on the sidewalk. Sure enough Beth was there before she could stand up, and she had to struggle to keep her balance. Maggie laughed as Beth hugged her tightly, and Maggie buried her nose in the curls on top of Beth's head.

Suddenly, Maggie noticed a pair of khaki pants and well-worn tennis shoes standing close by. She stood to greet the man whom she knew must be connected to Beth and nearly lost her balance again. "Dr. Bales!" she uttered with disbelief.

Those warm eyes that had first greeted her at his office door seemed just as surprised as she was. In a moment, however, he regained his casual manner and said, "Why, Maggie Gray. So you're the Maggie that Beth keeps saying when she points to all the posters in her room. Her enthusiastic chants tell me she thinks you're wonderful."

Maggie stammered a bit before she could regain composure. She hated herself for having him think she was surprised—no, stunned—to see him with Beth. Was he a relative? An uncle? A guardian of some sort?

"Yes, I'm doing an art therapy internship here," Maggie finally managed to say.

He nodded, and said simply, "I'm Beth's father." Maggie hoped her astonishment was not obvious.

"I usually spend every Sunday afternoon with Beth. But tomorrow I have to leave for a trip, so I made Saturday be our day together, didn't I, pumpkin?" he said, as he tousled Beth's curls. "Sunday is when she shows me her artwork. I can't tell you how grateful I am to you for doing this. Beth is my world, and anything that brings her happiness does the same for me."

Beth still had her arms wrapped around Maggie. "Beth is a darling and a delight to teach," Maggie said sincerely. "She seems to be a happy child, and I'm sure you're part of that happiness."

He didn't respond to her comment, but took Maggie aback with his next statement. "Miss Gray, it's my turn to ask for a favor. If you would be so kind, I would like to ask you some questions about our little student here—say, over another cup of coffee?"

"Well, sure," she responded. "Just tell me when and where."

"Is it possible to meet tonight? I'm leaving tomorrow to be out of town for nine days."

She sensed this meeting was important to him, so she gave a simple, "Yes."

"Is the Wolf Den still okay? Say, seven thirty?" he asked.

"That's fine."

"Well, see you then," and with that, he took Beth's hand and helped her toward the building while Maggie gathered her scattered supplies.

Maggie spent the afternoon working with her threesome and gave no thought to the coffee agreement until she was heading back to her apartment. She wondered where Beth's mother was. Perhaps she came during the week. Maggie remembered there was no wedding band on Dr. Bales's finger. Oh, well, it was really none of her business.

By Saturday evenings, she was always tired from her brim-full week. Now, she was wishing to just settle down with a good book and not have to go out again. However, she needed to repay his kindness to her, so she climbed into the car once more and headed toward campus.

He was waiting for her when she arrived. He stood up when she walked in, and somehow she found that quite charming. He was wearing the same shirt, khakis, and tennis shoes he had on when she saw him at Magnolia, but he had added a light jacket.

13

"Hi," he said. "And thanks for coming." He motioned for her to sit down in a casual, genteel manner.

The waitress appeared just as Maggie was settling into the well-worn cushion. They both ordered the same as before—black for him and lots of cream for her.

She could sense he was trying to find a way to open the conversation. She felt a bit uncomfortable, not knowing exactly why she was here, and in her effort to bridge the silence, she blurted out, "Beth is such a sweet child."

"That she is. You have no idea what a ray of sunshine she is in my life," he said. Maggie thought of this child with her extremely limited abilities. She found it difficult to see how Beth could provide such inspiration for him.

He slowly began to talk. "I asked you to come for coffee because I want to discuss Beth's progress with you. She was diagnosed as profoundly retarded soon after she was born. Profound retardation occurs in only 1 or 2 percent of those with any form of retardation. She was a pretty unlucky little girl, I guess. Anyway, I want to get your opinion about how much she is learning in art class. Her achievements in other classes have been meager. However, I've been very impressed with her posters. I guess I'm hoping you see some ability to express herself through shapes and colors—some ability we haven't seen in the other classes." He waited with a question mark in his eyes.

"Well, I think Beth is an adorable little girl with a great heart for learning new things. She touches all the shapes and traces their outlines before she selects any for her poster. I'm not certain why she does this, but it may have something to do with understanding space and how things fit together. She always picks bright colors. I loved her flower last week. Did you notice that one?"

"Yes, and I thought it was her best one yet. You must be a very good teacher, Maggie. What prompted you to go to Magnolia?"

"Oh, don't give me credit for my altruistic spirit," she laughed. "Actually, the professor of one of my classes chose me for this internship. Honestly, I guess the two hours of credit that I won't have to pay for was my real motivation."

"Ah, the starving grad student." He smiled as he said it.

"Well, beginning teachers don't earn a lot, you know, so I do have to count my pennies," she replied defensively. Truth was, Maggie had always had to count her pennies.

"Anyway, you have to be a special person to be willing to spend every Saturday afternoon at Magnolia. Not much reward there."

"I do confess I was dreading it in the beginning, but each week it has gotten easier. Now, I actually look forward to my time there. It has its own kinds of rewards," she said and meant it.

It was obvious he wanted to return to Beth. He asked Maggie if she noticed any behavior problems or social inappropriateness. Maggie quickly assured him she had seen neither.

Maggie was becoming more and more curious about Beth's mother. Did she dare to bring it up? Probably not a good idea. She had great respect for their academic differences, as well as the fact she hardly knew him. Besides, that seemed a bit too personal.

As they finished their coffee, he began to make small talk about the warm days April had brought and then asked her when she would graduate. "That's at least a year away and perhaps more, depending on how the classes are offered in the evening," she told him.

"Yes, scheduling for night students is always tough. Well, I'd better let you go," he said. "And I have to go home to pack. I won't be here next weekend, and I wondered if it would be too much of an imposition if I call you when I return. I would just like to know that Beth was okay when you saw her last."

"Sure," Maggie replied. She began to look for a piece of paper to write her telephone number on when he quickly produced a small book from his coat pocket and thumbed to the G's.

"Here we go, Maggie Gray. What's the number?" She had forgotten how he had always used both of her names. Well, she might not feel comfortable to ask about Beth's mother, but she certainly thought it was okay to ask him about her name.

"I'm curious, Dr. Bales. Why do you always say both of my names?"

"Oh, I have a habit of doing that with students so I can remember their last names." He laughed. "Guess I'm getting to be that absent-minded professor after all."

She wrote her number in the book and felt that was the signal to take leave. She scooted to the end of the booth and stood up. He quickly followed. He extended his hand, and she was surprised by its warmth and firmness.

She walked out in front of him. They waved as they pulled out of the parking lot. Maggie drove back to her apartment thinking she had not even asked where he was going. Oh, well, none of her business.

Ten days later on a Tuesday evening, Maggie's phone rang. Dr. Bales's voice gave a cheerful, "Hello. Is this Maggie Gray?"

"Yes. Oh, hi," she replied.

He asked several questions about Beth before he asked how Maggie's week had been. He seemed very upbeat during the conversation. Maggie decided to be bold and ask, "How was the trip?"

"I came back with such renewed energy. It was an international conference, so I heard lots of papers on new topics, but also I got in some sightseeing. It was held in London. Charming city. Have you been there?"

"Oh, no. I've never traveled beyond North Carolina. But I really hope to see much more of the world someday. That's my big dream. It will probably be on a shoestring budget, but that won't matter. I would love to see the great art museums and cathedrals."

"Hey, I bought a book while I was in Westminster Abbey. It has lots of pictures of statues and windows that might interest you. Would you like to borrow it?"

"Oh, I would love to," she replied enthusiastically.

"Good. Can I drop it off where you live or would you be interested in another cup of coffee? I would love to tell someone about my trip— you know, bore you with details and pictures and all that stuff."

Aha! She had an answer to at least one question. He didn't have a wife at home. She felt a tug of sympathy for this man with the warm smile who appeared to have no one to talk to but a severely handicapped daughter.

"I would love to hear about your trip. And I promise not to be bored with the pictures so long as there are fewer than a hundred. Shall we meet at the usual place?"

"Sounds great. But how about I buy you a sandwich to go along with that coffee for your indulgence? Seems like a small price for having a captive audience," he chuckled. "Say, Friday at seven o'clock?"

"Fine. See you there," Maggie answered.

After she hung up, she had a small feeling of delight and no idea where it came from. He was a lonely professor who just needed to show someone his pictures from a trip. That was it.

Friday night was one of those balmy spring nights that Maggie would love all the rest of her life. In the South, one had to enjoy springtime before the humidity set in, in early summer and weighed you down until late September. She wore a yellow cotton skirt that rippled around her ankles and a matching sleeveless top with a modest scooped neckline. Her sandals had been dragged from the back of the closet for their debut of the season.

Maggie arrived first. Never a good thing to do, she thought. But this wasn't a date, she reminded herself. She watched Carson walk across the parking lot. He was wearing a blue shirt and khakis that weren't exactly new but showed signs of a recent pressing. And she guessed he had just buffed his brown loafers. There was a spring in his walk as he came through the door carrying a book and large envelope under his arm.

"Hi." His tone was jovial as he arrived at the booth.

"Hi to you, world traveler," she responded with equal enthusiasm.

"Well, not quite the world, but for me anywhere out of the country is a big deal," he laughed.

As he sat down, he seemed to take notice of her in a way he hadn't before. She could see a flicker of recognition in his eyes, as though he was really seeing her for the first time. "You look very nice tonight," he said. Then, as if he felt that an inappropriate statement, he stammered on the next sentence, "Well . . . you've always looked nice . . . but especially tonight."

Maggie smiled. "Thanks. This nice weather makes me want to poke all my woolens into the back of the closet until next winter. I know our weather is considerably milder here than up north, but I still am winter weary by March and eager for warm evenings and all the blossoms of spring."

They ordered subs. While they were waiting for the order, he scooted the book across the table to her. "Please keep it as long as you wish," he said.

"Thanks so much. With exams and projects all due soon, I may not have a chance to read anything until the end of May."

Dr. Bales nodded.

Maggie decided if she initiated the topic of his trip, he would feel less like he was burdening her with his travel log. "So, tell me all about London," she ventured.

"London was all I anticipated and more. I spent a lot of time in presentations and seminars but managed to hit the high points of the city. At least, now I will have my own mental images of most of the famous places when I hear about them next."

She asked the usual questions. What historic site impressed him most? How was the food? How did he like the accents? Was anything a disappointment? He talked with eagerness about each question.

The food came, and they each focused on eating for a while, with occasional murmurs of how good it tasted and how hungry they were. After the waitress cleared the table, Carson placed the large envelope on it and began to lay out pictures. Starting to explain them, he paused and then asked if he could move and sit beside her.

"Guess I'm not very good at looking at things upside down. I can barely tell Westminster from the Tower of London," he laughed.

Maggie slid over without a reply, and he quickly scooted in beside her. She was surprised by the sense of warmth that casually flowed through her.

She quickly turned her attention to the pictures as he pointed out all the features of each. She wasn't bored in the least.

"I have lots more," he said with a smile, "but I didn't want you to develop a sudden headache and rush out."

"Oh, I truly have enjoyed seeing them. As I told you, my dream is to travel someday when I can afford it, if that ever happens. I envy your job that allows you that kind of freedom," she said with some hesitation.

"On my own, I could never have afforded the trip. I'm on a grant, and I'm required to present at least one paper a year. The grant pays my expenses to the conference where I present. It's a great deal," he said, smiling. Then in a more somber tone, he offered, "Beth's care is very expensive. It takes all of my resources above the basic expenses of living. I don't mind, of course, but it keeps me pretty strapped."

They were both quiet for a moment. He turned to her, and she noticed a tinge of red in his cheeks. "I must be keeping you from a date tonight. After all, it's TGIF, and I'm sure you have better things to do than listen to my ramblings."

She couldn't stifle a laugh. "I'm afraid there are no dates in my life right now. Actually, dating is pretty far down on my list of things I want to accomplish. I had to work two jobs to support myself through undergraduate school, and almost as soon as I finished that, I started grad school. So between classes here at the university and teaching twenty-eight fifth graders, my days don't allow for much of a social life. And going to Magnolia takes my Saturdays." By the time she finished, she hoped it didn't seem like she was whining.

"You sound like a very serious student, and I admire that greatly," he said with solemn eyes. "And going to Magnolia is definitely a demanding responsibility."

"Well, I'm afraid Magnolia has made me a little less tolerant of my fifth graders these days and some of their goof-off behaviors. They just don't know how fortunate they are," she said sadly.

He was watching her intently as she talked. When she finished, he leaned an elbow on the table and looked her directly in the eyes. She noticed a slight hesitation before he said, "You aren't a student in my department, and you aren't an undergraduate. So, Maggie Gray, would you reconsider that dating moratorium and go out with an older man who can't take you to any fancy places?"

At first, she thought he sounded so analytical she was almost put off, but his warm eyes waited for an answer. An unexpected feeling engulfed her, and she could only think how nice it was to sit beside him. She flushed just a bit before she answered.

"Yes, I would like that. And fancy places haven't been my fare before now, anyway. They can just wait a little longer."

Maggie remembered Carson had laughed with genuine pleasure at that statement.

"So, could I take you on a real date tomorrow night after you get back from Magnolia? There's a good movie this week at the Union, I'm told. Don't remember the name just now, but we could give it a try, if that's okay with you?"

"Sounds great. I haven't seen a movie in ages."

"Good. I'll pick you up at seven." She gave him directions, and they parted at their cars, waving with a new found eagerness.

Wow! thought Maggie. Driving away that evening, she had felt a lightness in her heart that had never surfaced before.

This morning, as she placed a piece of bread in the toaster, Maggie was amazed she could still remember that feeling more than thirty-six years later. Without warning, the vivid contrast of her happiness then with her ever-present sadness now caused Maggie's eyes to overflow. Tears mingled with her coffee as she thought of the wonderful days they had spent getting to know each other.

CHAPTER 3

Maggie and Carson dated every weekend after his return from London. That summer they took picnics to the nearby lake where they watched the boats, they went to movies, they watched television at her apartment, they drove to the coast for long days in the sun, and once they stayed for a lovely dinner with a window view of the ocean. They were getting to know each other in a comfortable, relaxed way, and Maggie loved the pace.

One Saturday they drove to Pinehurst to spend the day seeing the unique Sandhills region of the state. After an afternoon of exploring, they sat in wooden rockers on the porch of the lovely old Pinehurst Resort Hotel, gazing out across the manicured croquet grounds. Carson turned to Maggie with a very serious expression.

"Maggie, I've been thinking that maybe you need to know about my first marriage, that maybe it will make a difference in how you feel about me. I don't want it to be a problem for us later." He waited for a minute until Maggie nodded for him to continue.

"Clara and I were high school sweethearts. I graduated first and went off to Chapel Hill and the University of North Carolina while Clara was still a senior. She wrote me every day, pleading with me not to fall in love with someone else and leave her," he said softly. "I never understood why she was so worried. She had been my girl for three years.

"When I went home to Hudson on breaks, I spent every minute I could with her, but she always cried when I left. I didn't know how to reassure her there was no other girl for me. On my spring break, Clara

21

seemed more reluctant than ever for me to return to school. The evening before I went back to UNC, we went to a local park with a picnic Clara's mother had packed. Maggie, I'm not proud of this, but after it got dark, we started making out on our blanket. We'd always put the brakes on in the past before things got out of hand, but that night, for whatever reasons, we didn't stop. We were both virgins, and the experience sure wasn't what I'd heard it was. I had no idea what to do except for my basic instincts. Afterwards, I noticed Clara was quiet on the ride home, and I knew she was disappointed, too. Tears welled up in her eyes when I kissed her goodnight. I wasn't sure if the tears were because I was leaving or because of what had just happened. I promised her it would be just a few more weeks, and I would be home soon for the summer. I would make everything okay for us then. Later, as I lay in the bed I had slept in since I was four, I knew I had to learn some things about lovemaking before I saw her again."

Maggie noticed the furrow on Carson's forehead as he talked.

"I could hardly wait to get home at the end of the semester, but as soon as Clara opened her front door, I knew something was wrong.

"She looked pale and her eyes were bordering on puffy. I spoke to her parents who were standing behind her with welcome-back smiles, and then I grabbed her hand and suggested we go for a soda. Once we were in the car, Clara burst into tears. Something was wrong all right. She was pregnant." Carson paused. The furrow was still there, only deeper.

"I drove to the park—the scene of our 'crime'—and held her a long time until there were no tears left to fall. I told her there was only one thing to do. After all, I loved her and the baby was ours. She only nodded.

"We drove the agonizing five miles back to Clara's home. Her parents were on the patio, so we went out and sat down with them. Their expressions of greeting instantly evaporated when they noticed Clara's puffy eyes. I had never been so nervous in my life. Clara kept sniffling. I took her hand in mine and blurted out the truth. At first, her parents were angry and said some harsh things to both of us. Then, they were mortified when we explained to them that we had to get married as soon as possible. They asked if my parents knew about this, and I begged them to give us a couple of hours so we could go and tell them.

"Only my mother was home when we arrived. She was expecting her youthful, hungry son to come home, and she would spend the long summer vacation making all his favorite dishes. Instead, there I was telling her about the unplanned pregnancy and the hurry-up marriage. Mom had always been my best advocate, supporting me in any sport I ever tried, cheering me on when I got good grades, encouraging me when I didn't—all that stuff. Now I had to witness the pain of disappointment in her eyes. It broke my heart.

"But she recovered enough to hug Clara and then me and said we would all get through this. Her voice broke at the end, and I knew she wondered how we would make it. I guess she called my father because when he came home that night, he gave me a hug but his usual exuberance wasn't there."

Maggie could tell how painful this story was for Carson. She could tell by the sad look on his face and by how many times he paused and looked at the floor. He seemed determined to tell her, however, so she sat quietly, waiting for each burst of information.

"Our mothers hoped people would see a summer wedding as nothing more than two impulsive kids who wanted to go off to college in the fall as a married couple. And both our mothers tried to find ways to explain to their social circles why they supported such a youthful marriage. I know our parents were embarrassed, but after the first shock wore off, they never chided us again. I think their looks of disappointment hurt the most."

His words were choked with emotion.

"In the end, our families accepted what they labeled 'this unfortunate event' and agreed to help out with the finances until I could get my degree. Soon after Clara's graduation, we had a small wedding in the Methodist church where we had both been baptized. Clara's dream of a big wedding with lots of bridesmaids just wasn't to be. I felt sorry for her when she walked down the aisle behind her one attendant. Guess we never really talked about it though. We lived with her folks until school began, and then we moved to campus.

"I was in a history class later that fall when a woman came to the room and spoke briefly to my professor. Dr. Daniels nodded and motioned for me to go with the woman.

"Outside the door, she told me my wife had called and said there was an emergency. Clara wanted me to call her immediately. The woman pointed in the direction of an office and hurried me down the hall. But no one was home when I phoned. Frantically, I ran out of the building, grabbed my bike from the rack, and raced across the lawn to the street. When I bounded into our apartment, I saw a note on the kitchen table that said, 'Gone to the hospital. Please come!'"

Carson's voice was tight.

"When I got there, Clara had had a miscarriage. She was pale as a ghost. I held her as she cried for hours. Her parents arrived that evening, and my parents came the next day. After I got her home, Clara cried every day, and nothing I could do stopped her tears. I was just too dumb to know how to console her, I suppose.

"At one point later on, I thought maybe another pregnancy would be the solution. However, since the miscarriage, Clara had kept to her side of the bed. Whenever I tried to hold her, her body would suddenly stiffen. I wasn't sure how to approach her about another baby, so I finally dismissed that idea and concentrated on my studies. Oh, we were polite to each other, but I guess we both knew the early longing was gone.

"We muddled through the next few years. Clara took a job as a receptionist in a law office to help with finances. She refused to enroll in university classes, saying she didn't feel she could concentrate and really wasn't interested in school any longer. I felt responsible for her lack of motivation. She had been a good student in high school."

Carson's countenance changed, and Maggie noticed a sheepish grin. "I finally graduated with top honors in chemistry, and I was tapped by my department chair to receive a full assistantship if I would consider grad school.

"I went home that evening and asked Clara how she felt about my continuing with college. I told her it could mean a better future for us. She simply shrugged and said I was free to do whatever made me happy. So, after a summer of stocking groceries, I returned to classes that fall.

"I learned I could finish my doctorate in three years if I took an extra class each semester, plus summer school. I set my course and pursued it with dogged determination. My graduate assistant stipend and Clara's salary paid the rent and bought groceries. No frills, of course."

In spite of the pain, Maggie noticed his voice was stronger, and she detected notes of pride as he talked about his studies.

"I suppose our marriage wasn't either wonderful or terrible. Somehow, it existed. I was mostly too busy with classes to think about it. Later, I regretted I didn't try harder to communicate with my wife."

Carson rocked for several minutes, gazing out over the wickets on the croquet court. Maggie thought he was counting them.

"I don't like telling you the rest of the story, Maggie, but I believe you need to know this. Occasionally, Clara would allow me to make love to her. I hated the idea that it was some kind of 'gift' and she was just the benefactor. Although sex wasn't the first thing on my mind any more, I certainly never stood on principles or refused her favors. Early on, the pill had given her headaches, so she insisted that I use condoms. I know those aren't very reliable now, but I was pretty ignorant about contraception back then."

Maggie felt herself blush. A clear picture of her grandmother invaded Maggie's mind.

"Finally, graduation day came. It was a huge accomplishment for me. My parents and sister and her family came two days early with lots of gifts, dinners out, and good wishes. Although my in-laws came the day of the ceremony, I knew something was different. Guess I had failed to notice earlier that they had grown distant toward me.

"After the diplomas had been handed out that morning and the pictures had been snapped, we all spent the afternoon celebrating. Finally, everyone left, and Clara and I were alone in our apartment. The wine had been plentiful, and I had that mellow feeling, you know. In addition, I was suffering major fatigue from final exams, completing my dissertation, and the whole shebang. All I wanted to do was go to bed. Clara had had her share of the wine, too. I could tell she was a little tipsy when she walked unsteadily to the sofa and plopped down beside me. She nestled closer and began to kiss my neck. I knew that was the signal for another one of her 'favors.'

"The apartment was packed for our move to my new job at NC State

University. I racked my fuzzy brain for which box had the condoms. I sure didn't want to break the mood by digging around in boxes, so I hoped the wine would keep her from noticing until things had gone too far. Later, I realized she didn't notice at all."

Maggie squirmed in her chair. She felt like an intruder on this very personal story. Moreover, she hated the stab of jealousy she felt. After all, she knew Carson had been married, and Beth made it obvious it wasn't a sexless union. Still, the details of that night left her feeling unsettled.

"Two months later, we learned Clara was pregnant again. This pregnancy was troubled from the beginning. Clara was very sick, not just in the morning, but all day. At one point, the doctor feared she might have an ectopic pregnancy. Later, she developed gestational diabetes. Her doctor worried about how much fluid she was retaining. The problems never stopped. In addition, I had to spend long hours in my new position as assistant professor at State. When I was home, nothing I said or did for her made any difference. She clearly viewed me as the enemy who got her pregnant.

"This time, she made it until the eighth month. Beth, named for Clara's grandmother, was born on January 10. At first, we were both overjoyed with the tiny bundle the nurse brought us—wrapped all snugly in a blanket and wearing a cute pink cap. Clara cooed to our baby, and I know I was all smiles. My own little daughter, so tiny and new."

Maggie's heart ached when she heard those words. Images of Beth flashed before her.

"Soon after the nurse left, two doctors came in. I knew by their expressions that the news wasn't good. The doctors began telling us Beth wasn't a normally developed infant. One of them removed the pink cap and pointed out her slanted forehead and unusual, low-set ears. They said these symptoms needed investigation. I could see Clara growing paler with each comment they made. I reached for her hand, but she withdrew it immediately, shoving it under the sheet. The doctors asked for permission to begin tests. Clara nodded slightly toward me, so I signed the forms.

"I took Clara home a few days later, but Beth stayed in the hospital. We visited her every day. I knew it was a terrible strain on Clara. She barely said anything on the drive over and less when she saw Beth. Clara grew thinner by the day."

Carson's story was interrupted when a waiter appeared on the porch in his white dinner jacket and asked if they would like something to drink. Maggie ordered lemonade and Carson ordered iced tea. They made small talk until the beverages came. Carson paid the waiter and took a long, slow drink from the frosty glass. "Guess I didn't realize just how thirsty I was." By the time the waiter reappeared with his change, Carson offered up his glass for a refill. He sighed and began to talk again.

"After extensive tests, the doctors called a meeting. I left the University early that afternoon and picked up Clara. The verdict was devastating. Beth appeared to be suffering from a very rare form of a chromosomal disorder—trisomy mosaic 9. She had three of the number 9 chromosomes instead of two. The locations and percentage of cells with the extra chromosome determined the severity of Beth's abnormalities. To the best of their knowledge, given the scarcity of medical information about this genetic aberration, the doctors believed Beth would be profoundly retarded and have physical disabilities that would prohibit normal development. Her mobility restrictions would prevent her from ever crawling or walking, in their judgment.

"They told us it probably meant a short life span, also. Most infants don't make it to their first birthday." Carson stopped rocking and leaned forward, studying the wide, wooden boards on the old porch.

"Then one of the doctors dropped the biggest bombshell. He said we should consider putting her into an institution.

"I argued until I was blue in the face, but they wouldn't relent on their recommendation. They were just as adamant that it would be easier to place Beth somewhere right away rather than for Clara and me to develop an attachment to her when she would ultimately have to be placed there anyway. Clara said nothing during that entire conversation. I watched her intently, and her whole body seemed to shrink into the shadows that kept growing larger as the sun faded through the windows.

"But I steadfastly refused to sign the forms that would send my little daughter away. How could I? We were her parents. She belonged to us. I had no idea how she would be cared for anywhere else. So we took her home later that week. I remember struggling to imagine what the months and years ahead would hold as I carried her into the house and put her in the tiny bassinet. Clara was colorless. Her lips looked blue, pursed in a thin line. Later, I noticed she stood for over an hour looking down at Beth before I finally convinced her to go to bed."

Carson put his glass on the table beside his chair and folded his hands. Maggie sat very still. Finally, he took a deep breath. Maggie noticed his clenched fingers had turned white.

"Three days later, I came home and heard Beth crying and gurgling as I walked in. I started for the bassinette when I saw a note on the table by the door. I couldn't believe what I read. Clara told me she couldn't raise a retarded child, that she had to have some life of her own, that she had left us. She signed it, 'I'm sorry, Clara.' I just stood there rereading the note until Beth's cries grew louder and forced me out of my trance.

"I picked her up and noticed she was wet, so I went to the drawer and got a diaper and changed her. Clara had never planned to breastfeed, so there were bottles in the refrigerator. I held Beth close to my heart as I fed her. Then I rocked her back and forth until she fell asleep. Every clunk of the old rocker seemed to be driving the reality of what had just happened deeper into my brain.

"After I put Beth back in her bassinet, I sat at the kitchen table and wept for what seemed like hours. I wept for Clara. I wept for Beth. And I wept for myself, I suppose. Finally, I dried my face with a dishtowel and called my mother. She promised to come the next day.

"I also called my in-laws to see if they were aware of all that had happened and to ask if Clara was with them. My father-in-law told me they knew and understood why their daughter left. He said he and her mother felt terrible about Beth. They also thought I needed to face reality and put her in an institution where she could be cared for by people who knew how to handle such a 'deviance of human development.' He also asked me never to contact Clara again. I had a gut feeling he had rehearsed what he would say to me."

A shudder went through Maggie, and she had an instant dislike for Clara's father. How harsh. She swatted at the fly hovering near her lemonade with extra vengeance.

"Mom took care of Beth during the day, and I took over in the evenings. However, we both knew that arrangement couldn't last.

"We talked about my options. Finally, I made an appointment to see Beth's doctors as soon as I could get a break in my schedule. They strongly recommended placing her at Magnolia Hospital, which they said was much better than state-controlled facilities. They made all the arrangements, and just like that, my precious little daughter and my wife were both gone."

Carson was struggling to hold back the tears. His voice broke on the last words. When he regained his composure, his voice was soft.

"I visited Beth several times a week in the beginning. She defied the doctors' predictions and lived past her first birthday. However, living longer certainly didn't mean that Beth learned more, unfortunately. As her second year rolled past, I realized she had little comprehension of whether I was there or not. And the sixty-mile round trip three or four times a week was taking a toll on both my budget and my level of fatigue. Gradually, I stopped going except on Sundays.

"Fortunately, as Beth grew older, and with the help of a skilled staff, she seemed to know I was someone special. She would smile at me when I arrived and give me a hug. I often took stuffed animals for her, and she would cuddle them the entire time I was there.

"I can't praise the physical therapists enough. In spite of the doctors' dire predictions, they were able to give Beth a level of mobility that has allowed her to propel her body in that funny, lop-sided walk. I don't know the untold hours they spent with her, but I will forever be in their debt. At least she can walk beside me and hold my hand, and you will never know how much joy that gives me."

Maggie noticed that for the first time that afternoon, he was beaming. They sat for a long time in silence, watching the sun sink lower behind the stately pine trees in the distance. They held their cold glasses, with damp napkins wrapped around them, in their hands.

His weekly visit to Beth was what had brought him to Magnolia on that fateful day in the spring. Now, every Sunday after church, Maggie accompanied Carson to see her. Each visit, Maggie marveled at the pure joy that shone through Carson's eyes as he played with Beth. He stroked her hair as she held up her stuffed animals and hugged her tightly as they were leaving.

Two weeks after their trip to Pinehurst, they left early on Saturday morning and drove to Grandfather Mountain near Blowing Rock. They took a picnic in a cooler. Once they arrived, they set off hiking on one of the easier trails, but the day soon grew hot even in the tree-covered mountains. They joked about their lack of toughness as they returned to the car and went in search of a picnic table.

Maggie unpacked pimento cheese sandwiches and Carson's favorite—roast beef with tomatoes and horseradish. As she took the lid off her homemade potato salad, she noticed an admiring glance from Carson. He had brought the plates, utensils, and chips. "Thought *I* could handle this part," he said with exaggerated seriousness. "I even managed to provide some drinks for us." He produced a couple of cans of soda from under the ice in the cooler and pulled the tab on one, handing it to Maggie.

They ate slowly, enjoying the beauty all around them. The views were magnificent. Seemingly, nature had provided every shade of green in the spectrum right before their eyes. Maggie tried to capture it all in her memory in hopes of recreating it sometime on canvas.

Later, after all the food was stowed away, Carson pulled an old blanket from the trunk of the car and spread it under a large oak tree some distance from the picnic table. He took Maggie's hand and guided her to the blanket. They sat down, and Carson settled close to her. He kissed her softly for several moments. When he finally took his lips from hers, she laid her head on his chest.

"Mysterious Maggie," he mumbled into her hair. She rose abruptly.

"Why on earth do you say that?"

"Well, we've been dating almost three months, and I don't know anything about your childhood. I'd love to hear about your growing up years and your family. Or, my dear, did you just sprout from under some cabbage plant?" he teased.

Maggie had dreaded this day. She moved away from him and sat forward. As she looked out into the distance, she said, "I'm afraid my family isn't quite like yours, Carson."

He noticed the sadness in her voice. "Maggie, I'm sorry. I didn't mean to pry. You can tell me later." He reached for her hand.

"No, it's okay. It's not a very happy story, but I guess it's only fair you know who Maggie Gray really is." She scooted back until she sat against the trunk of the oak tree, purposefully looking for something solid to lean on. Then she began to tell him about her life growing up in Ahoskie, a small town in eastern North Carolina.

"My mother was a beautician and my father was a maintenance worker for the county. They spent most of their weekends at bars or riding tandem on Daddy's motorcycle, along with lots of their biker friends. I had . . . have . . . an older sister, Betty. My sister and I always knew we were pretty far down on Mama and Daddy's list of priorities. The only thing they required of us was to be quiet, stay out of trouble, and graduate from high school. When we were young, my parents usually dropped us off at my Granny's house on Friday afternoon and picked us up late on Sunday night. I can remember being so sleepy on the ride home, but sleep wasn't allowed until we had gotten ourselves into the bed Betty and I shared. There were never any goodnight hugs for us.

"I loved my grandmother. Granny was always so kind. She didn't give us a lot of hugs either, but I knew she loved us. *She* never yelled at us or hit us. On Sundays, Granny took us to church. On the way, she told us stories about Jesus and reminded us we had to be good because Jesus didn't love bad girls. Our parents never said a word about Jesus. Their threats were a far different kind if we ever stepped out of line."

Maggie shuddered when she finished the last sentence. Carson had moved back to the tree trunk to sit beside her. He put his arms around her and pulled her against his chest for several moments before she straightened up and continued.

"When I was eleven, Betty got pregnant by her twenty-one-year-old boyfriend. I knew she was sneaking around, but I never told anybody. I was too afraid. I warned Betty once, but she slapped me, so I just kept it to myself. My parents were furious when they found out about the baby.

"This is the worst memory of my childhood. Daddy took off his belt and beat Betty until Mama screamed at him to stop. Mama was certainly no stranger to using the belt herself, so I knew he must be half killing Betty. I had hidden in the closet the minute I heard Daddy unbuckling his belt, pulling Mama's coat over my ears to try to muffle Betty's screams and the slashing sound of the belt cutting the air—a sound I still dream about sometimes." Maggie's shudder was so obvious Carson immediately reached to hold her again, but she resisted.

"I decided at that moment I would never date a boy as long as I lived!" Her voice reached a crescendo.

"May I just offer here that I'm sure glad you changed your mind on that one." Maggie looked to see if Carson was teasing, but his expression was very serious.

"Betty had refused to tell any of us the father's name or where he lived, but Daddy had his ways, I guess. Anyway, Daddy went to the boy's home and found him alone. He jerked him out into the driveway and threatened to beat him within an inch of his life if he didn't marry her. That weekend, Mama, Daddy, and I witnessed Betty's marriage in front of the local magistrate at the county jail. Betty was crying, and her new husband—named Harold, we learned—looked like he wanted to be anywhere but standing there.

"Afterwards, we all went for pizza, and Betty and Harold spent the night at our house. I had to move out of the bedroom Betty and I had shared for those eleven years and into a small loft over the front porch. I actually liked being away from everyone even if I could barely turn around in that little cramped space. I remember making a vow that night. When Granny wanted to emphasize something, she would say she was going to 'turn heaven and earth.' Well, I decided I would 'turn heaven and earth' to get a good education so I could get away from my family. I was a pretty good student, and my fifth-grade teacher had told me once I should set my sights high. That was just what I decided to do!" Maggie's clenched fists were pounding the ground beside her.

"It's easy to see your determination has followed you for a long time, Maggie."

"After the baby came, I convinced Mama I should go and live with Granny so the baby could have my room. Mama actually seemed relieved. The house was nowhere near adequate for two families living there, and Mama and Daddy spent even more time in the bars or on the open road now that there were three others in the house. I suspect the baby's crying nearly drove them crazy, too. Anyway, all they cared about was being certain the same fate didn't happen to me.

"When Mama dropped me and my one battered suitcase off, she gave Granny strict orders not to let me out of her sight unless we were at church. Mama certainly didn't care about my soul, but I guess she figured church was a place where there wouldn't be any 'hanky-panky,' as she called it."

Maggie pulled her knees close to her body and tugged at the hem of her slacks. She paused for a long time before she continued.

"From then on until high school, my days were spent either at home with Granny or in school. On Sundays, we put on the freshly ironed clothes Granny had sweated over the Friday before and went to Sunday school and church. Granny was a Pentecostal. Boy, by the time I was thirteen, the fire in those sermons convinced me I sure didn't want to make Jesus mad. So one Sunday, I went down to the altar of the First Pentecostal Church and 'got saved.'" Maggie drew the quotes in the air.

"Afterwards, Granny just kept hugging me and telling me how proud she was. Many other members of the congregation came up, too, and hugged and congratulated me. I wasn't sure why there was such a to-do about being saved, but I smiled at everybody anyway. Carson, I didn't even know what I had ever done that I needed to be saved from, but I sure didn't want to take any chances," she said, laughing.

"Maggie, it's awfully hard for me to imagine you, of all people, could have had many transgressions."

"Anyway, I have to hand it to Granny. She made it very clear that Jesus wanted me to be 'pure and undefiled,'" and again Maggie made curves in the air. "She must have said those words at least once a day. I figured Jesus had a really good emissary in my Granny." Carson had laughed with gusto.

"I would love to tell your Granny what an impact her admonitions still have on you, my dear," he said as his laughter subsided.

"I didn't date in high school. In my junior year, the captain of the football team—who walked like he owned the world, and I secretly hoped would fall flat on his face—asked me to the prom. Well, I knew there was only one reason for that invitation. He had quite the reputation for his 'conquests,' so I knew he just wanted to brag to his friends the next week that he had seduced the biggest prude in school. I looked him square in the eye and told him to drop dead. I still get tickled when I think of the expression on his face. He just stared at me as if I had said the world had quit spinning, and then he finally stomped off."

Maggie thought she saw a flicker of relief in Carson's eyes.

"I worked hard on my studies in high school. My English teacher in the tenth grade made me believe I actually might be able to make it into college. So I started working at the local burger joint with hopes of saving as much money as possible towards tuition.

"In my junior year, Miss Stivers, the guidance counselor, helped me fill out applications and write the accompanying letters to several of the state's universities. That next fall I received acceptance letters from three of them," Maggie said shyly. "I showed them to Granny, but I never mentioned them to my parents on my few visits home. My parents fully expected me to get a job and start making what amounted to 'real' money as soon as I graduated. And I still hadn't saved nearly enough for college, so I didn't figure I was going to go anyhow. No reason to get them all upset.

"A couple of months before graduation, the principal called me into his office. Miss Stivers was there, too. They were both smiling.

"Mr. Rollins held out a letter. I started to read it and couldn't keep the tears back. It seems they had nominated me for a scholarship to North Carolina State University. The letter told me I had been selected! It would pay my first semester's tuition, and if I could keep a B average, the scholarship would continue to pay each semester. I just stood there staring at the letter in disbelief as my tears started to fall on the paper. Out of the blue, I hugged both Mr. Rollins and Miss Stivers. I saw tears in Miss Stivers's eyes, too. As I was walking back to class, I realized because I didn't have a car and it was over a hundred miles to Raleigh, I wouldn't be expected to go home on the weekends. I think that idea might have been as exciting as the scholarship."

"Maggie, I'd love to meet those two and shake their hands. Their faith in you has certainly been rewarded. Every teacher's hope."

Maggie nodded and continued, "Graduation night was on a Friday.

Besides Granny, Mama, Daddy, and Betty showed up. Harold had long since left, but not before Betty got pregnant for the second time. Little Bobby was just a toddler, and I was worried he would start fussing. I didn't trust Betty to take him outside. Harold Junior was in school already, so I figured he could sit still for a while. He was such a scrawny little guy. Actually, my heart went out to him. I could only imagine what kind of life he had living with my parents.

"I smelled the familiar whisky on Mama's and Daddy's breath. I knew they were probably pretty uncomfortable at an event like that, so I guess it was no surprise they fortified themselves beforehand. Betty was trying to corral Bobby with the words we had heard over and over from our parents, 'Wait til I get you home.'

"No one but Granny knew I was going to give the valedictorian's address, and my stomach was churning. I stood there silently, hoping it would soon be over for everyone's sake.

"Following all the welcomes and speeches, the principal rose to give out the diplomas. I was completely unaware he would also list awards and honors each student had received as he called our names. My cheeks burned red hot when he called 'Miss Maggie Gray, recipient of the Dorton Scholarship given by North Carolina State University.' I knew trouble was ahead.

"After the ceremony, I just wanted to run from the building and not have to face my parents, but I gritted my teeth and went to find them with a smile plastered on my face," Maggie said sadly.

"My daddy thundered, 'What in the hell is goin' on here?'"

In spite of the heat, Maggie shivered as she went on. "My mother started yelling in a loud voice that I had been sneaking around and not telling them things. People standing nearby stopped conversations to look at us. I just wanted to die. The night that should have been so special was becoming a nightmare.

"Thankfully, Granny—frail, passive Granny—spoke up. I remember her saying, 'You just go on home, Victoria, if you can't be proud of your little girl here. Shame on you for acting this way.' Mama shot Granny a killer look and stalked off without another glance in my direction.

"As I lay in bed that night, I figured I must have mattered so little to my parents they didn't think it was worth continuing the fight. Daddy's parting statement was that I shouldn't expect anything from them if I wanted some 'damn, big education.'" Maggie noticed the muscles in Carson's jaw were set in a rigid line.

She told him with the help of the scholarship that continued each semester, and working two jobs, she had managed to graduate from college with a degree in elementary education and no student loans to repay.

Carson had stopped her story and said, "Maggie, you're the most amazing woman I've ever known." Then he had kissed her until they both had to break away to breathe.

As the afternoon wore on, Maggie told Carson she had dated three boys in the four years she was at NCSU. They had each stopped calling after a few dates when Maggie held firm to her resolve of no more than three kisses per date. "I never quite figured out why I thought three was the magic number between affection and runaway lust, but it seemed to me that was the point where the boy started getting ideas there was more in store for him."

"Hey, three kisses were more than enough for those guys, honey. I get jealous just thinking about you kissing someone else," and they had both laughed.

"Two months before my graduation day, Granny died. The one and only telephone call I got from home during the four years I was away was Mama telling me a neighbor found Granny lying on the ground by the crooked, metal mailbox. That mailbox was the reward at the end of the quarter-mile walk she took every day of her adult life to get what few letters and flyers might come her way. Granny loved the mail, and now I was filled with guilt because I hadn't written more often to this gentle, kind woman who had given me a safe place to live and stuck up for me at graduation.

"I had no desire to stand in some funeral parlor with my disreputable family and make small talk about Granny's virtues to people I hardly recognized anymore. I knew my parents still hadn't accepted the fact even four years later that I had gone off to college, so any conversation with them was bound to be hostile and futile. I decided to arrive just in time for the funeral."

Maggie stopped again and gazed off into the distance. She was resurrecting memories that had not surfaced for quite a while.

"I gave Mama a quick hug and patted Daddy's arm—he was no hugger. I met Betty's new husband and third child. Growing up, I had always envied Betty's good looks. She had silky blonde hair and a creamy complexion, whereas my brown hair was nondescript and my skin was darker. Now, her hair was limp and clung to the collar of her too-tight jacket and her skin had a grayish cast. She was only twenty-six, but I thought she looked ten years older. I decided husbands and children were certainly taking their toll.

"After the graveside service, Daddy mumbled a few words about it being good to see me. He quickly found his way over to a corner where some men were laughing in a way that indicated now the deceased was in the ground, life had returned to normal.

"I had to hold back the tears. My precious Granny was hardly buried, and I suspected the men were back to telling their dirty jokes. I wanted to yell at them—at my father, most of all—that Granny mattered. That she deserved better. Instead, I squelched my anger and walked over to where Mama was standing with a group from the beauty shop.

"In front of her friends, Mama asked me when I was coming home after graduation. She told me Betty needed help with the children," Maggie spoke with uncharacteristic bitterness.

"I remember her asking if I couldn't get a job at Ahoski Elementary and babysit in the evenings for Betty.

"I wanted to yell at Mama that these weren't my children—that I wasn't the one who had gotten into such a mess! I had been their 'good girl' and here Mama was denigrating all the long hours of study I had put in, the two jobs I had worked, and the never ending fatigue. Did she really think my goal in life now was to be an unpaid baby sitter for my sister who had broken all the rules?" Maggie's voice had raised at least two pitches. She sat for a moment collecting her thoughts before continuing.

"However, I tried to smile through gritted teeth and said I wasn't sure when I would get home. I had been too busy with senior projects to think of life after graduation. Mama give me a brutal look and called me 'Miss High and Mighty,' I remember."

Maggie told Carson her parents didn't bother to come to her graduation. Of course, that wasn't completely their fault, Maggie admitted, because she didn't send them an invitation.

"Why did I want them to ruin a second graduation, for Pete's sake?" she asked Carson, without expecting an answer. "If Granny had been alive, I certainly would have wanted the only woman who really loved me to be there. As for the others, I have to admit I had a much happier celebration without them."

She didn't go home. Her good grades, along with glowing letters of recommendation from her advisor and her supervising teachers, meant she had no problems getting her first teaching job in the Raleigh area. She decided on an elementary school in Cary. She settled into a tiny, rather bleak apartment not too far from her school.

"I told myself it wasn't so bad for a first apartment. With my second paycheck, I went to the Goodwill store and picked out most of the furniture you see now. Someday, maybe I'll be able to afford a nicer place," she said wistfully.

A breeze had begun to whisper through the leaves on their solid oak. Maggie looked up at the gently swaying sea of foliage. She felt exhausted. Carson seemed in deep thought. Finally, he turned to her and said, "Maggie, don't *ever* be ashamed of your story. You have my unending admiration."

Today, those words rang in her mind as clearly as they had all those years ago. She looked at the clock. How long had she been standing there reliving the past? She wanted to believe there was a future that held some treasured moments, too. But today, she wasn't certain.

CHAPTER 4

Off Maggie trudged to pull on the jeans lying on the closet floor where they had fallen last night. She prided herself on neatness, but a week of teaching fifth graders at this age of her life always left her drained, so occasionally clothes didn't make it to hangers. She grabbed a sweater from the top shelf and rummaged for her sneakers. Dressed, she headed off to start the Saturday chores—the time when Maggie tried to cram a week's worth of errands and household tasks into one day.

Soon after Carson went to Carolina Manor, a neighbor asked Maggie what she did with all her free time now—suggesting life was much easier without a husband around. Exasperated, she had replied, "What do I do with my *time*? Everything I did before Carson became ill, and now, all of his work, too!" She never forgot the surprised look on his face.

Car maintenance had always been Carson's responsibility. Maggie remembered his diligence in keeping records of service and repairs. She faithfully tried to follow his example.

Today, she hurriedly settled behind the wheel of her modest car. The drive to the dealership was less than ten minutes. She parked the car and tried to put on her most confident expression as she strode to the service area. Besides the oil change, she asked the young man behind the counter to check out a strange noise. "It's a tick-a-tick-a-tick sound, and that's the best I can describe it," she said defensively as she handed the keys to the youthful service manager with the puzzled look. She knew Carson would have used terminology that was far more sophisticated.

She always cringed at the feelings of inadequacy that came over her when she couldn't fill his shoes.

She headed for the waiting room. She surveyed the well-worn, unkempt area with its overflowing ashtrays, stained upholstery, and ragged, outdated magazines that had who-knows-how-many germs from all the hands that had held them. She decided not to pick one up as she settled into a frayed, overstuffed chair.

With nothing to read, Maggie's mind wandered back to the summer of their courtship. Carson had told her one Friday night he would pick her up at seven o'clock the next morning. He had said the day would be a surprise. He arrived in a jovial mood, whistling as he accompanied her down the walk. Backing the car out of the driveway quickly, he said, "Time to spray gravel!" On the outskirts of town, the car headed west. That was the only clue she got. An hour later, they stopped for pancakes in Kernersville.

"Okay, mister, I can tell from that smug look you're really enjoying this secret mission," Maggie said just before the blueberry syrup she was pouring slipped and drenched her pancakes.

"Yes, indeedy, I am!"

Maggie's sudden guffaw caused the people at the next table to glance their way. She had not heard "indeedy" since Granny passed on. "Okay, I'm determined to be a good sport, but this better be worth it," she said with a taunt in her voice.

Carson's ebullient manner faded for a moment. "I'm hoping it will be a good day for both of us," he said in a slightly somber tone.

After breakfast, they headed west once again—making small talk, admiring the scenery. They passed Winston-Salem and Statesville. Maggie decided they were going back for another day in the mountains, but she didn't see any provisions for a picnic. As they neared an exit for Hickory, Carson turned on his signal light, followed the ramp to the intersection, and turned north. Maggie was seeing new territory.

Finally, after Carson had wound his way through several turns off the main road, he took a right onto a tree-shaded street and slowed the car. "Honey, this is Hudson. I thought you might want to see the town I grew up in." He looked at her with hesitation as if he was beginning to doubt this had been such a good idea after all.

She squealed with delight. "Why, I'd love to see it! How sweet of you to bring me here!" Maggie's heart felt full.

Carson reached for her hand and squeezed it. "Maggie, Maggie . . . you're a special woman."

They drove slowly down the street and turned onto Autumn Lane. "Third house on the left up there is where I grew up." Maggie leaned forward so she could get a better view. And there it was—a two-story, white frame house, not large but comfortable. There were several pots of red geraniums on the porch and steps. The lawn was immaculate. Carson pulled to the curb and sat there in deep thought, still holding her hand. Maggie decided to remain silent, too. She wondered, did his parents still live here? Was she going to meet them? Finally, he spoke.

"It was a good place to grow up. I had two great parents. They were both schoolteachers, and Dad worked on construction crews in the summers to supplement their income. We weren't rich by any stretch, but my sister and I always had what we needed. Katherine was ten years older, so I was only in the second grade when she went off to college. But we got along great when she was home. I do remember a few times when she didn't want a kid brother tagging along with her and her friends. Can't imagine why," Carson said, smiling. "On those occasions, Mom would send me off to play with one of my buddies down the street.

"By the time I was out of high school, Katherine was married and had two children. They're wonderful kids—well, they're teenagers now, of course. Maria just finished her freshman year in college and Scott will be a senior in high school this fall. I've always enjoyed being around them. However, Maggie, I feel small when I admit this, but I've had moments of jealousy when I see how bright and normal they both are. For me, it makes Beth's condition even more painful." Carson's eyes often misted over when he spoke of Beth. Maggie never knew what to say.

"Three years before I met you, I was lecturing to an auditorium full of freshman chemistry students. The department secretary came to the door and pointed to me. I had a sinking feeling when I saw the somber look on her face. I excused myself and stepped outside into the hallway. She told me I had an urgent call from my sister who was waiting on the line. I literally ran to the office and grabbed the receiver. I yelled 'What's wrong?' into her ear.

"Katherine's voice was trembling. She told me Mom and Dad had been in an automobile accident. I had to wait so she could compose herself enough to go on. She said they had been visiting our aunt in Georgia and were on their way back home. Some guy doing twenty miles over the speed limit had clipped their van from behind as he pulled around them, and they had flipped over twice. They were both thrown out and killed instantly."

"Oh Carson, that's horrible! How sad . . . how tragic," and Maggie shook her head, having difficulty imagining that phone call.

Carson stopped talking and stared at the white house. He swallowed several times.

Finally, he continued. "I vaguely remember dismissing class and standing in that empty auditorium trying to absorb the news. It felt like my blood had turned to slush, and I started shaking with cold.

"I loved Mom and Dad, and I knew they loved me. They stood by me throughout my marriage and all the years in college, and Mom was wonderful when Clara left. After that, they came to visit me often, and we always went together to see Beth.

"On the day of the funeral, I remember standing at the cemetery in total disbelief—like I was in a dream. They were both gone—both! You just never expect that. Katherine and I held on to each other while the minister said the last words over their identical caskets."

He was quiet for a long time, just staring at the house. Maggie kept patting his arm with her free hand. He seemed lost in fresh pain. She noticed the knuckles on his left hand were white as he gripped the steering wheel.

Finally, Carson pulled away from the curb and headed down the street. A couple of young boys were passing a football in a yard as they drove by, and Maggie imagined that could have been Carson as a child. She smiled.

They spent a couple of hours exploring the town. At the high school he attended, they had gotten out of the car and walked into the building. After Carson explained he had been a student there once, the custodian had waved them on in. Carson showed her his classrooms, the cafeteria, even his locker. She didn't ask, but she bet this was the first time he had gone back to the school since Clara graduated.

They ate lunch at one of his favorite childhood restaurants. It was a low, brick building with green and white awnings. Inside, customers called to each other and chatted loudly over their luncheon specials. Carson introduced her to his fifth-grade teacher and one of his father's Rotary Club friends who hailed him as they were leaving. Of course, both wanted an update on his life, and Maggie could sense the curiosity toward her. Small town at its best, she thought as they pulled away from the parking lot.

Carson even showed her Clara's house. She wondered if he knew what happened to Clara. She wanted to ask, but then decided she really didn't want to know if he still kept up with her. However, as they were leaving Hudson, she realized he had not driven her to any parks—and she was glad.

Maggie sat in the car shop waiting room letting the warm memories of their drive back to Raleigh that day long ago wash over her. She remembered knowing that Carson was letting her into his life, and that meant she was special to him. The thought wrapped itself around her like warm sunshine even today in this most unlikely place.

As the summer progressed, so did their affection for each other. Maggie had long since relented on her three-kiss rule, and often she could sense the urgency in Carson. One night, as she pulled away from the passion, he said, "You said Granny was frail, but she sure packed a wallop on your resolve, my dear."

"Sometimes, I think her voice is growing fainter," Maggie had said with hesitancy.

But contrary to all her other dates, he never insisted. When they both knew kisses weren't enough, he would stop and simply wrap his arms around her and hold her tightly. Neither of them said anything, but they both knew their feelings for each other were growing deeper.

Sometimes she thought her most precious moments that summer were when Carson held her against his heart and she felt its steady beating. She sensed a closeness she hadn't known existed.

Suddenly, her reverie was interrupted by the service manager's voice telling the customer across the room his car was ready. The faint smell of aftershave lotion that lingered in the room as the man left to claim his vehicle reminded her of Carson.

In October of that year, he had come for their usual Friday night date. She noticed he had on a new sport coat, a departure from his navy blue he always wore with khakis. Mentally, she had dubbed that his uniform. The only thing that ever varied was the shirt and maybe an occasional tie.

But tonight was different. The jacket had an ecru background with a subtle navy and rust plaid design. He had on navy slacks and penny loafers. She thought him quite handsome.

She wished she had chosen something a little nicer from her own wardrobe, although he had certainly seen every item she owned that was fit for public viewing.

Suddenly, she realized he was handing her flowers from behind his back. "My goodness!" she exclaimed. "Well, thank you very much. Aren't they lovely!" She was fumbling for words. She thought that gesture only existed in old movies. She opened the door wider, motioning for him to come in while she hurried off to find a vase. As she sat the bouquet of red and yellow mums on the worn coffee table, she said, "Look how much life they breathe into the room. I don't think I've ever had fresh flowers in this place before, but don't they look nice!" Carson had seemed very pleased with himself.

"I took the liberty of bringing dinner for us tonight," he said, as he walked back out the door. She was mildly surprised. Unless it was a picnic, they always chose some local restaurant. He returned carrying several bags, and she recognized the logo from the nicest Chinese place in town.

She found two black and white checkered placemats and put them on the small table in the kitchen. It was her only eating space. The ad in the newspaper had said the apartment had an "eat-in kitchen." However, that was true only if you didn't mind your elbows hitting the wall behind you on one side or your knees poking the base cabinet on the other.

She took two scratched, plastic plates from the cabinet. Funny, she had never noticed the scratches before. She rummaged for silverware and wished she had some nice fall napkins.

"Do you have wine glasses?" he asked.

"I'm sorry, I don't. I never drink wine here," Maggie said—suddenly feeling inadequate in her own kitchen.

"No problem," he assured her. "We can use any glasses you have." And with that, they drank their first wine together out of two chipped water tumblers. Carson's easy acceptance of her contributions to the meal—plus the wine—soon smoothed Maggie's earlier fluster.

They ate in an unhurried manner, talking mostly about their respective classes, the fall weather, some political news. But Maggie sensed something was different. She kept waiting to hear the reason for this deviation in their routine. Maybe he had gotten the grant he had written recently.

After dinner, she started to put the dishes in the sink. "No, let's let those go for now," Carson said, pulling her into the living room. "This is how we handle the dishes tonight," as he closed the door on the messy kitchen.

He sat her down on one side of the sofa and pulled up the small Victorian chair she had bought at the Goodwill store. He scooted the coffee table out of the way so he could sit in front of her. He had a very serious countenance. She was getting nervous. Was he going to tell her something she would hate to hear?

He took her hand in his wonderfully warm one, no doubt made a little warmer by the wine.

He began. "Maggie Gray, I first need to tell you I have fallen in love with you, but before I go any further, you must know there is a caveat that comes with this declaration. I want you to hear me out, and then I will give you as long as you need to think about it." She sat very still, looking into those brown eyes she sometimes wanted to drown in, afraid of what might come next.

"I have no idea why Clara miscarried or why Beth was born in her condition. It may have been my wife's fault, but it may also have been mine, or perhaps a combination of our genes. I will never know. But I will never attempt to create another life. I couldn't go through that trauma again, and I certainly would never put you through it. Also, I could never risk losing you like I lost Clara.

"I want you to think very seriously about what I've said. If having children is the priority for you that it is for most women, we will just have to realize this relationship must end—for me, a very sad end. However, it is only fair to you to know how strongly I feel about this matter. Maggie, think hard about what you really want. It will be something you live with for the rest of your life."

She started to speak, but found no words. She knew her feelings for him, though she kept them in a dark place in her heart, hoping they wouldn't grow any bigger. She had feared if she allowed them into the sunlight, he might suddenly walk away and leave her with more pain than she could bear.

Before she could form any sounds in the back of her throat, he rose from the chair and took her hand, pulling her up. He kissed her very gently. "Let's go for a ride, and no more discussion about this for tonight," he said, breaking all the tension that had suddenly mushroomed inside her body.

She held onto him, wanting to feel the safety of those arms once more. They stood locked together for what seemed like a long time. She could feel his breath ruffling her bangs. Her mind was struggling to absorb his words.

"Yes, let's," she finally offered. She knew she had to think about what he had said. Maggie was too logical to dismiss such a grave decision in spite of all the feelings to the contrary that welled up inside her.

They drove for a while, making small talk. They laughed at silly jokes. They held hands across the front seat. They admired the harvest moon. She knew they both were enjoying the reprieve from the decisions that lay ahead.

When they returned to Maggie's apartment, Carson promptly headed for the kitchen, tossing his jacket across a chair on the way. "Now to those dishes," he said. He washed and she dried. Their first chore together, and it had felt so right to her.

Standing in the kitchen, he seemed reluctant to leave. She knew it wasn't because he wanted an answer. As he held her close, she didn't discourage him.

Just when she thought they were heading some place they had never been, he suddenly stepped back and looked deeply into her eyes. "No, Maggie, I want you to decide if we have a future before either of us has regrets about tonight. I could never be your first if I wasn't going to be your last. And besides," he said, with a twinkle in his eye, "I don't want Jesus mad at me either!" She giggled. He gave her a quick hug and said he would call tomorrow.

As she lay in bed that night, sleep never came. Instead, she thought of not having children of her own. She loved her students, but she also found them draining some days. She thought her sister's children were loud and whiny, though she had to admit she had seen them very few times. But would she miss holding her own babies? Then she thought of Beth. Her heart broke each time she saw this darling child with so many limitations. What if Beth were her child? Would she be sorry she ever had her?

Finally, Maggie got up, went to the kitchen, and made some hot tea. Cradling her cup, she sat on the sofa—the place where Carson had told her he loved her a few hours before. She thought of his earnest face, his warm eyes, his honesty. Would she choose to give up this man so she could have children someday with someone else? He hadn't proposed, but she felt that was the next step if she accepted his edict.

As dawn cast its pale light through the kitchen window, she knew she had the answer. Carson had surprised her last night; she would surprise him this morning.

Picking up coffee and bagels from the local bakery, she headed her car in the direction of his house. She had never been inside before, and she wondered if she should call first to give him time to get out of bed and do whatever he did in those first five minutes. Maggie's proper self finally won out, and she stopped at the phone booth two blocks from his house and placed the call. Instead of the sleepy voice she expected, Carson sounded wide awake.

"Hi," she said, timidly.

"Hi back," he said and she could hear the smile in his voice. "Couldn't you sleep either?"

With those words, she breathed a sigh of relief and began to gush with enthusiasm about her own little surprise for him. "No, I couldn't, so I decided to bring breakfast to you. Coffee and bagels. Hope you like blueberries."

"Nope, can't stand them," he teased.

"Well, guess you'll just have to watch me eat two then. I'm at the corner service station. Be there in less than five." She noticed her eagerness had definitely won out over her reluctance to seem impulsive.

After a hug in the doorway, they walked toward the table on his screened-in porch. It was chilly, and Maggie had only grabbed a sweatshirt. She shivered slightly, and Carson immediately went to get a windbreaker.

While he was gone, she looked around. Everything was very neat, but the place looked gloomy. The color scheme, if one could call it that, was all beiges and browns. His furniture didn't look any newer than hers. She had dreams of a home with lots of sunlight and bright, bold colors everywhere. She wondered if Carson would find that appealing, too.

He returned, placed the jacket over her shoulders with a gentle squeeze, and held her chair while she sat down. "So Maggie, this is a total surprise. Are you always such an early bird?"

"No, but then I don't always have such profound questions to wrestle with all night," she replied. Now she was wondering how she was going to continue. He waited, providing no verbal fillers for the quiet that followed. He was watching her eyes intently. She knew he was trying to see what lay beyond them. She dropped her gaze to the table—swallowed—and began.

"As you know, my family didn't exactly give me a good roadmap for what love looks like. Anyway, I learned a long time ago that I needed to take care of myself—not count on others. I hope that doesn't sound like I'm being a martyr, but it just worked for me. I've liked a couple of boys, but it never got close to love."

She stopped for a moment to see if he would respond, but he just kept a steady gaze in her direction. She took another bite of her bagel and swallowed two sips of coffee. Still he said nothing, but he did reach for her hand.

"Okay, this is the hard part." She paused and returned his gaze. "I've made my decision. Not having children is better than the alternative. Carson Bales, I love you, too. How do I know that, given my history? Because you are the kindest, finest man I have ever met, and I do not want to live my life without you. If you feel the same way, please say so. But if you don't, please allow me the dignity of walking out of this house, getting into my car, and driving from here to who-knows-where. Just stand up right now and walk into your bedroom and shut the door, and I will leave with no goodbyes," she said with defiance, but suddenly feeling more vulnerable than ever before in her life.

Carson dropped his gaze, released her hand, and slowly rose from his chair and padded across the tile floor—not toward, but away from her! Her heart fell into the pit of her stomach, and she couldn't catch her breath. What a fool she had been. Her face burned with shame. I will never say "I love you" to another human as long as I live, she cried silently.

But before he reached the hallway, he stopped at the cluttered desk in the tiny den. He opened the top right-hand drawer and removed something. His back partially hid the drawer from her view. She heard the rattle of paper. Then he turned and walked toward her with a small blue bag. He set the bag on the table, off to one side, and took her hands in his. Her heart climbed several steps toward her chest.

"Maggie, this is not what I had in mind at all. But then maybe we just need to let life lead us into its precious moments instead of trying to produce them." With that, he reached for the blue bag and pulled out a black, flocked box with a gold fleur-de-lis on top. He cradled it in one hand, and Maggie's heart knew. Her heart knew he did truly love her, and he didn't want to spend his life without her either. And then her heart sang its loudest and strongest song ever. It almost drowned out his next words.

"Maggie Gray, if you will marry me, I will never use your last name again because it will be mine. I want to live with you for the rest of my life. And if you can't say yes to that, then please walk out that door, get in your car, and drive away because I don't want you to see me cry."

He still had not opened the box. It didn't matter. Whatever was in the box was of no importance compared to the gift he had just given her. He had asked her to be his wife, but much more significant to her was his declaration that he would love her until death.

"I may never move from this spot," she said, "because it's the best place I've ever been. I never knew happiness like this even existed, Dr. Carson Bales. Being Mrs. Bales will be my greatest honor."

With that, he opened the tiny box. What she saw inside was completely unexpected. There was no diamond ring. Instead, lying on a small velvet pillow was a beautiful, wide, gold band, intricately carved. It was lovely beyond any she had ever seen. He held the box in his hand.

"Maggie, I would like to get married as soon as possible. However, if you want to invite your family, then I will acquiesce to a convenient time for them."

Just thinking of the problems that would ensue if her parents and sister came to the wedding caused Maggie to shudder.

"No, no. I want it to be just our time—just us," she said.

"Good," he replied, "because I really don't want to wait another day. What do you say about next weekend?" Wow! She could hardly believe her ears.

"Yes, absolutely yes," she said, amazed at her own eagerness.

They sat at the table and made plans. They would ask Reverend Adams, the new associate minister of Carson's church, to marry them. They would get the marriage certificate and the blood test on Monday. Maggie would ask her best friend, Marty, to be her attendant, and Carson's best man would be Dave, one of his colleagues. If those two were free on Friday evening, then the wedding party was complete.

The minister was taken aback when they asked him after the worship service on Sunday if he would perform the ceremony. "Well, it's my policy to counsel couples at least three sessions before the wedding. I need to be convinced that you two are suited for each other," he said, solemnly.

"Would it be possible to have one very long session?" Carson asked.

The minister laughed. "In other words, you want the short course!" he exclaimed. In the end, they met with him twice that week, and he seemed satisfied they were good candidates for a life of matrimony.

Maggie had gone to the doctor to get birth control pills, but the doctor warned that she had to use them at least thirty days before they would be deemed reliable. She had explained this to Carson afterwards while they were loading some of her things into his car to take to his house, and he had only nodded.

One afternoon, Maggie shopped for wedding attire and lingerie.

She shuddered at the thought of her groom seeing her present ragged assortment of undies.

The week was a blur. Maggie hardly remembered being in her classroom. She knew her heart was somewhere else, and the students loved to correct her when she told them to turn to the wrong page, or she forgot to take up their homework.

When the dismissal bell rang on Friday afternoon, she grabbed her things and was on the heels of the last student out of her classroom door. She was almost running when she reached the parking lot and jerked her car door open, flinging books, purse, and coat across the front seat. In a flash, she was out of the parking lot and headed to her apartment.

Once there, she started the shower because the water took forever to heat. After throwing off her school clothes, she plugged the curling iron into the outlet on the counter and stepped gingerly into the shower. She shampooed her hair and felt the water continue to warm as it cascaded down her body. Suddenly she wondered if Carson would like her body. She had always been rather slender. She certainly wasn't as curvaceous as many of the women she saw on television or in the movies—the so-called sex symbols. Would he be disappointed? She could hardly believe this would be her wedding night. In the flurry of the week, she hadn't given the honeymoon much thought. Now she shivered under the steaming water with just the idea of being close to Carson's naked body. How she hoped he wouldn't be disappointed with her!

She toweled off and put on her new rosebud pink bra and panties. She used the blow dryer on her hair and carefully applied her usual modest amount of makeup. With her curling iron, she turned strands of hair at vertical angles and then fluffed them out to frame her face.

Next came her new navy suit. It was ironic she had not bought a white suit. She would bet she was more entitled to wear white than most brides. However, white was just too impractical. She would have to wear this suit many times in the future, so her frugal self had nixed any light color. However, she had bought a frilly white blouse, which would have to do. Adding blue pumps and a clutch purse, she surveyed herself in the long mirror behind the door. "Carson Bales, meet your bride," and with that she snapped her suitcase shut and carried it to the front door. Carson was to pick her up in exactly five minutes.

Maggie stood wondering what it would be like to live with someone else. She prayed with all her might that she would be a good wife, that Carson would never regret marrying her, that they would be happy.

Her thoughts were interrupted by a rap on the door. She almost jumped. She knew when she turned that knob her life would be changed forever. And that thought brought such a wave of joy she started tugging at the knob before she had unhooked the safety latch.

There he stood—her bridegroom—so handsome in a new navy pinstripe suit. He took a long look at her, and she wondered what he was thinking. He gathered her in his arms and whispered against her hair, "You're the prettiest bride ever, Maggie, and I am the luckiest groom." With that, he handed her a corsage of white roses, and they were off to the church.

They stood before the altar in the church's small chapel. Maggie, Carson, Marty, and Dave, along with Reverend Adams. The vows were soon over, and Carson placed the lovely gold band on her finger. The minister pronounced them husband and wife. Carson kissed her quickly, embarrassed they were being observed. "Hello, Maggie Bales," he had whispered.

The service manager's voice brought her back to the present. "Your car is ready, ma'am. The technician couldn't find the noise you mentioned. If you hear it again, bring it back." Maggie knew it was futile to argue, so she paid in silence and headed out to her car. She grew angry as she settled into her seat because she knew if Carson had been there, the problem would have been fixed. As it was now, she was certain she would have to return—and what a bother! Still fuming, she turned left into the street and headed to the drugstore for Carson's supplies.

CHAPTER 5

Maggie finished her dinner that night standing at the kitchen counter watching the news on her small television set. She ate in a hurry, eager to get on the road to see Carson. She was always surprised her eagerness had been sustained over all the nights where he had been asleep when she arrived and had never awakened before she left. Or the nights when he was very angry with her. Or the nights when he didn't know who she was.

But there was always that single evening when he would smile as she walked into his room, and she could see recognition deep in his eyes. That evening nudged all the others into the shadows of her memory where they were not so painful.

She followed the same ritual—close the blinds, turn on some lights, gather whatever supplies he needed, and finally, set the security system.

She drove through the inky streets and already wished for summer's long days when the trip didn't begin and end in darkness. Tonight, the symbolism disturbed her.

Carolina Manor sat at the end of a long drive off a street lined with Bradford pear trees. It always reminded Maggie of a movie set. The front looked like a replica of a slightly aging Southern mansion with tall white columns growing out of a flagstone veranda. However, beyond the reception area, the rest of the building was a long, low structure that was strictly utilitarian and institutional. It didn't seem to belong to the elegant façade.

Maggie pulled into a parking space. She always had her choice of spaces at night in the visitors' parking lot. She walked up the brick walk and onto the veranda. The tall, double front doors were showing signs of wear. White paint was chipping around the large antique brass doorplates, and the many hands that had turned those knobs had left darkened smudges.

Inside the doors, the lobby floor was covered with a slightly faded blue carpet. The furniture was decorated with floral upholstery, which helped to hide both wear and stains that had occurred over the years. Mahogany tables of various types seemed in keeping with the antebellum exterior.

Maggie assumed the reception area was intended to impress families who were looking for a place that seemed homey and less institutional for their loved one. There was a receptionist's desk to the right, and several offices funneled off the main lobby. This place was always empty at night. Those who worked in the offices during the day eagerly went home in the evenings to escape the constant reminders of aging and its infirmities, she was sure.

The scene changed as Maggie walked into the hallway beyond. Her flats made a clicking sound on the tile floor as she walked by the staff station. Each wing had its own station because each had occupants with different needs. Carson's wing was specifically for those with Alzheimer's disease and other forms of dementia.

The hallway was brightly lit with florescent fixtures in a long row down the seemingly endless corridor. Maggie had walked this corridor maybe two thousand times since Carson came here nearly two years ago. The rooms were like dorm rooms, with one door after another opening off the corridor. Carson's room was almost at the end.

As she came closer to his door, she felt the familiar sensations of excitement and dread. She loved being with him when he was more lucid. On the nights when he didn't know who she was, or worse yet, when he was angry at everyone, including her, her heart would break with every exchange between them.

She gently pushed the door open and saw the flickering light of the television. Carson was often asleep in his recliner, so she waited a moment to see if she heard his gentle snores. Yes, he was napping.

Maggie sat down in the small Victorian chair she had always loved.

She had insisted Carson have it in his room just for her when she visited. It was the same chair Carson had sat in the night he had told her he loved her. She couldn't bear to let it go, so she just kept having it re-upholstered. She used it these days to pull in front of his chair so she could talk directly to him as she held his hands.

Suddenly, Rose, the woman across the hallway, began calling, "Somebody! Somebody! Help!" Maggie jumped and ran into the corridor to find Rose coming through her door, leaning heavily on her walker, and looking bewildered.

"Somebody help me! I got lost, and I can't find myself. Help me find myself!"

Maggie moved swiftly to her side and began to stroke her arm. "Rose, I'm here, and I will help you."

"Who are you?" Rose screeched and tried to retreat.

"I'm Maggie, and I know you're Rose. My husband is Carson. I've seen you before, and I will be your friend," Maggie said in her most soothing voice, as she moved away a bit to seem less threatening.

"Well, help me find myself then!" Rose screamed. Just at that moment, one of the staff members Maggie recognized as Ruth came quickly down the hall and took Rose by the arm.

"I'll handle this," Ruth said in a sharp, commanding tone. She quickly maneuvered a resistant Rose back into her room and shut the door.

Maggie felt helpless. The staff was used to this type of behavior, so they handled such incidents in a brusque, no-nonsense manner. The gentleness and understanding Maggie had so wished for Carson when he first went there had been the exception, not the rule. She had quickly realized, more often than not, staffers were either authoritarian or condescending to the residents, often treating them like children.

In the beginning, she had wept night after night on the drive home, praying that God would help Carson's caregivers treat him with the same kindness and compassion she did. Gradually, she—like most of the other families—just accepted the system. The energy she had spent trying to change the staff's understanding of Carson's needs and the Alzheimer's disease in general had not produced significant change. She suspected "the system" accounted for why many family members spent less and less time with their loved ones. They had little control over the care in these institutions, and that only exacerbated their sense of guilt.

Once, Maggie had seen a man whom she assumed was Rose's husband when she had come in the daytime, but he was never there at night. That particular day, the door to Rose's room had been open, and as Maggie sat in her chair, she could see directly into it. He seemed pleasant enough to Rose and asked lots of questions about her health—questions that Rose could not answer, of course. That was another thing Maggie observed. Loved ones tried to carry on normal conversations, including "Mama, do you remember…," and they would end the question with some obscure fact. Of course, Mama didn't remember! Maggie always wanted to yell at them, "If she could remember, why would she be here?" Anyway, she noticed the man had hugged Rose kindly when he left, and that had touched Maggie's heart.

Maggie would love to call him tonight to tell him Rose needed comfort, but she had no idea what his name was or how to contact him. And, she supposed, it was really none of her business.

She had almost nodded off in her chair when Carson stirred. His afghan fell to the floor as he moved.

"Hi there, honey," she quickly said, so he wasn't startled by her presence. She retrieved the afghan and smoothed it over his lap.

He looked at her with eyes that were uncomprehending. "It's me . . . Maggie," she offered. He continued to stare at her. She took his hand, but he gave no response. "I'm your wife," she went on, trying to help him find a niche for her.

Slowly, he began to focus, and a smile started to form around his mouth. "Hi," he said. On the good nights, he would respond to her with great affection, telling her over and over that he loved her. "When did…?" he asked.

Carson had lost the ability to speak in full sentences, so Maggie was endlessly anticipating what he was trying to say. She was pleased she got it right most of the time. Otherwise, he grew more frustrated searching for the words he wanted.

"Just a few minutes ago. You were sleeping, and I didn't want to disturb you."

"You don't…," he said, and then words failed him again.

Smiling, Maggie said, "Guess what. We were married thirty-six years ago today."

"We were?"

He looked at her with the expression she had come to call the "lost" look. He simply couldn't find the information in his memory bank, so he just shook his head.

"That's okay," she assured him. "It was a nice wedding, and we have had a good marriage."

"I'm glad," he said in a soft voice.

They talked for a while in the odd sort of way couples communicate when one has Alzheimer's disease. The conversation usually went in circles with the same things said many times and Maggie finishing his sentences. It would seem inane to others, but it worked for keeping Carson engaged in some sort of dialogue and making Maggie feel connected to the man she loved with all her heart.

With little left to say, she asked if he would like help putting on his pajamas. He usually preferred her to help him instead of staff members. She thought it was probably a modesty issue.

He nodded, with a smile. "You are one," he said.

She rose and held out her hands to him. He didn't respond, so she tapped each folded hand with her fingers until he slowly lifted them into the air. She took one hand in hers and gently pulled forward. He began to rock back and forth in an effort to get momentum for rising. As he did so, she moved so she could put two fingers of her other hand on his back belt loop and tug. After several tries, he was upright. She then moved in front of him and took his other hand to steady him.

She walked backward, leading him into the bathroom where he could hold onto the bar in the shower. She quickly pulled pajamas out of the dresser drawer and found the adult diapers stacked in the closet—double for nighttime.

She unbuttoned his elastic-waist jeans and let them drop to the floor. Carson had to be prompted to raise his feet. She did this by tapping them with her fingers until his brain got the message. As Maggie tapped, she would also utter encouraging phrases. "Up we go." "Let's kick that ball." "You're marching in the band." Whatever helped Carson's brain respond and send a message through his body. Slowly, he would raise one foot. She could remove his pants from that leg and quick as a flash slip on one leg of the pajamas. After she helped him lower the trembling extremity to the floor, tapping would begin on the other one. She repeated the process with the second leg. Before she pulled the pajamas up, she positioned each diaper and fastened the tapes on both sides. Next, she slowly and painstakingly guided his feet into his bedroom slippers, again tapping each foot until his brain got the message to lift. Carson's memory cells that controlled the leg muscles were compromised, his doctor said. Putting on the pajama top was always easier.

Finally, they were finished, and he seemed tired and ready for bed. Her conversation had dwindled to the standard phrases of "That's good," "You're doing great," "There you go."

Maggie held his hands and walked backward with him to his bed. He sat down slowly, and she helped him swing his legs in place. Then she removed the bedroom shoes that had just been put on. She would not dare have him move barefooted across the wood floor because he might fall, one of her biggest fears. A fall often meant a hospital stay, which could lead to serious complications. She knew some patients never recovered. Finally, Carson was tucked in. She noticed the clock on his bedside table. The nighttime ritual had taken exactly thirty-four minutes. She leaned down and kissed his forehead. "Sleep tight," she whispered.

He smiled that warm smile and said in a sleep-filled voice, "Don't let…"

Softly, she finished for him, "…the bedbugs bite!" She kissed his forehead again and smoothed his hair.

Maggie turned out the lights and gently closed his door behind her. She leaned against the wall for a moment as weariness settled into every part of her being. The nighttime routine was physically taxing, but she suspected the mental component of coaxing the delayed responses was just as draining.

The drive home was always filled with emotion. She has happy tonight because he seemed to know who she was. He had said "Love you" several times. That was a phrase he could still remember. And that was as good as it ever got.

Later in bed, she thought about this night thirty-six years ago. They had spent their brief honeymoon on the Outer Banks. Not the ideal time to be at the beach, but they had only the weekend to be away from their jobs. And, anyway, they weren't there to sunbathe!

They ate seafood at the most famous restaurant on the island, though Maggie noticed that neither of them finished their dinners. They checked into the hotel where Carson had booked reservations, which were probably not necessary at this time of the year, but he was always one to plan ahead. Maggie remembered feeling very shy as Carson unlocked their door. She kept looking at her blue pumps. He tipped her chin up so he could look into her eyes.

"Welcome, Mrs. Bales, to the threshold of our new life." She melted against him as he kissed her for a long time. "Maybe we don't want to become a spectacle out here," he laughed as he took her hand and they scrunched through the door together.

Carson carried their luggage from the car and set it on the floor before wrapping his arms around her in an embrace that lingered on and on. The intermittent kisses were warm and soft. He stroked her hair. Maggie could hear his breathing grow louder and faster.

Carson suggested she use the bathroom first. She felt awkward when she stepped in and shut the door. It seemed straight out of some Victorian novel. She would be quick about it, she decided. She was eager and she wanted him to think she was eager, but her natural modesty prevented her from ripping her clothes off in front of him. She changed into the white chiffon gown and peignoir that had taken quite a chunk out of her paycheck. However, she was proud to present herself as a virgin to her husband and decided the money was well spent for the statement it made.

She opened the door and stepped quietly into the bedroom. Carson was reading through the visitor's book but looked up as soon as he heard the door open. He just stared for a moment. Her newly styled ringlets lay softly just above the cloud of white ruffles. He rose and came and gathered her in his arms.

"You are the most beautiful bride in the world!" he exclaimed for the second time that day. "And I am the luckiest husband." He kept holding her, but she could sense that something had changed. Finally, he moved back so he could look into her eyes.

"Maggie, I realize I didn't talk to you about tonight, and that is all my fault. I'm afraid this may not be the night you had planned. Or the night I wish it could be. But I can't take the chance of a pregnancy and nothing is safer than the pill—I've checked it out. Your doctor said it won't be dependable for about a month, so I believe . . . I know . . . we need to postpone the consummation of this union. Will you be disappointed if we wait for a few more weeks?"

Maggie had no idea what to say. In spite of her prior apprehensions, she was looking forward to finally being loved and loving back in the way her body had been directing her for months now. She dropped her head and said nothing. He pulled her close to him again and tried to hold her, but she moved away. He looked stricken as she moved toward the bathroom. And stricken was pretty much how she was feeling, too—rejected on her wedding night!

She took off her white negligee and folded it carefully, replacing it in her luggage, followed by the more revealing gown. She reached for jeans and a sweatshirt she had brought for walking on the beach and put them on. Tears welled in her eyes. She took several moments to regain her composure. Then, with resolve, she stepped back into the bedroom. She was *not* going to argue on their wedding night.

Carson's face was ashen. "Maggie, I've let you down. I should have told you earlier this week that we have to wait until it is safe. In all the hurry, I just didn't. I'm so sorry!"

She looked at his kind face, those pleading eyes, and saw such despair. Her heart melted.

"It's okay." Then she began to giggle. "After all, I've waited twenty-four years. How bad can it be to wait another few weeks? But, Dr. Bales, I am *not* wearing my expensive white gown tonight. The next time you see that, it will not be for nothing." She moved toward him and punched him on the arm.

"Are you really going to sleep in those?" he asked, both puzzled and relieved.

"Well, that all depends on what you sleep in," she murmured into his ear.

So Maggie Gray Bales and her new husband spent their wedding night clothed only in each other's arms. She awoke in the morning to the realization she had indeed married the most wonderful man in the world—the only man for her. She looked at his tousled hair and the beginnings of a shadow on his face, and the love she felt for him was so exhilarating she could scarcely breathe. Welcome to married life, she exclaimed silently.

When they returned on Sunday, they drove first to Magnolia to see Beth. They did not try to explain their marriage. It wasn't a concept Beth could understand. They stayed with her for an hour and then said goodbye. Beth had always seemed to accept their departures without emotion. She simply went back to whatever she was doing when they came in.

They drove to Carson's house where they had agreed to live. Maggie only had enough time last week to bring over a few of her things; but as Carson unlocked the door and ushered her in, he looked at her with total love and said, "Welcome to our home, Maggie Bales!" And Maggie knew, perhaps for the first time ever, she really *was* home.

On their one-month anniversary, Carson came home with a single, long-stemmed, red rose, tied with a white velvet ribbon, and a bottle of sparkling wine. Later that evening, Maggie gently removed the white chiffon gown from the bottom drawer of her dresser.

CHAPTER 6

Sunday was the day Maggie missed Carson the most. He had always made his special pancakes while she showered. They would eat and read the Sunday paper until time to dress for church. This morning as she lay in bed garnering resolve to leave its protective covers, she wondered if the lonely feelings that greeted her each Sunday would ever go away.

Later that morning, Maggie closed her hymnal and gathered her purse and coat as the choir sang the final benediction. She always dreaded the questions by their friends after the service. Of course, they meant to be kind and caring, but she had no words that could capture Carson's state on any given day. She would always say the same thing every Sunday. "He's doing well, thanks." They would always smile, mumble, "That's good," and seem thankful they didn't have to continue the conversation. Maggie understood illnesses that held no happy future always made people uncomfortable.

Perhaps the hardest question of all was, "And how are *you* doing?" That was a question she never knew the answer to. Odd that she had as much difficulty explaining her state as his. She sometimes asked herself how she was doing but never found an answer that felt adequate. Coping. Perhaps that said it best. However, she always put on her most pleasant smile and replied to those queries with, "I'm just fine, thanks." Then she hurried to greet the minister and get out the door quickly. It was easier for everyone.

Most Sundays, Maggie enjoyed having lunch at one of the local restaurants. She felt less alone watching other diners come and go—a young couple trying to shush a crying baby, an older couple laughing about some shared memory, teenagers suffering through the meal with parents and siblings while seeking refuge on their cell phones.

Maggie knew it might be easier to go home and eat a sandwich, but Sunday was the one day they had *always* dined out. She could tell when Carson was bored with the sermon. He would write on his church bulletin, "Where's lunch?" and pass it to her. Sometimes he included a smiley face.

Now, Maggie usually chose restaurants far from church, where other members were unlikely to go. While she hated the pitying looks toward a single diner, she equally disliked being asked to dine with people who really wanted to have their Sunday lunch alone. One such event had occurred soon after Carson went to Carolina Manor, and the memory still upset her.

She had gone to Carson's favorite restaurant—one close to the church—and as she stood waiting to be seated, a man from the congregation, whom she barely knew, came over and asked her to dine with his wife and him. Maggie really preferred to eat alone, but she had no ready excuse for not joining them. She offered a smile, said how nice it was of them to ask her, and followed him to the table.

The reception she got from his wife quickly told her this was *not* her idea. She was so frosty that Maggie wondered if it would be possible to develop some sudden illness and leave. The husband was obviously ill at ease by his wife's coldness. What a mess, Maggie thought. They don't want me here, and I don't want to be here. How did this happen? From that time on, she had simply said, "No, thanks," unless the offer came from really good friends, and hoped she wouldn't forever be labeled as rude.

Today, she was lucky. She saw no one she knew. She ordered quickly and ate half of the entrée, taking the other half home for dinner tonight.

She graded papers in the afternoon, resenting this intrusion on her time when she could have been reading a good book. Most of the original group of Maggie's teacher friends had retired several years earlier. Five years ago, when she could have retired, they had first learned of Carson's Alzheimer's disease after he had finally consented to go for an evaluation. Besides being devastated about the disease and its prognosis, Maggie knew their financial state would not allow her to stop teaching.

Two years before the diagnosis, Maggie had noticed Carson was very forgetful. He also became quarrelsome at times, which was so uncharacteristic of him. He had planned to teach at the University until Maggie retired, and then they joked they would finally get their chance to "see the world." Extensive travel had always eluded them, but their time was coming soon, they thought.

First, it was little things. Sometimes the department chair would call and ask if Carson was ill because he had missed the faculty meeting. Or the conscientious students would complain to the dean that Carson gave the same lecture three times during the semester.

Maggie would find pots on the range that had boiled dry because he was attempting to make their dinner when he got home before her—something he had always done in the past. He would be sitting in his tiny office at home, completely unaware of the burning smell. She was scared because his behavior wasn't just confined to academic negligence; it could cause safety issues as well. It was then she became adamant he go for testing. He had protested vigorously but finally relented after she asked that he do it for her.

Sitting in the neurologist's office, Maggie was amazed at the questions Carson couldn't answer—and those he could. He could not tell the examiner who wrote *Macbeth*, but he recited every word of its most famous soliloquy from his high school memory. He didn't know the month of Lincoln's birthday, but he voluntarily recited two paragraphs of the Gettysburg Address. Most odd, he could not name the numbers of most of the elements on the periodic table—a table he had taught for well over forty years. When asked to draw a clock face, he drew a meticulous image complete with Roman numerals. However, he could not put hands on the face that pointed to 1:45.

Further tests revealed changes in the brain itself. Although most of the medical profession believe that Alzheimer's disease isn't really verified until an autopsy following death, his doctor still labeled Carson's condition with certainty. Maggie remembered sitting with Carson in the doctor's office when he gave them the diagnosis. Afterwards, the kindly doctor reached out and patted Carson's arm and said, "Ol' buddy, I'm sorry this is the news I have to give you." She noticed a flicker of sadness in the doctor's eyes. She wondered how many times he had given other families the same devastating verdict.

Carson was mortified and immediately wrote his letter of resignation. The dean and department chair reluctantly accepted it. Carson had been a valued member of the faculty, achieving full professor status in the shortest time possible. Students loved him and colleagues thought him a solid citizen in the department. He had received several federal grants, been awarded the University's outstanding teaching award, and served as chair of the faculty senate. All who knew him were in disbelief that this accomplished man could no longer find his classroom.

Friends began to notice changes. Maggie and Carson were grocery shopping one day and almost bumped into their neighbor's cart as they rounded an aisle. The neighbor began her usual cheerful chatter, and Maggie realized Carson did not recognize her. Quickly, Maggie said, "So good to see you, *Kathy*. We would love to catch up, but we are hurrying today because I have a dental appointment." With that, she grabbed Carson's arm and propelled him quickly down the aisle, leaving Kathy with a puzzled look. The same quizzical looks were occurring at church and Carson's Rotary Club. Maggie knew word would soon spread about his peculiar behaviors, and she braced herself for all the questions.

Carson's doctor suggested he have a driver's test, given mostly to people who are rehabilitating from such illnesses as strokes. It was a five-hour test that included three hours answering questions from a computer screen and ninety minutes of actual driving. The attractive young woman, whom Maggie guessed to be in her midtwenties, sat down with both of them at the end of the test and gave Carson the bad news. She would have to report to the Division of Motor Vehicles that Carson was no longer capable of driving. Most glaring, he was unable to recognize road signs, even the Stop sign. She remembered he had wept softly all the way home and gone to bed immediately after they arrived. It may have been the hardest day for him in the entire insult of Alzheimer's.

For over two years, Maggie took care of Carson at home. She watched him vigilantly, hiring someone to stay with him during the day while she was at school. When she was home, she stayed by his side. She gave up her book club, her church committees, her once-a-month dinners out with other female faculty, and she accepted no social engagements. She never minded these sacrifices because she knew she was spending precious time with a husband who was gradually slipping away from her.

Then Carson began to wander. That first occurred while the daytime caregiver was there. She wasn't negligent—just not accustomed to watching him every minute. Even under her vigilance, twice he slipped out the door, but luckily, neighbors noticed him and brought him back. One night, Maggie awoke to the ringing of the doorbell. As she struggled to understand what was happening, she realized Carson was not in bed. She ran to the door, throwing on a robe in full stride, and there stood Carson between two police officers.

"We found him walking about half a mile from here," one said. "He couldn't tell us his address, but he knew his name, so we looked you up in the phone book." Maggie saw the frightened expression on Carson's face. She gently pulled him in the door and stepped outside to thank the officers, apologizing several times for not hearing him leave their bed. The officers were very kind and assured her that she could call them anytime she needed them.

Next, she had a security system installed to warn her when he left the house. His wanderings became so frequent she was getting very little sleep, and the security alarm at all hours of the night was disturbing the neighbors, though most were very gracious about it, telling her not to worry. Carson had been a very good neighbor himself, often raking the elderly Mrs. Gardner's leaves in the fall or mowing Mr. Benjamin's lawn all summer when he had a broken leg.

Finally, Maggie realized she could not continue to watch over Carson at night and work all day. The hardest decision she ever made in life was the one that put him in the place he now resided. Only through the encouragement—no, insistence—of her friends and her minister did she finally crumble and decide she was only human, and it was imperative she stay healthy for Carson's future.

She cried for weeks after he left. It had been a difficult adjustment for him, too. He didn't sleep well for several months. He would yell out in the night or ring his call bell over and over. The staff told her he constantly asked where she was. Those words were like daggers in her heart.

However, finally the unfamiliar became familiar to him. He never asked about their home anymore. She believed he had forgotten where they lived. Actually, that made it easier on both of them.

She finished grading the papers and glanced at the clock. In forty-five minutes, she would need to leave the house to make her nightly trip. She ate her leftovers from lunch, looked at the newspaper briefly, and left the house promptly at six thirty.

Tonight, when Maggie entered Carson's room, she could tell he was having a bad day by the vacant look on his face. He stared at her as she said, "Hi, there," in her usual effort to sound cheerful. He didn't respond. Instead, he watched her in silence. She moved toward a chair and started to remove her coat.

Suddenly, he smiled. "Mother!"

On these days, he often confused Maggie with his mother or his sister. When Maggie had mentioned this incident in a caregivers' group meeting, a social worker told her it was because he had known them before he knew her. Maggie knew the woman had told her this theory in an effort to comfort her. However, it was no comfort at all.

Sometimes Maggie corrected Carson, and other times, she just let it be. Tonight, she needed him to know who she was. "No, it's me . . . Maggie . . . your wife."

At this, he jerked his head in the other direction. "She go!" he yelled. It would be of no use trying to explain that was Clara.

"Well, then is it okay if I stay with you for awhile? Would you like that?" she asked, trying to console him. He just stared at her.

She sat for a few minutes and made idle comments—about the maple tree in the back yard, the cool weather, the football team. He didn't respond.

"Could I help you with your pajamas? They would be more comfortable for you," she offered. Finally, he nodded.

They went through the same procedure as the night before. He was less responsive than ever so the whole ordeal took even longer. She had him sit down in the shower chair, hoping to make him more comfortable. She was limp by the time she got his bedroom shoes on. She had repeatedly encouraged and cajoled, but she knew he was becoming more agitated as the process continued. She was trying to hurry.

To get his shirt off and his pullover pajama top on, she started to remove his glasses. "NO!" he roared, and with that, he slapped her squarely across the face. She fell back on the tile floor and heard the crack of her elbow. She lay there, stunned. He had been difficult to handle before, but he had never hit her. It took a few seconds to comprehend what had just happened.

Maggie slowly sat up and rubbed her throbbing arm while the side of her face burned. She was having a hard time controlling herself. She wanted to yell at him, she wanted to slap him back, she wanted to run away. Instead, she rang the call bell for the nurse.

"Please come now. I need help getting Dr. Bales into bed." Maggie's voice had a shaky, urgent tone.

Promptly, the nurse appeared in the doorway. "What happened?"

"I guess he didn't want me to take his glasses, so he hit me," Maggie responded. "My arm is really hurting. Can you please take over?" Maggie noticed a large lump growing on her elbow.

Maggie turned to Carson who sat there expressionless, "I am going," she said through clenched teeth. "I will come back tomorrow night." He said nothing. She did not move to hug him or to say, "I love you," as she had done every night before. Instead, she walked out the door.

Once in the car, Maggie sat while tears rolled down her cheeks. She knew that in Carson's mind his action was rational. He wanted to keep his glasses. Those warm, brown eyes had suffered vision loss as he grew older. He had required special lenses with prisms, so he was very careful about scratches. His glasses had been so important to him before he began the journey with his Alzheimer's disease. He saw her as a threat to their safety, and he wanted to remove the threat. His only defense was to hit, probably something he had done as a child.

Still, that knowledge didn't take away the shock of being struck by the most gentle, loving man she had ever known. Carson had made her his primary concern for over thirty-six years. He had fiercely protected her. Now, he had also hit her.

Slowly, she found her car keys and pulled out of the parking lot into the dark night. When she got home, she located the ice pack and filled it from the tray in the fridge. The cold against her elbow felt as icy as her heart, but finally the numbing effect on her growing lump began to ease the pain. As it did, she slowly let go of her sadness and frustration. Tomorrow—she prayed silently—tomorrow, please make him more lucid.

As she dressed the next morning for school, she almost laughed when she felt the aches in her elbow and jaw. "I'm one sorry sight," she said aloud, remembering Granny's favorite phrase when her arthritis flared up. When Maggie backed the car out of the garage, she noticed the Carolina blue sky, and her spirits rebounded. The unpleasantness of yesterday's visit had already begun to fade. Each day brings its share of challenges and rewards, she thought. She hummed as she drove toward her undauntable fifth graders.

CHAPTER 7

Five days later, Maggie straightened her desk and shoved homework into her book bag. She looked around the empty classroom as she walked out the door. She had an after-school dental appointment before she stopped by the grocery to pick up a few things for the weekend. When she finally walked into her house, the phone was ringing. She quickly set down the bags and her purse on the kitchen counter and picked up the receiver. Almost before she could say hello, an urgent voice said, "Mrs. Bales, you need to go to Memorial Hospital as soon as possible. Your husband has been taken there."

Maggie paused. "Excuse me . . . who is this?" she managed.

"I'm sorry, Mrs. Bales, but we have been trying to reach you for over two hours, and I was getting frantic. This is Joyce at Carolina Manor." Maggie did not recognize the name.

"One of the nurses went to check on your husband following lunch and noticed something was wrong. A doctor was here visiting a family member, so the nurse asked him to step in and look at Dr. Bales. He immediately told her to call the paramedics and get him to the hospital."

Maggie gathered her thoughts enough to ask, "So, do you know what's wrong?"

Suddenly, a crisp voice took over—a voice Maggie recognized as one of the head nurses. "Mrs. Bales, your husband has been taken to the emergency room. That's all we know." Her no-nonsense manner jerked Maggie into action.

"Thank you," Maggie replied just as crisply and hung up the receiver.

She grabbed her purse and rushed out the door, catching her coat on the handle. "Let me go!" she yelled at the door, without realizing the absurdity of her words.

The drive to the hospital took a good twenty minutes when all the traffic lights were in her favor. Today, they all taunted her with yellow as she approached, and then they turned red before she could make it through. Maggie was shaking from fear and the chilliness outside, and her coat suddenly seemed paper-thin. She turned up the heat as she waited, desperately willing the light to change.

Finally, the hospital parking lot was in sight. She grabbed the ticket rolling toward her from the metal box, begged the gate to open faster, and took the first spot she found.

Maggie raced into the lobby and searched the hospital directory. Too late, she realized she was on the wrong side of the building. The halls seemed endless as she sailed by arrows directing her down yet one more corridor. At last, she rushed through the Emergency Department doors, signed in, and asked the attendant where her husband was. He paged someone. An older nurse appeared and led her to room sixteen where Maggie saw Carson lying on a narrow bed. He appeared to be sleeping, and she thought how small he seemed under the sheet.

"What's wrong? Has the doctor seen him? Who's taking care of him?" The words tumbled out of Maggie.

"Three doctors have seen him, Mrs. Bales," the nurse replied gently. "Dr. Stevenson will be his primary physician, and he asked me to let him know as soon as you arrived. I will find him now." And she left the room.

Maggie moved to the bed. She nervously patted Carson's foot while she waited.

Very soon, Dr. Stevenson hurried in. He introduced himself, shook her cold hand, and told her they were still running tests. "The other doctors and I agree your husband has probably had a stroke. We have given him medicine to break up any clots."

Maggie felt her knees begin to tremble. She reached for the bed rail to steady herself.

"We might have operated on some patients, Mrs. Bales, but your husband's Alzheimer's disease isn't in his favor. Anesthesia can be very harmful to people with dementia. Anyway, we are hoping the medication will be successful in destroying the clots.

"Your husband is lucky that it was recognized quickly," he said. "Actually, the doctor who noticed your husband's symptoms is on our staff here."

"I need to thank him," Maggie managed weakly.

"I have ordered a room in our stroke unit. The test results should be back any time now, and then someone will take him there, unless we all got it wrong. Because of space, we usually don't allow relatives to stay in those rooms, but due to your husband's disease, I can arrange for you to be with him. As we work with him in the days ahead, you will need to help us understand what his abilities were before the stroke occurred. Let the nurse know if you need anything, and I will see you later." With that, he shook her hand again and moved quickly out of the room.

Maggie's feet seemed rooted to the floor. She willed herself to make some forward motion. She found a chair, scooted it close to the head of the bed, and forced her words to seem normal. "Hey there. You've been up to mischief today, I hear. You caused quite a commotion at the Manor. Just wanted a little attention, eh?" She managed a smile, hopeful he would know she was teasing.

He opened his eyes and his lips moved slightly. She leaned closer to his face so she could hear him. She noticed the distortion on his right side. He tried to make the sound again. On the third try, she thought he was saying, "Maybe." She smiled, took his hand and held it tightly.

"You better behave and not give me such a scare," she said lovingly. "And I promise to stay right here with you until you are all well again."

The nurse stuck her head in and told Maggie the gurney was on its way. The tests had confirmed the stroke.

Time passed in a blur. Machines beeped, tubes dripped, noises clattered in the hall. Maggie made quick phone calls to Carson's sister and a few of their friends. Nurses and doctors moved efficiently in and out of the room, and finally, night settled in with all its darkness. Darkness also gathered in Maggie's heart.

She realized it was past nine o'clock and she hadn't eaten. Suddenly, she was starved. Carson appeared to be sleeping again. She rose from the chair and felt the stiffness in her bones. Taking her purse from the locker on the wall, she began the trek to find food. She discovered only the coffee shop was open at this hour. It offered sandwiches and a few snack items.

Maggie ordered a grilled cheese and a cup of coffee. The caffeine shoved her numbed brain into action. She realized she needed to go home and get some toiletries.

She hurriedly finished her sandwich, gulped down the last sip of coffee, and walked quickly back to the nurses' station. "I'm running home to get some things. If my husband wakes, please tell him I will be back soon."

"Yes, and we will keep checking to see that he is okay while you are gone," a pleasant, older nurse responded, reassuringly.

The house seemed cold when she walked in. She checked the thermostat, but the temperature was where she always kept it. However, that didn't stop the shiver that engulfed her body.

Maggie quickly found her overnight bag and began to stuff items in that would see her through the next couple of days. No need to take pajamas. Instead, she changed out of her school clothes into a stretchy warm-up suit. After brushing and flossing her teeth, she hurried to close the blinds, check the lock on the back door, and set the security system.

Maggie glanced at the clock and saw it had taken her twenty-eight minutes. She grabbed her overnight bag and tossed it into the back seat of the car. For the second time that day, she headed toward the hospital.

Settling into the recliner once again, Maggie studied Carson's face closely. He appeared to be resting. The strain of the day began to subside. Even the coffee couldn't keep sleep from overtaking her.

The next thing she knew, a nurse was quietly checking the machines on the other side of Carson's bed. Maggie stirred, and the nurse smiled at her. "Looks good," she whispered. Soon Maggie drifted back to sleep though her dreams were sinister and disturbing.

Early the next morning, as the light outside began to erase the darkness in the room, Maggie was awakened by Dr. Stevenson when he stepped through the door. She was chagrined to be found sound asleep. She coughed in an attempt to clear her husky, morning voice.

"Good morning," she managed. "Guess this chair is more comfortable than it looks."

"Well, most people don't share your feelings on that," he answered with a half laugh.

He moved to Carson's side and examined him briefly. Then he asked Maggie to step into the hallway with him.

"We will be checking many things about your husband today. I would like to get him into rehab as soon as possible, but stroke victims who have other physical problems, including speech, present a different scenario for us. We'll do all we can to get your husband back to where he was yesterday before the stroke. Okay?" He smiled at her.

"Thank you. He's been through so much with the Alzheimer's. I don't want him to suffer any more ravages to his body." Maggie felt the tears begin to well.

"Of course not. We will be very busy with him today. Take breaks periodically. Walk outside in the fresh air. Eat to keep up your energy and watch the junk food."

She felt like she was in a fifth-grade health class. Nevertheless, she smiled, misty-eyed. "Thanks. I will remember that." He shook her hand, turned, and moved with purpose down the hall.

Maggie went to the small basin in the room. Looking into the mirror, she saw all the lines she had counted before, plus a few new ones. She brushed her teeth, washed her face, and applied light make-up. Her hair showed the marks of a night without a pillow. She frowned at herself in the mirror, and then the frown made her smile. Never one to fuss about her appearance, suddenly she was concerned about how she looked to people she didn't even know. "Strange how we focus on the inane when we have so little control over the significant," she said softly to the mirror.

Maggie slipped out of the door to find the coffee shop again. It was seven o'clock and the hospital was still quiet. She liked it that way.

"I'll have a large coffee and a blueberry bagel with cream cheese," she said to the pony-tailed, young woman behind the register. It had been her standard order at Bobo's Bagels.

She and Carson used to go there every Saturday morning, taking the newspaper so they could discuss the latest current events. After they finished reading all the sections, she tried working the crossword puzzle while he read the sports' statistics. Looking back on those serene mornings, she would give anything to relive just one of them. A sudden wave of nostalgia caused her to push the rest of the bagel aside. Her appetite was gone.

She paid the cashier quickly. She just needed to be back in Carson's room—to see him, to know he was still breathing, to believe he would talk to her again.

All through the morning, various people in white coats came and went. Maggie tried to make herself small in the crowded space. Most smiled at her as they left but offered no information.

As the day wore on, there was less activity in the room, so Maggie curled up on the recliner once again. She had nearly drifted off to sleep when the door opened and another doctor stepped into the room.

She pulled herself upright and nodded to him. Then she realized she had seen him before. Where, she wondered. He was tall, slender, and his hair was tinged with gray. He quickly rescued her.

"Hi," he said. "I'm Dr. Holton. My wife is in Carolina Manor across the hall from your husband's room. I was visiting her when the nurse asked me to take a look at him. I knew he needed to be seen here right away. How's he doing?"

"Oh, Dr. Holton, how can I ever thank you?" she said, jumping to her feet. She rushed to shake his hand. "Yes, I've seen you there. Her name is Rose. She's such a sweet lady." He kept a steady, puzzled gaze toward Maggie. She realized she was making no sense.

"I'm . . . I'm sorry," she stammered. "I really don't know how he is or what the prognosis is. He had several tests today and many people have examined him, but I haven't heard anything yet. I hope his doctor comes by before he goes home."

"I'm sure he will. I know him. He's a great guy," he stated calmly. "If it's okay with you, I will stop in occasionally to see how your husband is doing. By the way, my first name is Bill. And yours?" He waited.

"Oh, sorry. I'm Maggie Bales." She felt flustered.

"Nice to meet you, Mrs. Bales," he said.

"No . . . no . . . please call me Maggie," she stammered.

"Okay then, Maggie, I will be stopping by later." With that, he was gone.

Maggie settled into her chair once again. She had picked up a magazine in the gift shop after lunch, noticing they all had similar story titles on their covers—promises of great beauty, great figures, great wardrobes, or great sex. She began to turn the pages without much enthusiasm.

She had almost finished leafing through when Dr. Stevenson walked through the door. Her heart lifted as she looked at his smiling face.

"I have some encouraging news," he said. "Your husband shows potential to make a good recovery in terms of motor skills. All his neurological tests indicate there's probably no insurmountable damage. Of course, we don't know what role his Alzheimer's disease will play in this, but we will trust it won't interfere with normal progress. The stroke will be a temporary setback for him in terms of memory loss and disorientation, however. You can expect to see more confusion in the days ahead."

"I just want him to talk to me again. In the past, the confusion has given way to some lucid moments, and that's what I have lived for," Maggie said, as her voice choked.

Dr. Stevenson continued. "Tomorrow, various therapists will be looking at him more closely to see if we can get the speech restarted. We got his records from Carolina Manor, and it seems he already had limits on his mobility. Is that correct?"

"Yes," she replied.

"He will need a good bit of therapy for his right arm and leg, but I think we can restore most of what he had before. We'll move him to rehab on Monday. How does that sound?" he asked.

"Wonderful," she said happily. "Thank you so much!"

"Remember, the doctor who sent him here deserves the most credit. We don't know where he would be without early intervention."

"Yes, he stopped by today, and I did thank him," Maggie said.

"Okay. Be sure to get some rest. If you're determined to stay with your husband tonight, then ask for a pillow and a blanket. See you tomorrow." And with that, he was gone. Maggie sat there wondering if she really appreciated all his fatherly advice.

A couple of their friends stopped by and Carson's sister called. Maggie phoned her principal, and he told her to stay put. He would get a sub for her classes. For the next few days, at least, she would remain at the hospital.

On Sunday, Maggie began to worry about Carson's move to rehab. Change was hard for him. When he had surgery three years earlier, he had experienced "sundowning" after they moved him from intensive care to another wing. She prayed that wouldn't happen again.

As she sat wide-awake on Sunday night, she recalled the horror of sundowning. The night they had moved him to a new room Carson had gone to sleep but had awakened shortly afterwards. He methodically began pushing the covers away from him to the foot of the bed, a few inches at a time. When she had asked what he was doing, he wouldn't answer but stared straight ahead, never stopping the rhythmic effort to push away the thin blanket and sheet. Next, he slowly moved toward the rail, and she knew he was determined to get out of bed. He had tubes attached, and she begged him to stop, but he did not respond. He began to talk in sentence fragments. "Class charts. Roll isn't there. Second one. Watch out!" His eyes were glazed and unseeing. He appeared to be in some trance-like state.

She stood by the bed to block his exit, but he started to push harder against her. As his almost superhuman efforts to get up began to overwhelm her strength, she rang the bell for the nurse. Quickly, one appeared.

"I need help," she managed. "I can't get him to stay in bed, and I'm afraid he will pull the tubes out."

"Mr. Bales, Mr. Bales," the nurse said with great authority. "You need to lie back in the bed, sir." She tried in vain to remove his hands from the bedrail. They seemed frozen in place.

"Selenium isn't there!" he yelled. "Bring it!"

Both Maggie and the nurse tried to move him back onto the bed, but his amazing force resisted all their efforts. He kept moving off the edge. The nurse quickly used the call bell and summoned help.

A large, burly man appeared. Maggie's heart sank. "Please don't hurt him . . . please," she whimpered.

To the contrary, Maggie had never seen such a gentle man. He spoke very kindly to Carson as he held him firmly, but considerately.

"Sir, I am here to keep you from getting hurt. What is your name?" he asked.

"Dr. Carson Bales!" Carson yelled.

"And, Dr. Bales, who is this lovely lady standing here?" he asked gently, as he pointed to Maggie.

Carson stared blankly in her direction. He said nothing.

"Okay, sir, I need to help you get back into bed so you won't hurt yourself."

The nurse turned to Maggie and said apologetically, "This is called 'sundowning,' ma'am. It happens at night sometimes for older people who have had some trauma to their bodies such as surgery and anesthesia. It especially happens to those with dementia. Unfortunately, doctors forget to warn families about the possibility. It looks like we will have to restrain your husband for his own safety. I hope you understand."

"Do what you need to," Maggie said in a small, trembling voice.

The rest of the night was the worst in Maggie's life. Carson never stopped struggling against the jacket that held his arms to his chest. The jacket straps were tied to the bed rails and headboard, keeping him stationary. He kept saying repeatedly he had ruined Christmas and how sorry he was for doing that. She had absolutely no idea what he was talking about.

Maggie remembered staying motionless in her chair, not wanting him to look at her or plead with her for help. As much as she wanted to, she could not release him from his bondage. Soon, however, he turned his head in her direction.

"Bring me the pliers," he commanded.

"I don't have any pliers."

"Can't you get some?" he wailed.

"No, I don't know where they are."

"Are you tied up, too?" he asked.

Having no idea what to say, Maggie responded, "Yes, I am."

Carson began to cry. "Now I've done it! Now I've done it! What can I do to get us out of here? I'm so sorry."

Maggie tried to think. How could she distract him? It was 3 a.m., but she started singing. Carson had always loved hymns. She could barely carry a tune, but that didn't matter now. As she began the first verse of "Softly and Tenderly," he joined in. She sang hymns the rest of the night. Carson would sing until the song ended, but before she could search her memory for another, he would begin to chant again. "Now I've done it. Now I've done it."

At last, she noticed the room growing lighter. Carson noticed, too. "What's that?" he demanded. She wasn't certain what he meant. He pointed in the direction of the window.

"I think the sun is coming up," she answered.

"Well, look!" he ordered.

She moved to the window and opened the blinds. As the rays of a new day illuminated the room, Carson began to smile. "Okay . . . okay," he said, and promptly fell asleep!

That scenario repeated itself for many nights as soon as the sun faded from the sky. Finally, he adjusted to the new environment. But Maggie would never forget that experience—not ever. His terror was matched by hers as the sun set, and she watched him struggle to get away from whatever haunted him until the morning brought relief.

However, this time when he was moved, both Carson and she were spared the insult of another such episode. He seemed not to even notice the difference in the rooms. Maggie knew, in its own way, that wasn't good either.

In the days following his move to rehab, Carson's progress was extremely slow. Even his optimistic doctor seemed concerned. His speech was still incomprehensible. The sounds reminded Maggie of those Beth had made. She learned if she pointed to different objects and asked him what they were she could detect some differentiation of sounds. However, if he tried to tell her something of his own choosing, she got none of it.

One night, as she stood beside him holding his hand, she felt a light pressure. Then he whispered something so low she couldn't hear it. She bent closer to his face and asked him to repeat it. This time, she clearly heard him utter one word, "Tight."

"Yes, yes," she cried. "Oh, darling, you've got it!" She squeezed his hand very hard hoping he might say it again. However, he closed his eyes and soon was making snoozing sounds. "Well, it wasn't much," she whispered to him, "but you've made me one happy woman tonight."

One Friday afternoon, after Maggie had been at Carson's side for two weeks, Dr. Holton stopped by. It was his third visit to check on him. Maggie was writing lesson plans.

"Hi, Maggie. Dr. Stevenson told me yesterday you were still keeping a vigil. He is worried about you." He paused, then continued. "While I admire your stamina, I'm going to take advantage of my white coat here and prescribe a night out for you. You look like you need some fresh air. And selfishly, I have several questions about Rose and Carolina Manor I thought you might answer. I finish rounds at eight. How about getting some coffee? Remember, doctor's orders," and he smiled.

Maggie was caught off-guard, so it took her a moment to respond. He waited.

"Well, I suppose it would be all right." She later thought how lame that sounded, but at the time, it was the best she could do.

"Great. Let's meet at the new coffee shop over on Cassidy Street. Do you know where it is?"

"Yes, I've been there before."

"How about eight thirty?"

"Okay," she said simply.

After he left, she realized she was in her scruffy jeans. She decided to go home and get a quick shower and change of clothes.

Once at home, she looked into the mirror and thought Dr. Holton must have agreed she was on the verge of illness, too. She couldn't believe how pale she looked. There were dark circles under her eyes. Her hair was limp. Her jeans hung loosely. "You *are* a mess," she chided.

She took a long, hot shower. As she toweled off, she realized she had lost weight. No wonder her jeans didn't fit. She hung the towel over the hook beside the shower, sprayed mousse on her wet hair, and began to blow it dry. Hopefully, she could bring some life back to it. It had always been one of her better features.

She chose a pair of navy wool slacks with a turquoise sweater. She had a navy and turquoise tweed jacket, but she decided that might be too dressed up for the occasion, so she removed her black, short coat from its hanger. She applied her usual dab of make-up. Her hair responded nicely to the brush tonight.

"Okay. At least I look like I'm among the living," she voiced as she glanced in the mirror. Maggie almost felt like herself again, even though it was a weary self. Maybe the doctor had given her the right prescription after all. She knew she needed a good, hot meal. She glanced at the clock and saw she had time before meeting Dr. Holton. She picked up her coat and purse and headed for the car. Pulling into the parking lot of the restaurant, she even noticed hunger pangs.

CHAPTER 8

Maggie lingered over her favorite pasta dish—angel hair, scallops, and asparagus—slowly coiling the angel hair around her fork, a strand at a time. She didn't want to be the first to arrive at the coffee shop. She wondered what questions Dr. Holton had about Carolina Manor. Should she tell him about the earlier episode with Rose? Perhaps not.

She checked her watch, paid the check, and pulled on her coat. She braced for the chilly air. As she walked to her car, with the wind stinging her face, she decided if Dr. Holton thought she needed fresh air, she had just filled the prescription.

She drove into the parking lot and hoped her ten-minute delay had given him time to arrive. Indeed, she could see him through the window at a small table in the alcove. He stood as she entered and motioned to her.

"Hi," he said, and she could tell he was taking notice of her change of clothing. He was in navy slacks, too, and a lovely plaid sweater in shades of navy, gray, and cream, over an open-collar cream shirt. Quite a dresser, she thought. She guessed his age to be midsixties.

She felt awkward as he moved to help her with her chair. She realized she hadn't spoken since she came in. Quickly, she said, "If fresh air was your order, doctor, I got quite a dose just coming in from the car."

He laughed. "Well, it has certainly put a blush on your cheeks that wasn't there this afternoon."

She was glad when the server appeared. He ordered black coffee, and she ordered hers with cream. Maggie realized this was the same order the night she first had coffee with Carson. Her eyes misted at the thought.

Dr. Holton noticed immediately. "Hey, are you okay? Did I say something out of place?"

"No, no," she responded. "I just had a moment of déjà vu. I'm sorry. The first night I met my husband, we had coffee, and it was cold outside. I just realized that our order tonight was the same as that night long ago."

"I understand, Maggie. Sometimes I can be in the most unlikely places and have some flashback of Rose and me that leaves me feeling weak. It's hard to let go of the people they were, isn't it?"

"I'm . . . I'm not sure I have," Maggie said in a soft voice. "I've grown used to living alone, but I haven't grown used to being lonely. Does that make sense?"

"It certainly does," he sighed. "I walk into the house after a long day with patients or residents and almost call out for Rose in hopes she will come to meet me so I can just feel her presence and her serenity. I always have a letdown feeling when I realize she isn't there."

They continued with similar stories until their coffee arrived. She quickly picked up her oversized cup and let its heat penetrate her icy fingers.

Dr. Holton—Bill, he insisted—asked about Carson. They discussed the slowness of the recovery. She asked about Rose. Bill explained that Rose suffered from early-onset Alzheimer's disease, just as her father had. He was worried about her. She had not been as lucid recently. They both knew Alzheimer's patients showed more confusion when there were physical problems. Bill believed Rose's jumbled thoughts could be a signal of something more sinister.

They talked slowly at first, but as each of their stories seemed to overlap with loss and grief, the conversation gained momentum. They both seemed hungry for another person who truly understood what they were going through. They sometimes talked over each other and had to stop and apologize.

She learned he and Rose had had one son, William. Maggie could hear the pride in Bill's voice as he talked about him. He told her about William's trophies in soccer throughout high school and college. He had studied law at Duke University. Later, William, his wife, and two daughters had moved to Germany where he was a junior member of the diplomatic corps, with a promising future.

"He was just crossing the street one day in Hamburg—like any other day—when he was struck by a car. He died within a few hours after he arrived at the hospital. Rose and I were trying to get airline tickets when Betsy, our daughter-in-law, called to say he was gone. One of the great regrets of my life is not being there with him." The deep sadness in Bill's eyes grabbed Maggie's heart.

"Rose never recovered from the grief. She often had on fresh make-up when I came home from work, but I knew she was trying to hide the evidence of the tears she had shed earlier. She always met me at the door with a smile, however. We talked about William sometimes, but for the most part, we each tried to hide our grief from the other. It was just so painful."

He told Maggie he often wondered if that had been the right approach after all. "Lord knows, I wanted to cry until I was empty, but I always felt I had to be brave for Rose. And I'm certain she felt the same about me, as I look back."

Bill said Betsy had been good to keep in touch, and she often sent pictures of the granddaughters. However, she had married again three years ago, so Bill didn't feel comfortable making frequent telephone calls anymore. They only talked when Betsy called to get an update on Rose. Both girls were teenagers now, and he found he was out of touch with their lives. Maggie noticed the pain on his face as he talked.

Maggie told Bill she and Carson had no children, but she didn't tell him why. Instead, she told him Carson had a daughter from a first marriage, and Beth had lived her life in a private hospital for the mentally handicapped, defying all odds of doctors' predictions. Maggie recounted Beth's funeral four years earlier when Carson's Alzheimer's disease was already noticeable. Maggie had ached for him when he stood at the graveside with tears streaming down his cheeks as Reverend Adams offered the final prayer over his precious daughter. Bill could tell from the softness in Maggie's eyes that Beth held a special place in her heart, too.

Each story was accompanied with tones of love for their spouses and the helplessness of their situations. And each understood the other perfectly.

Finally, she realized the customers had dwindled to only one man who sat studying his laptop in a far booth. She looked at her watch. It was almost eleven. She was jarred back to the present.

"Oh, my," she exclaimed. "Look at the time!"

Bill, too, seemed surprised. "I'm sorry I've kept you so long. You may never follow doctor's orders again," he said with a grin.

"Well, the doctor should have ordered a muzzle," she quipped. "I can't believe I've talked so long."

"I hardly think it was a one-way conversation, Maggie. What I do think is that we both needed a listening ear—someone who knows the face of Alzheimer's. And speaking for me, I would like to do this again. Maybe we can be our own small support group," he said with a smile.

In a quiet voice, she said, "I feel almost guilty about the calmness this evening has brought. People who haven't experienced the disease firsthand mean well, but their comments are so general and unrealistic in dealing with the situations and worries it brings." She stopped, unsure what to say next.

"I know, Maggie, I know. Even my medical friends don't understand. That's why it would be nice to talk with you again, if you agree." He waited for her response.

"Yes . . . yes, I would like that, too," she said slowly.

"Would you like to meet again next Friday night, say, here at the same time?"

"Yes, that would be good," she answered.

On her way to Carson's room, she suddenly realized they had not discussed Carolina Manor at all. Perhaps next Friday.

Carson was asleep, issuing a gentle snoring sound. His mouth still drooped on the right side and a small trickle of saliva eased down his chin. She wiped it away with a tissue. She leaned over his bed and kissed his forehead. "I love you," she said softly.

Carson stirred and she took his hand. He did not open his eyes, but she could see his mouth working a bit. Some sound came from it that was inaudible to her ear. She leaned closer.

"What did you say?" she whispered.

He made one more effort, but it was useless. She took his hand and kissed it tenderly before releasing it. Carson was already snoring gently again as she curled up in the chair.

On the following Monday, Maggie went back to her classroom. It was unfair to the students and to the school to stay away any longer. After all, she had to carry her weight, she told herself. Teachers and students seemed glad to see her, and she held back tears as different ones told her how much she had been missed. The day passed quickly.

She continued to teach during the day, go home just long enough to change into more comfortable clothes, return to Carson's room and the recliner where she slept at night. She still wanted to be near him when he woke during the night to give him a sense of security and familiarity. In the morning, she returned home to shower and dress for the day. She could feel the fatigue in every bone of her body.

By Friday night, she was so weary she wished she knew Dr. Holton's telephone number so she could call and cancel their meeting. She didn't find it listed in the phone directory, so she splashed some water on her face and ran a brush through her hair. She didn't even change her clothes.

He was sitting at the same table when she walked in. As he rose, she saw a look of concern cross his face.

"Are you okay?" he asked quickly.

"Oh, I'm fine," she responded, trying to sound cheerful. "Just the end of a long week. I went back to school, and I'm still staying with Carson at night."

"I'm afraid I'm going to have to give you yet another prescription," he said, half smiling.

Strangely, his statement sent a shot of anger through her. Last week, she had accepted his "prescription" with good humor. But tonight she was reeling from the hectic pace of the week. She really did not need to be treated like a patient! Bill noticed her frown.

"I'm sorry. I was kidding, but I can see you didn't appreciate my attempt at humor."

Maggie was chagrined her emotions had been so obvious. "It's okay. Maybe my fatigue and worry keep me from seeing the funny side of life just now," she said with a weary voice she tried to disguise. "Don't worry. A cup of coffee will raise my spirits, I'm sure."

He summoned the server, and they ordered. She was right. The steaming, caffeine-loaded coffee had at least a temporary euphoric effect on her mood. Soon they were chatting as they had a week ago when they had sat in this same spot.

Bill and Rose had met when they were both sophomores at Wake Forest University. He was a biology major, and she had a scholarship to study piano. He had loved to hear her practice and had attended every performance she gave for the next two and a half years. She also played for St. Paul's Episcopal Church on Sunday mornings. He was present at every service, though his presence was for Rose rather than an indication of his religious fervor, he admitted.

"On Christmas Eve of our senior year, I gave Rose my grandmother's engagement ring, which my parents had generously had reset for the occasion. We made plans to marry the following summer after our May graduations."

Rose was from Greenville in Pitt County and the second daughter in her very affluent family, but she was the first one to marry. Her family's social circles were buzzing with anticipation of the wedding. Bill recounted that he wanted to marry in June but was quickly told by Rose's mother they must have more time to properly prepare for the most important event in their lives. Sure enough, they were feted all summer with parties of every imaginable sort—showers, pool parties, North Carolina pig pickin's, formal dinners at the Greenville country club, shag dances, and the list went on. Rose's wardrobe for all those events would carry her through several years of their early marriage when he could ill afford to buy nice clothes for her, Bill conceded.

Bill told Maggie all about the wedding. It was a lavish affair. The church was overflowing with both people and flowers.

"Rose had twelve bridesmaids, and her mother insisted each one have an escort for the recessional. I had to round up every friend I had in both high school and college to be groomsmen. I spent the next five years going to their weddings as payback.

"When I stood at the altar with the minister and my entourage, the aisle became a sea of mint green as the bridesmaids floated down to the altar railing. The dresses had these giant flounces, I think they're called. Anyway, as the bridesmaids walked toward me, the hoops propelled the flounces like pendulums on clocks. I thought I was going to be hypnotized." With that, Maggie broke into giggles.

"I'm sorry," she said when she gained control. "I know it was lovely, but I just pictured you in a trance with glazed eyes. Anyway, I love your descriptions, so please continue." Bill was smiling, too.

He told her the bridesmaids carried huge bouquets of calla lilies, tied in mint green satin ribbon. Their skirts filled every inch between the railing and the first pew. The groomsmen wore black tuxedos with mint green boutonnières.

"Yes, to this day, I don't like pistachio ice cream," he chuckled. "Nothing against the marriage, but I can still see those mounds of mint green moving toward me like ocean waves that might suck me under. I remember wondering just how many yards of fabric it must have taken to make those dresses. But at least Rose's mother loved every moment. Rose was sick at her stomach the night before—a bug, her mother said—but I always figured it was a bad case of nerves."

Bill said Rose had walked down the aisle in her grandmother's wedding dress that was all lace. The train swept behind her some ten feet. Her long veil was so poufed he was not certain he was marrying the right woman until her maid of honor lifted it for him to kiss his bride.

"I was sure relieved when I saw I had married Rose." They both chuckled.

"I'm amazed you can remember all those details," she said.

"Oh, the reception was equally grand and lasted well into the evening," Bill continued. "At that point, I just wanted to take my bride and ride away, but I endured toast after toast and dance after dance. I remember how much my feet hurt in my rented shoes, yet Rose told me I had to dance with every dowager in town *and* her nubile daughters to satisfy my social obligations. Finally, sometime past midnight, we left for our honeymoon. Of course, we were both too exhausted that night to feel anything akin to romance."

Maggie told her wedding story reluctantly. She certainly could not match the grandeur of his event. However, Bill seemed almost envious of the simplicity of her marriage.

"It really should be about just the bride and groom," Bill said. "In my assessment of weddings back then, many were supposed to reflect the status of the bride's family in the community—the bride and groom just supplied the reason to pull out all the stops. But then maybe I'm a bit jaded, or only a man, as Rose used to tell me," he said, grinning. "Was your family angry that you didn't have a big affair?" he asked.

"No," Maggie said quietly. She had no intention of revealing anything about her family or her early years. When Bill realized she wasn't going to say more, he began to tell her about his own family.

Bill's parents had very modest means compared to Rose's family, though he had never experienced any sense of deprivation while growing up. His father owned a small printing company in Asheville that was moderately successful, and his mother was a bookkeeper for a law firm. Bill was an only child. His mother had had several miscarriages before he was born.

His parents insisted on paying his expenses in college so he could focus on his studies. They knew his dream was to go to medical school, and they hoped his grades would be good enough to get him admitted into a topnotch program. He was accepted at Duke University, where William would attend later.

"My parents were so proud of me. And I have to admit, I was pleased, too. I honestly wasn't sure I could do it," he confessed to Maggie.

Soon the conversation drifted to Carson and Rose. Bill thought Rose was holding her own now. No big improvements, but she wasn't continuing to slide. Meanwhile, Maggie feared Carson was not getting better and worried about the ramifications that his declined state would have on his stay at Carolina Manor. He would not be able to return to the Alzheimer's wing if he needed the same intense care he had in rehab.

"He should qualify for the skilled care unit," Bill said.

Maggie had completely forgotten about that wing. "Oh, do you think so?" and she guessed her voice had such a sound of hopefulness he was quick to respond.

"Yes, yes I do. Definitely! When they release him from the rehab unit, he should be able to move directly into skilled," he said.

The relief in her voice was touching. "Oh, that would make it so much easier. I want him out of the hospital, but I have been so worried about where he will go. I know he can't go back to his old room because those residents must at least be able to walk with assistance. The staff members aren't allowed to lift them. Thanks so much for this information. It gives me some hope." She was smiling broadly.

Their conversation didn't last as long this time as the first, but as they stood to go, he put his hand on her shoulder. "Maggie, I'm going to try this again without any humor. As a physician who looks for signs of stress in people, I truly think you should stop spending the nights with Carson and sleep in your own bed. You look not just tired, but haggard, and you're pale. I noticed a slight tremor in your hand as you stirred the cream into your coffee cup. These things tell me you need more rest. But please know I respect your right to make your own choices," he said gravely.

Maggie smiled, "I have to admit you're on the right track. I know I'm tired. I have a hard time concentrating, and easy decisions seem like mountains to climb. I promise to consider your sage medical advice," she said with a feeble smile.

"That's all I can ask," he offered. "Same time next week?"

"Yes, and I hope to look and feel perkier," she said trying to put a lilt to her voice.

As she pulled out of the parking lot, she felt aches in every bone. "I *am* tired," she conceded. However, she could not bring herself to leave Carson alone all night, at least not tonight. Maggie's conversation with Bill had wrapped her in all the memories of the past, and she just wanted to sink into the recliner beside Carson's bed and listen to him make wonderful sleep sounds—to know he was still there, and she could reach over and touch him.

Maggie slept fitfully. Her dreams were of a young and healthy Carson. But each dream was interrupted by scary shadows that appeared. She was thankful when she noticed the first glow of daylight, and she walked once more to the small sink to splash some water on her face. She looked at Carson who still appeared to be sleeping. She decided to hurry home for a quick shower and change of clothes.

But on Sunday morning, she felt so tired she didn't even try to go home. Carson slept more than usual, so she made out lesson plans, graded two sets of papers, and worked crossword puzzles. Bill's words kept running through her mind all afternoon. How long could she continue to stay by Carson's bedside at night? Each week, she hoped for some news from the doctors about his progress that would indicate how much longer they thought he would be hospitalized. Dr. Stevenson offered little information now except to say his progress was much slower than expected. The thought of stretching out full length on her own bed with real sheets made her bones ache even more. Was her presence in Carson's room every night helping his recovery even a little? Apparently not.

Finally, at seven o'clock that evening, she made a decision. As Bill had said, it does Carson no good if I exhaust myself to the point of illness. She visibly nodded her head in agreement. With that thought, she packed up her books, papers, and overnight bag, kissed a dozing Carson on the forehead, and slipped out the door. She alerted the nurses she would not be staying overnight.

Later, when she crawled into her own bed, every fear and worry she had stifled since that ominous phone call washed over her. She slid down under the cool sheet and began to cry. Her tears became giant sobs as she fought to catch her breath. Maggie sensed Carson was not going to get better—not going to walk again or even speak again. The pain of that realization kept fueling her tears until they finally washed away every ounce of hope she had clung to.

She had no idea how long she lay like that, but finally there were no more tears inside her. She felt drained, but calm. She lay quietly until sleep took her into another dimension.

Maggie slowly became aware of a shrill sound, but she seemed to be in some dense fog she could not escape. Finally, ratcheting herself above the shroud, she realized the phone beside her bed was ringing. She could not remember where she was, but she instantly felt overwhelming alarm. "Carson!" she cried. She grabbed the receiver and screamed, "What's wrong?"

"Maggie! Maggie, are you okay?" her principal asked.

"Oh, Carl, it's you," Maggie gasped, and then confused, asked, "Why is it you?"

She heard him laugh. "Because you aren't at school, and you usually are on school days, that's why."

She looked at the small clock that had kept her on schedule for the last twenty years. "Oh my goodness—8:51 a.m.! Oh, Carl, I obviously overslept. No, I know what happened. I came home last night for the first time since Carson went to the hospital, and I forgot to set the alarm. I've become accustomed to the nurses coming in at six o'clock in the morning, and I haven't needed an alarm. I'll be there as soon as possible." She was stammering and slightly incoherent, she knew.

Carl, who had known her for many years, said in reassuring tones, "Don't worry. I was just concerned when you didn't show up and didn't call. I knew something was different. I have Jayne Markowski with the students now. She has a planning period. We can cover until you get here. Just take your time, and don't do any crazy driving."

"Thanks, Carl. I'll be there within the hour. I'm so, so sorry."

Even in her haste to get to the shower, she felt an unexpected sense of pleasure because she had slept so soundly. How long had it been since she had had that much sleep in one night?

"Dr. Holton, you just might have been right after all," she trilled.

Chapter 9

Maggie had a spring in her step as she approached the table where Bill was waiting Friday night. He was reading a paper but immediately rose when he caught sight of her.

"Look at you!" he said, smiling. "I see color in those cheeks and sparkles in those eyes." He held out his hand, and when he took hers, he didn't let go for a moment.

She laughed. "I'm sure you're congratulating yourself on your diagnosis and prescription. And, yes, I have been sleeping in my own bed this week."

"Well, well, and you're reaping the benefits of such wise counsel, my dear."

After they ordered the usual coffee, Bill became more serious. "How's Carson?"

"Dr. Stevenson told me on Tuesday he is not showing any real improvement, so he will be moved back to Carolina Manor next week. I called the social worker at Carolina during my lunch period yesterday, and she will begin the process of reassigning Carson from the Alzheimer's wing to skilled care. I do look forward to his being out of the hospital. I've come to hate hospitals and all the endless noise of machines, equipment, and people. At least Carolina Manor is more peaceful."

She stopped. "Sorry," she said. "Guess I am just a little wound up tonight."

He laid his hand on her arm and said earnestly, "Maggie, you've been through an awful ordeal. No need to stifle any emotions with me. I understand so well that, as caregivers, we try to wrap all of these changes into neat little bundles we can carry with us and never take the paper off. But it just doesn't work like that. Sooner or later, the bundles will grow larger, and the wrappings will fly apart."

The sincerity in his eyes, the gentle pressure of his hand, and his soft words were more than Maggie could bear. Tears began sliding down her cheeks.

"Whoa! I certainly didn't mean to make you cry," he said, leaning toward her.

She reached for a tissue. "No, that's okay. I guess some of the tape on the fancy wrapping paper just gave way. You're right. I always try to seem so 'together' when people ask about Carson. I just don't want their sympathy. Bill, it's such a relief to talk to someone who knows the challenges."

"Same here."

He took his hand back, and she felt a small chill cross her arm.

"How is Rose?"

"Not well this week. I continue to have some feeling—medical or just gut—that she's changing. She is almost uncommunicative now and seems listless."

"I'll try to stop in and see her when Carson gets back."

"Thanks. She . . . and I . . . would like that. She always enjoyed company. She was very sociable. Got that from her mother, I suppose. However, I can't promise she will say much, if anything, to you now."

"I certainly understand, but I will look in on her anyway," Maggie offered.

During coffee they began to talk of the past again. Memories of happier times seemed to keep the present at bay, Maggie had realized earlier.

She told Bill about always wanting to travel and never fulfilling that dream. "Carson and I promised each other we would see the world together. When we married, I knew he had a big financial responsibility for Beth's care. He was just making ends meet, but we thought two incomes would take care of Beth and give us some extra money for trips abroad.

"Carson lived in a small house near campus, so after the wedding,

I moved in with him. In our second year, the University started buying property around us to use for a new classroom building. We didn't want to be surrounded by pavement, plus having students traipsing through our lawn, so we sold that house.

"Of course, that meant buying another home. We decided to move to the side of town most accessible to Magnolia, but the homes were more expensive. So we put our travel plans on hold and started making double mortgage payments, believing we would pay for the house as soon as possible and then satisfy our wanderlust.

"However, first, my car dropped dead one day in an intersection on the way to school. There was no resurrection of my old faithful. Later, Carson's bit the dust, too. Then we had two car payments *plus* the mortgage.

"Just after we finished the car payments, the roof leaked during a heavy rainstorm, and the result was a new roof. Two years later, the heating system waved good-bye.

"So, one thing after another took precedence over our elusive travel. Four years ago after Beth died we could have traveled, but Carson was beginning to wander. I couldn't take the chance of a trip." She stopped, suddenly feeling weary and wrung out.

Bill had listened intently to her. She loved the fact he never took his eyes from hers. He never seemed restless or bored with her chatter. He seemed to let it soak in as thirsty soil accepts rain. Only Carson had ever given her such complete attention. A faint warmth spread through her.

"Rose and I loved to travel, too. I feel sad you and Carson didn't enjoy that together because some of my best memories involve our trips. I hope travel is in your future, Maggie."

"Yes . . . well . . . not anytime soon," she said wistfully.

As they were leaving the table, Bill held her coat as usual, but this time, he let his arm linger around her shoulders. He turned her toward his face and said in a soft voice, "You are a fine woman, Maggie. I'm glad you're my friend."

To her total dismay, Maggie almost wished he would kiss her. She moved quickly away from his arm, pretending to look for the gloves she had not worn.

As he walked her to her car, he asked, "What about dinner next week? I think we could be a bit more imaginative than coffee every Friday, don't you?"

Maggie wasn't certain how to answer. Yes, she would love to have dinner, but was that moving in a new direction? Still, she found it hard to say no.

"I guess one cannot live by coffee alone," she said in a vain attempt at humor.

Bill smiled. "I've heard good things about a new place close to Southern Seasons. Would you like to give it a try?"

"Sure," she said, trying to sound casual about the whole matter.

"Shall we meet there . . . or shall I pick you up?" he asked tentatively.

"Oh," she hesitated. "I'll meet you there. Just give me directions."

Bill nodded, and she guessed they both understood why. "I'll have to call you this week with the exact location."

He opened her car door, and they said brief good-byes. Maggie's thoughts were jumbled on the way home.

Monday morning, Maggie was handing back homework papers when her intercom alerted her to a phone call. Dr. Stevenson was calling to tell her he was writing orders for Carson to return to Carolina Manor on Wednesday. He seemed apologetic that rehabilitation had not produced the desired results. Maggie asked him what he saw for Carson's future.

"Probably more of the same," he said. "I think he could live for quite a while without walking or talking. He seems to be in overall good health. I believe the Alzheimer's disease played a major role in his inability to respond to rehab, but we will never know. There just isn't enough research to help us on this one."

Maggie thanked him for his care of Carson, and they hung up, each knowing that was probably the last time they would talk. Maggie walked slowly back to her classroom, pondering the future.

The social worker at Carolina made all the arrangements for moving everything from Carson's room to the skilled care unit. Maggie didn't have to go back to his room, but she wanted to see it one last time. She decided to do that on Friday so she could tell Bill during their dinner she had stopped in to see Rose.

On Wednesday, Maggie went immediately after school to see Carson in his new room. She arranged his clothing and toiletries in drawers, connected the cable to the television, hung his two favorite pictures, and put boxes of tissues in accommodating places while she chatted about her day, knowing he would not respond. But he did follow her around the room with his eyes. Those eyes had seemed to warm a few degrees when she had first come into the room and kissed him hello. She believed he, too, was glad to be away from the hospital and that made her heart lighter. The staff brought his dinner, and Maggie helped feed him.

Finally, at nine o'clock she noticed he was asleep. She tiptoed to his bed and kissed his forehead. "Sleep tight," she whispered. He did not awaken, so she picked up her coat and purse and gently closed the door behind her. A new chapter had begun.

Thursday afternoon, she stopped into a local women's boutique to look for a blouse. She told herself she had needed a few wardrobe additions for awhile. It had nothing to do with dinner Friday evening. She had never spent a lot on clothing. She preferred classics to fads, and she usually shopped when clothes were on sale. However, a bright blouse or sweater gave new life to her tailored pants suits—her teaching uniform—so she occasionally indulged.

She found a pretty coral blouse that would be great with the gray pinstriped pants and jacket. The clerk told her the blouse was just her color. Never mind the sales pitch, Maggie thought, but it did bring out her hazel eyes. After paying, she walked jauntily to the car, swinging the pink plastic bag.

She decided to drop by to see Carson before she went home. He was awake when she entered the room. The stroke had affected Carson's smile. She saw his face make the funny, screwy motion that caused her to smile in return.

"Hi, sweetheart!" she sang out. "Don't you look good today." She leaned over to give him a big hug. He never hugged her back anymore, and sometimes Maggie thought that was the hardest part of this disease. She had treasured their lovemaking, but throughout their marriage, there had never been anything as comforting as Carson's hugs.

She sat by his bed and held his hand while she told him about her day. Maggie loved her students and told him about each one's progress—and occasionally, the lack of such. He had known she always agonized over those students who were having difficulties, believing there was a key that would unlock their abilities if she could just find it.

She heard the dinner cart coming down the hall, so she decided to say goodbye. The nurse's assistant would feed him. Maggie kissed him lightly on the cheek. "See you tomorrow," and she made her way to the door. She blew a kiss and stepped into the hallway. Carson had not uttered a sound during her visit. She sighed.

Friday afternoon, after Maggie visited Carson, she walked to the other wing to look at his old room. As she approached, a woman in her early forties walked out of "his" door. Maggie stopped abruptly and realized someone was already occupying the room. She was surprised Carolina Manor had so quickly moved someone else into Carson's space. But she smiled at the woman and extended her hand.

"Hi, I'm Maggie Bales. My husband used to be in this room, and I was just coming by to be sure we didn't leave anything behind." Not quite true, but Maggie wasn't ready to explain to a stranger she wanted one last look at a room that would forever be etched in her mind.

"I'm Mildred Cross. My mother was just assigned here. We haven't found anything that isn't hers, but if we do, I'll turn it in at the nurses' station." She was curt but in a weary sort of way, like this whole situation was too overwhelming. Maggie's heart went out to her.

Maggie thanked her and walked the four or five steps to Rose's room. She knocked lightly and got no answer. The door was slightly ajar, so she peeped inside. Rose was wrapped in a pretty quilt and appeared to be sleeping peacefully in her chair. Maggie decided not to awaken her.

As she walked to the car, Maggie struggled briefly with seeing Rose and having dinner with Bill. Well, it certainly wasn't a date. She and Bill simply shared a common enemy. The conflict vanished at the same time she turned the key in the ignition.

Later, at home, she showered and dressed, putting on the new blouse. She admired the color again. Dressed for the evening, she backed the car out of the garage, temporarily holding the piece of paper with the directions between her teeth.

The air was cold, but clear. She enjoyed the evening skies in fall.

The stars were more vivid, and there was nothing like a Carolina harvest moon on a crisp night. It seemed to sparkle as its reflection danced through atmospheric ice crystals.

She could see swirls of exhaust fumes coming from the cars ahead of her as she waited to turn into the restaurant parking lot. The lot was full, but she found a parking place by waiting for someone to back out. She looked for Bill's car, but didn't see it. Darn! She did not like to arrive first.

Just then a horn honked, and she looked in the rear view mirror. She saw Bill waving to her from his car. She rolled her window down, and he said, "Hey, you got lucky. I've driven around twice, but I'll keep trying. Just wait and I will escort you from your car, ma'am, after I get this rig parked." He gave a playful bow.

Maggie smiled, waved in response, and rolled her window up to keep out the cold. Bill drove a Mercedes—a large, black one. Maggie sat there wondering if he also lived in a large house.

Soon he was at her door. She grabbed her purse, stuffed the keys inside her coat pocket, and stepped into the frosty air. She quickly decided she was ordering coffee this evening, along with dinner. Or maybe not. She knew coffee was usually ordered only with dessert in nicer restaurants, but cold water certainly had no appeal to her right now. With Carson, she would never have given it a thought. If she wanted coffee, she would have ordered it. A slight sadness reached her heart.

The hostess showed them to a table along the wall. Although the room was crowded, the sounds of clinking glasses and low conversations created a pleasant ambiance. On the way to their table, Maggie took note of the yellow walls, the black lacquered chairs and tables, and the white tablecloths. The chair seats were upholstered in black and white tweed while yellow cloth napkins folded like crowns sat on top of the tablecloth. A square, black glass container held live yellow mums with some eucalyptus. Trendy, she decided.

When the hostess placed the menus before them, she asked if they wanted to see the wine list. Bill turned to Maggie. "Would you like some wine?" Ordinarily, Maggie didn't drink wine unless it was a special occasion such as a birthday or anniversary, but her cold hands reminded her wine had always warmed her insides. Still she paused. She suddenly felt awkward. She had not dined alone with anyone but Carson for so long, and for that moment, she missed him terribly.

Bill noticed her hesitation. "I enjoy red wine with dinner and believe it has some good medicinal qualities, but it is certainly your choice. However, a glass might be very therapeutic after a week with your students," he said with a twinkle.

His easy manner dissolved the sudden uneasiness that had emerged from out of nowhere. "Well, I'll have to leave the ordering to you. I do know I like white wines, though, and ones that aren't too tart. Beyond that, I'm lost."

"Fair enough," he said. "I think I can pick something you'll like." With that, the hostess placed the wine list in front of him and wished them a pleasant evening.

When the server came, Bill had already chosen the wines. After he left to fill the order, Bill asked about her day. Maggie told him she had stopped in to see Rose, but she had been sleeping in her chair.

"I didn't go by today," he said. "I had a late patient who works until five o'clock, but I have been her doctor for years, so I make an allowance for her hours."

They read the menus until the wine came. Maggie decided on the chicken and shrimp pasta with a small spinach salad. Bill ordered prime rib, the specialty of the evening.

After the server left with their orders, Bill lifted his glass and she responded in kind. "Here's to Carson and Rose," he said. She felt a sense of relief.

They talked about the past week. They shared snippets of information, each being attentive to the other. Conversations about their earlier lives had always come easy, but tonight they seemed more focused on the present.

Maggie learned Bill actually ironed his own shirts now. The cleaners made them much too stiff, he said. He was also handy with a vacuum cleaner. Bill discovered Maggie could repair the plug on a lamp cord, unstop a gutter, and caulk around a bathtub.

Their meals arrived, and they turned their attention to eating. They had just settled into enjoying the food when the sound of Bill's pager caused them both to look up. He took it off his belt and looked at the number.

"I'm sorry," he said. "Usually, I don't respond to these if I'm not on call, but it's a colleague of mine who's an emergency room physician. Ten to one, he wants a fourth for golf tomorrow, but in case it might be one of my patients, I need to return the call. I left my phone in the car. Please excuse me and continue eating."

Maggie didn't want to finish her dinner before Bill returned, so she idly watched other diners. Soon he was walking quickly toward her, negotiating the maze of tables. While he was still several paces away, she saw the stricken look on his face.

"I'm so sorry, but I have to go. It's Rose. They brought her into the emergency room about thirty minutes ago. Rick thinks it's her heart. I'll call you when I know something," and he dashed toward the door.

Maggie sat in disbelief. She had just seen Rose. Was she okay at that time? Was she really sleeping? Maggie's appetite was gone. She summoned the server and asked if he could put the food into take-out containers.

She paid the check with her credit card, picked up the cartons of food, along with her coat, and headed out the door. The drive back seemed long.

At home, she waited for Bill's call. She glanced through a new magazine, stared at the stack of ungraded homework, turned on the television but found nothing of interest, looked at the clock a dozen times, watered the plants, worked part of a crossword puzzle, took the clean dishes out of the dishwasher, and finally at eleven o'clock, put on her pajamas. At midnight, she turned off the light, both weary and awake with concern. Finally, she drifted off to sleep.

She awoke at 6:30 a.m. Pink light seeped in around the shades. It was going to be a sunny day—her favorite. The anticipation of the day helped her shake off the night's slumbers. She sat up in bed, hugged her knees for a few moments, and then tossed the covers aside.

As she headed toward the kitchen for her first cup of coffee, she tried to think of plausible reasons Bill hadn't called. She felt sure he had spent most of the night with Rose. She just hoped he was getting some sleep after they got her stabilized.

The phone rang at 8:20 a.m. Without a greeting, Bill said, "She died, Maggie."

She was not sure she had heard correctly. A long pause followed while she processed his words. Finally, she caught her breath and said, "Bill . . . oh, Bill . . . I'm so sorry. I just can't believe it."

"They did everything they knew to do until after two o'clock, but nothing worked. She breathed her last breath at 2:31 a.m. I held her hand and watched the monitor flat line." Bill sounded robotic, like a recording.

"I have no idea what to say. I feel numb. In my scenarios of what had happened, I didn't think of this one at all," she said quietly.

"I didn't want to call you during the night. Also, I needed to go home to get the phone numbers of her sisters, our daughter-in-law, and other relatives. I lay down for a couple of hours, but sleep didn't happen. So I made some strong coffee, and early this morning, I called everyone who is immediate family. Now I have to start planning the funeral. I guess I will wait until her sisters get here before I finalize the details. I want to honor their wishes, too." Then he paused.

"Please let me know if I can do anything to help—anything at all," Maggie offered, not sure what to say.

"Thanks, Maggie. I'm not sure what I need just now. It's such a shock. I'll be in touch—in the future." With that, he hung up.

Maggie held the receiver, staring at it for a long time. His last statement made her doubt he would ever call again. And, she thought, perhaps that was best.

CHAPTER 10

Rose's obituary appeared in the Sunday paper. Maggie saw it while drinking her coffee and noted the funeral service would be Tuesday afternoon at three o'clock at Christ Church in Raleigh where Rose had played the piano for services for almost forty years. "What dedication," Maggie said aloud.

Three o'clock. Maggie had a planning period at the end of her school day. She could leave during that hour without having to ask someone to cover a class and still get to the church on time. She would go to the service but not to the cemetery. She felt final rites should be reserved for the family and the closest of friends.

Tuesday afternoon, she stuffed the papers to be graded that evening into her well-worn book bag and locked her door. She had told Carl she would be leaving early, so she slipped out a side door nearest the parking lot. She noticed the day was not only sunny, but the temperature was milder than the past weeks had been. She was instantly grateful, thinking of those who would attend the graveside service.

As she drove through the church lot looking for a parking space, she was impressed with how many cars were already there, and it was still forty-five minutes before the service. Finally, she found a spot, pulled in, and checked her make-up in the visor mirror. Maggie never remembered to bring her small cosmetic bag to school. Touch-ups were not something she did on any regular basis. She could have used some blush as she noted her pale cheeks. Sorry, but the so-called twelve-hour make-up had failed before the seventh hour! It had never been tested on women who spent six hours a day teaching fifth graders, she guessed.

At least that morning, she had remembered to dress appropriately. She had on her good black suit, a sedate white blouse, and her black suede pumps. She hoped to blend in with the mourners.

She stood in line to sign the guest register and then was seated near the back of the sanctuary by an usher who looked to be in his nineties. The pews were filling fast. It was obvious to Maggie the Holtons had been important members of this very old, revered church. As she sat reading the program, she remembered Bill had said Rose was the one who attended regularly. Of course, she would, Maggie thought. After all, she had to be there to play the piano. Maggie wondered how important church was to Bill. They had never discussed religion.

Promptly at three o'clock, the procession started down the aisle from the back of the church. Those gathered stood for the singing of the first hymn. The cross bearer, the priests, and the pall-covered casket were followed by the family. Maggie was near the aisle side of the pew, so she had a good view of the backs of heads. She saw Bill pass by first and then tried to figure out who the others were.

Probably it was the former daughter-in-law and her new husband who came next, followed by the teen-age granddaughters. The two older women with neatly coiffed hair, accompanied by men in somber navy suits, she guessed to be Rose's sisters. Following next was an assortment of men and women probably in their thirties with a sprinkling of children and more teenagers, most likely Rose's nieces and nephews and their children, Maggie surmised.

At the end of the hymn, the priest asked the guests to be seated. According to the program, the service looked much like others she had attended in recent years—ritualistic and perfunctory—but a far cry from funerals she remembered at Granny's Pentecostal church. There, mourners cried out in grief as the minister droned on and on about the virtues of the departed until he finally began giving altar calls for those among the congregation who hadn't yet received salvation. She knew the minister figured this was a choice time to remind them of their mortal souls.

However, certainly Episcopalians and her Methodist church used a much more subdued approach to eulogizing the deceased. Today, the priests read scriptures, said prayers, and delivered a brief homily that mentioned Rose's family, her service to the church, her many good deeds, and her stay at Carolina Manor. Next, a soloist with a spectacular voice sang one of Rose's favorite pieces of sacred music, according to the priest. It was not familiar to Maggie. The service ended when the priest commended Rose's soul to God in his final prayer.

The priests led the recessional, followed by the pallbearers with the casket. Bill came next. He looked drained, with downcast eyes, as he approached where she was standing. Maggie started to look away when the elderly woman beside her dropped her hymnal. The unexpected noise caused Bill to glance in Maggie's direction. He gave her the briefest of smiles and a nod. She nodded in response.

It was almost over. As she heard the final benediction, she wondered when it would be her turn to be the grieving spouse. She shuddered at the thought.

The next months were filled with her classes at school and visits to see Carson who had few fluctuations in his days now. The staff got him up daily to avoid pneumonia and bed sores. They used a mechanical lift to raise him from the bed and into his wheelchair. As the days grew longer and warmer, often she would find him sitting on the screened porch if she went to the Manor directly from school. Even though he couldn't tell her, she knew he enjoyed being in the fresh air. Without attempting to speak, he seemed to listen to her endless prattle about school, weather, chores, and so forth, and some days she saw the lopsided attempt at a smile cross his face. On those days, Maggie's heart was happy, temporarily easing the frustration that so often accompanied her home on other days.

It was early May, and Maggie was looking forward to the end of school. She loved her students and had always found joy in teaching them, but after nine months, she was ready for a break. Because the students were ready for the break, too, they were more restless and less eager to spend their days at desks.

"It's time to wrap up the year," she muttered to herself, as she stepped into her car one warm afternoon. "We all need summer again."

Later that evening, as she graded the last set of papers, her phone rang. She always prayed it was not bad news about Carson, so each time she picked up the receiver late in the evening, it was with a tentative hand. "Hello," she ventured cautiously.

"Hi, there." It was Bill's voice.

"Well, hello," she said with more enthusiasm than the first greeting. "How are you?" Was that the right choice of words? Probably not. She was never good at knowing what to say to the bereaved.

"I'm beginning to adjust," he offered. "Some days are better than others, but as you know, the grieving process begins long before death occurs when your loved one has Alzheimer's disease. I lost Rose in small pieces over time. I know you understand that."

"Yes, I do—I truly do," she replied. "One becomes widowed by degrees."

"And how's Carson?"

"About the same. I see him every day, but there are few changes. He still cannot speak or walk, but he seems to recognize me some days, and I count myself lucky for that."

"Yes, you are lucky," he said in a somber voice. There was a brief pause where it appeared neither of them knew what to say next. Bill broke the silence.

"I believe I owe you a dinner. I remembered weeks later after I left so abruptly I had not paid for our food and wine. I would like to make amends for that social faux pas. Are you up to dinner this Friday night?" he asked.

She searched for a response.

Her hesitation prompted him to say, "Maggie, perhaps I am assuming you enjoyed our meetings as much as I did. I think we still have lots to share that others don't really understand. But if things have changed for you, just say so, and I will still consider you my friend."

She chose her words cautiously. "Dinner would be . . . nice." Suddenly feeling bolder, she continued, "Actually, I would like that very much because you understand Carson's condition so well. I'm just not sure what I can contribute to help your grieving process now. I know you have moved on from the days when Rose was at Carolina Manor."

"Well, let's say I'm trying to move on. Sometimes, for a split second, I still think about going to see her there before I remember what happened," he replied. "Let me buy you dinner Friday night, and we'll see if the conversation is still as worthwhile to both of us as before. Fair enough?"

They settled on a place and time. She would meet him at the restaurant. Maggie hung up the phone and shook her head. She hadn't expected this, and certainly she hadn't expected the warm feeling that stirred inside.

The soft breeze on Friday evening buoyed her good spirits even more as she walked into the restaurant. Bill was there and watching for her. He waved to get her attention and stood immediately to hold her chair. He looked a little thinner but immaculately dressed. She wished she had chosen to wear something a little more stylish.

Whatever apprehensions they each might have had about the evening were soon washed away with the wine they drank. They talked long after they finished eating. The server cleared the table, brought coffee and two refills, and they were still leaning toward each other in animated conversation. Bill talked about Rose's family and their grief. He told about his granddaughters' stories they shared after the funeral as they remembered their grandmother. He explained the long list of details that had to be cleared up after Rose's death. He did not talk about his grief, and Maggie decided against pinning him to the emotional mat with her questions.

For her part, she talked about Carson's new status, her visits, the end of school, and her love of summer. The conversation flowed in the same easy manner it always had with no awkward pauses as they changed from one topic to another. Bill still had the same engaging ability to seem absolutely engrossed in what she said—and she imagined he did that with everyone. A charming trait, indeed.

After Bill paid the bill and she collected her purse, he moved her toward the door with his hand at her waist. It was gentle, but every nerve in her body seemed to feel the pressure. As he opened her car door, he asked, "Would you object if I got in on the passenger's side for a few minutes?"

"Well . . . sure, that's fine," she responded, but his words caused a slight shudder to roll through her. What did he want to say he hadn't said in the restaurant?

He slid in beside her with ease. She had guessed him earlier to be in his midsixties, but he had the fluid movements of a much younger man. He rolled the window down, and the evening breeze stroked his hair. She watched the wavy strands of gray rise and fall as he settled in and turned toward her.

"Maggie, I told you I have had so many thoughts of Rose since her funeral. They are there when I wake up, when I fall asleep, and many times in between. What I didn't say to you is that you cross my mind, too. I would like to continue our friendship. It's as valuable to me now as it was when Rose was alive. If you want that, too, then we can just continue as we have been, but if you don't, please tell me. I'm feeling pretty fragile right now, and I don't want to call you in the future and be turned down."

Maggie tried to evaluate his words but didn't get any resolution before she felt compelled to answer. Slowly, she said, "Well . . . you are the only person who really understands my worries and trials with Carson."

She paused again. "Yes, meeting would be nice . . . occasionally." She chose the last word on purpose, hoping it sounded casual, emphasizing the friendship quality of their relationship.

"Thanks. Maggie, as I once said to you, you're a fine woman. I admire you very much." With that, he reached for her hand that was on the steering wheel and gave it a gentle pat. "I'll be in touch real soon," and he was out of the car.

Maggie lay in bed that night thinking of their last conversation. Why was Bill afraid to be turned down? It wasn't like they were dating, after all. Did that statement indicate some insecurity in Bill she hadn't noticed before? Was it related to the grief process? Surely, he had other friends to dine with, didn't he? She had no answers. And why could she still feel the warmth of his hand on hers?

As the questions kept her tossing about, she longed for Carson and the security of his arms. Life with him had been so safe, so predictable. Would she ever *really* get used to his absence? Like so many other nights, tears slid down her cheeks and eventually lulled her to sleep.

CHAPTER 11

The last day of school before summer vacation! Maggie had always loved the anticipations that came with the warm days of June. Driving away from the school parking lot every year, she always asked God to keep each child safe during the summer. Then she allowed the expectation of days of freedom and leisure to settle around her. "The vacation won't get any longer than it is right now," she sang out. And Maggie intended to cling to every precious moment.

Bill had called her last week after he noticed the date for the end of school in the newspaper. He wanted to take her to dinner this evening in celebration. His invitation caused her to turn down her colleagues' cookout where they would welcome summer with beer and burgers.

She stopped to see Carson on her way home and practically floated across the parking lot. He had known how much she loved the long, hot days when she read or painted without any restraints on her time. Summer was always a special time for them. How Maggie wished he could share in her freedom again.

"Hi, there," she said gaily, entering his room. His expression changed only the slightest bit. "Guess what—this is the first hour of my summer vacation!" Carson's eyes followed her to his bed, but that was the extent of his excitement for her.

Today, nothing could dampen her spirits, so she plunged ahead with conversation, telling him about the students' war whoops when pizza had been delivered. That was her special surprise for them in celebration of the end of school. She told him about her plans to set up the easel and painting equipment on the screened porch tomorrow so she could try her hand again. Maggie had not painted since Carson had gone to Carolina Manor. Today, the feel of the brush in her hand and the stiffness of her paint-smattered smock against her skin beckoned to her.

She plumped his pillows, went to get ice for his water container, added fresh water from the tap, adjusted his blinds so the sun wasn't so bright, and looked around for anything more she could do to make him comfortable. Seeing nothing else and being at the end of conversational tidbits, she kissed his forehead and promised to return tomorrow.

The crooked tilt on his face slumped back to its previous state, and he closed his eyes. She didn't know if that meant he was ready for a nap or he was angry she was leaving. That was just it—it was so hard to know what he was thinking. Sometimes, it was maddening!

After she arrived home, Maggie decided to take a shower. It seemed symbolic of washing away another school year and looking forward to a fresh, new summer. Afterwards, in her slip, she held her favorite blue dress in front of her and walked to the full-length mirror. Good choice.

She put on fresh make-up, used the blow dryer to fluff up her hair, and slid the dress over her slender frame. "Maggie, you'll do!" she exclaimed. She laughed as she remembered a smiling Granny saying those words when Maggie put on a freshly ironed dress before church each Sunday.

Driving to the restaurant, she thought of the days ahead. It was important to have goals for the summer so the days did not slide by without any accomplishments. On the other hand, it was such a thrill each morning to awake and know she could pull the covers over her head again and sleep another hour if she wanted. No goals—not even painting—would be allowed to interfere with that luxury.

Bill was waiting for her on one of the wooden benches outside the restaurant. The late evening sun formed a halo behind his head. Almost ethereal, she thought, walking toward him.

After they were seated and given their menus, Bill ordered wine to celebrate Maggie's freedom. They laughed easily as he told stories about supervising young residents who came with their zeal to cure the world of all diseases and then the letdown when they realized stomach aches, runny noses, and diarrhea might be their biggest challenges of the day.

Over dinner, Maggie mentioned she would be getting her painting materials out of the attic and seeing if her love for oils and acrylics could be recaptured. Bill only knew she had taken art classes in college, but she had not mentioned she used to paint before Carson began his descent into dementia.

"I would love to see something you've painted," he said with enthusiasm.

"Oh, you mean my etchings," she teased, then instantly regretted the familiarity of the statement.

Bill seemed to measure his words. "Well, that would be fine, too," he managed.

"I'm so sorry, Bill, that just popped out. I wasn't intimating anything. Just one of those catchy phrases that resides somewhere in the recesses of my brain and decided to sally forth for no good reason." She was blushing.

"No problem. Actually, that was pretty clever. Let's leave it that if you will allow me to see your work sometime, I would love to."

They split a slice of white chocolate cheesecake with raspberry sauce. Maggie ate few desserts, but she enjoyed every morsel of her half. The perfect ending to a perfect meal.

In the parking lot, Bill asked if he could take her to a new restaurant in Chapel Hill next Friday. Friends had told him the food was excellent, and he wanted to give it a try. Her happy mood contributed to her ready acceptance.

"Maggie, would you consider letting me pick you up? It's several miles away, and I hate for you to drive home by yourself afterwards." His expression showed genuine concern as he waited for an answer—the same look she had seen from Carson for so many years.

She hesitated, weighing her first impulse to readily accept his offer against some inner concern about propriety. Surely, though, Carson would not want her on unfamiliar roads alone at night, she reasoned. Amidst the warm evening and the warmth of the wine, she said with more enthusiasm than she intended, "Thanks. That sounds like a good idea." Bill was smiling as he wrote down directions to her house.

The next morning, Maggie awoke with more energy than she had felt since Carson's stroke. "Hello, world!" she sang out. "What do you have to offer Maggie Bales today?"

No covers over her head this morning. She wanted to taste the early sunshine and let it flow over her. Jumping out of bed, she hurried to the front door for the paper. The world felt fresh and new. She stepped out onto the porch in her pajamas, something she never did ordinarily; but her attire for bed was certainly not the frilly, see-through nightwear featured in certain store windows at the mall. Solid, substantial Maggie, she thought, with no lacy edges.

After her breakfast of cereal, juice, and coffee, she changed into jeans and an old blouse and headed for the pull-down stairs to the attic. She had not been up there since she put away the few Christmas decorations at the end of December. Maggie never liked attics. They seemed dark and menacing.

She found the easel and moved it over to the attic door opening. It was large and awkward to carry. She climbed down to the fourth rung of the stairs and began to wriggle the easel toward her. With the steps as a brace, she inched down each rung, being careful not to let the easel overpower her and push her off the ladder. Perspiring, she reached the floor, both the easel and herself intact.

Next, she went back for the paints, brushes, and palette. Her brushes were pristine, evidence of her meticulous care after each use. However, with the exception of two unopened tubes of white acrylics, all her paints were stiff and dry. Too much heat in the summers, she realized.

Maggie once again shuffled down the ladder and carried her gleanings to the screened porch. Her next task was spelled out. Purchasing new paints. Those would be quite expensive, but she was determined to do some painting, hopefully even today. She changed her dusty clothes and set out on her mission.

She always loved art supply stores. There was such a feeling of unleashed beauty in those rows and rows of oils and acrylics. What beautiful sunset or ocean waves lay within those oblong tubes or tiny jars? She began filling her shopping basket with one after the other. A feeling of pure joy washed over her as she anticipated the happy— perhaps frustrating—hours that lay ahead, mixing and remixing the contents of these purchases until the exact hue of peach or magenta or cerulean appeared.

Once home, she unwrapped the precious purchases and laid them in neat rows on the large round table she had used for years. She kept it covered with a white vinyl cloth that now had specks and swipes of a myriad of colors from other happy days spent in this room. The cloth was beginning to crack from age, but she was reluctant to part with it—it was an old friend.

Looking around, she realized there was an accumulation of dust from the winter months that really had to go before she could put one of the new canvases on the easel. Drat! She really was hoping to start painting this afternoon, but instead, off she went to the kitchen for cleaning supplies.

The rest of the day was spent scrubbing down the screens, walls, and floor until she was satisfied no dust was going to find its way onto the fresh paint. Wiping her forehead with the back of her hand, she surveyed the room and took pleasure in a job well done. Next, it would be a shower and off to see Carson. Her first day of summer break was winding down. Even though she was tired, all in all, she felt it was a day well spent.

After church the next day, instead of her usual lunch out, she picked up a sandwich at a drive-thru and eagerly hurried home. She would change clothes, eat quickly, and get her first canvas of the summer settled on the easel. She already knew what she hoped to create.

Maggie had always painted both things she could see literally and those things that were products of her mental images. When she finally picked up her brush and palette, she knew she would paint the beach scene that danced in her head. What a good way to start the summer. She could imagine what it would feel like to stand on the warm sands that sprang from her brush, and she would hear the rustle of the sea oats as she bent them toward the dunes in graceful arches.

The days ahead were spent diligently painting and repainting. Maggie realized how rusty she was. However, on Thursday evening, Maggie signed her name to the happy scene before her eyes. Children played on the sand, a kite flying from the hand of one; some distance away, sea gulls hovered over a spot where tourists had left part of a picnic lunch; lovers walked hand in hand away from the viewer; an older couple looked for shells; and a pier stood just at the edge of the picture with tiny images of people enjoying a day of fishing. Marshmallow clouds meandered across the blue sky, and sunlight tickled the tops of waves as they rushed across the ever-moving water. Maggie was filled with a sense of yearning to be on the beach with the others in the scene.

Friday, in preparation for Bill stopping by to pick her up, she found herself cleaning things in the house that ordinarily didn't bother her. She stood on a step stool and redistributed the gathers in the window treatments. She pruned all the leaves with dying tips from her plants. She rearranged the living room mantel twice and decided it was still too cluttered, so she removed the vase Carson had given her one anniversary. She thought a live plant would look nice, so she made a trip to the local florist and picked one out.

Although she didn't want to admit it, Maggie knew she was apprehensive about Bill seeing her house. She imagined he and Rose had a beautiful home, decorated with the elegant flair only money can buy. She didn't want it to seem she and Carson had scrimped quite as much as they actually had. Maybe with some fresh flowers on the coffee table, the furniture wouldn't look quite so dated. So she made another trip to the florist and selected a mass of yellow daisies. Yes, she had been correct—they made the entire room seem alive and happy.

Finally, she looked at her efforts for the day. The living room was welcoming, and all the rooms smelled of citrus from the cleaning supplies.

"Oh no!" Suddenly, she realized she couldn't make it to see Carson today and still get dressed before Bill arrived. If she had not decided to get the flowers, she would have been able to work it all into the day. But, now, she had no choice. It was time to get into the shower. She hoped the water would wash away her feelings of guilt.

The tepid spray from the shower was refreshing, and soon she was thinking about the evening ahead. She had splurged and bought a silk dress in a vivid apricot color. The saleslady had assured her it was the latest style, and she was meant to wear it. Maggie had never been one to fall for their lines, but she decided the cut and fit of the dress did flatter her. The saleslady babbled endlessly as she wrapped it, and Maggie knew she thought her inane sales pitch had borne fruit. However, all that mattered to Maggie was her anticipation of wearing it and feeling as vibrant as the people in her painting.

Bill arrived right on schedule. She would have expected nothing less. His usual instant eye contact was delayed this time by what she took as an appraisal of the new dress. She noticed his glance sweep over her, and she could feel herself blushing. Maybe she was *too* vibrant!

"That's a beautiful dress," he said, admiringly, and his eyes returned to hers.

"Thanks," she mumbled, feeling awkward now. They stood for a moment at the door before Maggie realized he was waiting to be invited in.

"Oh, I'm so sorry." The words tumbled out as she stood back and swept her arm inward, making a welcoming gesture. "Please come in."

Somehow, in all her cleaning frenzy, she had failed to have a mental run-through of just where they would sit, or if she should ask him if he would like something to drink. She made an instant decision. "Would you like a glass of iced tea?"

"Yes, thanks. I believe I would," he replied. She steered him into the kitchen, glancing with a small degree of smugness at the perfectly even gathers in the floral valances.

As she collected two glasses and began adding ice cubes, Bill wandered from the kitchen down the short hall and through the door on the left that took him onto the screened porch. She had not yet draped the painting for fear of smudging any wet paint. She thought she remembered turning the easel away from the doorway and toward the screens so it would catch the breeze.

Suddenly, she wondered if he would walk around to see the other side. She felt a twinge of apprehension. She realized she wasn't ready to show her work to him just yet.

He re-entered the kitchen. "Is that an easel on your porch? Were you serious when you said you wanted to paint again?"

"Actually, yes . . . I mean I did get everything out of the attic, and then I bought some new paints to replace the petrified ones." She could feel her old shyness awakening.

"So have you painted anything yet?" he asked.

"Well, sort of. I really love the beach, so I dabbled a little with sand and water, trying to capture that wonderful feeling I always have when I'm there," she replied.

"And did you?"

"Did I what?" Maggie was beginning to feel lightheaded. Why was she so reluctant to say she had painted a picture and then show it to him, for Pete's sake? Why was it important to her that he like it. After all, she liked it.

Puzzled, he said, "Did you capture the feeling you wanted in the painting?"

"Oh . . . well . . . somewhat. But then it only made me yearn even more to be digging my toes in the sand. I suppose it gave me some contentment when I put the happy people in the picture," she replied.

"Whoa. You only mentioned sand and water. Are there people, too? And, Miss Maggie, I would be running down the hall to have a look, but I prefer a guided tour by the artist who could tell me all the subtle nuances in her artistic approach." He was teasing her now.

Her shyness seemed to be mushrooming inside her. "Please, maybe another time. I don't think it's ready for viewing just now," she managed.

Bill's face grew somber. "Hey, I didn't mean to make you uncomfortable. Guess it's like the wine that has to age for a while, eh?"

She sighed. "I guess I'm more timid about my efforts than I realized." She noticed the condensation from the two glasses of tea she was holding was sending rivulets of water down her wrists. "Here," she offered. "Oh, wait until I wipe the moisture off." Grabbing a dishtowel, she dried the outside of each glass while he watched her intently. "Now, that's better," she said as she handed the green goblet to him. She realized she had not entertained anyone in her home for a long time, and she felt ill at ease in her own kitchen. And she was buying time as she tried to understand her unfamiliar emotions.

"I'm sorry, Bill. I guess it's the long hiatus away from a paint brush that makes me feel pretty uncertain about what I create. I'm feeling a little insecure right now, I'm afraid."

He put his glass down on the kitchen table and laid his hand on hers. Little shocks ran up her arm like tiny needles dancing over her skin. She had to get used to this gesture of Bill's that she knew was nothing more than a display of friendship.

"Maggie, you playfully offered to show me your etchings last week, and I thought you might be waiting for me to ask to see the picture. I certainly don't want you to feel I'm being pushy. I would love to see the painting, but only when you're ready to show it to me. I really do understand your reluctance.

"I have a woodworking shop where I used to enjoy spending my spare time. Actually, I made some rather handsome pieces, if I do say so, but I would definitely not want anyone to see a piece I would produce now after several years away from the lathe. Self-confidence doesn't always come easy to me either, Maggie. Truthfully, I can be very vulnerable in some areas of my life. I am sorry for asking you to show me the picture. Take your time."

For whatever reason, she felt an illogical sense of relief. So he had places in his life that left him feeling insecure, too. How about that? Somehow, she had never pictured Bill as anything but self-assured, and, in her mind, rightfully so. That he, too, could have insecurities gave her a surge of confidence. She smiled a little mischievously and said, "Grab your tea. You're going to the beach!" With that she walked ahead of him onto the sun porch where she turned the easel toward him with a flourish and then stepped back.

Bill moved beside her and stood looking at each component with great intensity. She watched his eyes shift from the sea oats, to the gulls, to the kites, and finally stop at the two people walking hand in hand.

He reached for her hand. Her breath caught in her throat.

"Maggie, it's beautiful! Your colors are so realistic. I can see why you feel like you are there. I love it! Would you consider selling it?"

That brought her back to her senses. She pulled her hand from his. "Goodness, I have never thought about selling anything I have painted. Why, the paint on this one isn't even dry." She was again in new territory, and an uncomfortable feeling eased into her awareness. She began to move toward the doorway. "I'm famished. Let's go eat, and we'll talk about any negotiations later," she said with more quiver in her voice than she wanted.

Bill followed, but she sensed he was surprised by how erratic her behavior had been this evening. Pull yourself together, Maggie, she silently whispered to herself.

She took his glass with what she hoped was a gracious smile and sat it beside hers in the sink. "I'm pleased you like the painting," she said rather formally.

She decided against a jacket. "Guess we're ready," she offered, still keeping her hostess smile plastered on her face. Bill nodded and quickly eased around her so he could open the door. She picked up her purse from the table and smiled as she sailed passed him and out into the warm evening air.

"Do you lock your door?" he asked. She realized how long it had been since she left her house by the front door. She felt chagrined as she fumbled in her purse for the deadbolt key. He took it from her, and she heard the familiar click.

She walked ahead of Bill to the car and paused while he grabbed the door handle. He put his other hand on her elbow to steady her as she slid onto the seat. She appreciated his gallantry and ignored the slight tingle that darted through her.

On the way to the restaurant, she felt more at ease. Even though it was the first time she had ridden in a car with Bill, she decided it was more comfortable than having him in her home—the home she had shared so long with Carson. They admired the scenery and the soft summer evening. They discussed their favorite things about the season and recalled summer vacations. Bill had far more exciting adventures to relate than Maggie did. He, Rose, and their son had spent two weeks each summer in Maine. He told her about fishing off the coast, hiking in the mountains, and Rose's favorite—staying in historic bed and breakfast inns.

She decided not to mention again that she and Carson never took extensive vacations. Instead, she talked about the places she would love to visit someday. Bill and Rose had been to several of those including England, Spain, and France. The miles passed in a hurry. Conversation seemed easy and fluid once again.

The restaurant's exterior was large and impressive. The parking lot was almost full. Suddenly, Maggie wondered if she would see anyone she knew and flushed at the thought of having to introduce Bill. Certainly, she could truthfully say he was a friend, but she knew unspoken questions would arise.

Mercifully, she saw no one familiar, and they were soon seated at a small table in the rear of one of the large rooms. Diners seemed jovial and enjoying a Friday evening of fun and good food. No one noticed them at all, she realized.

Again, Bill ordered wine. She had become accustomed to this and enjoyed it much more than she ever expected to. They both studied the menus after the wine steward left. It was certainly expensive. She wondered if she should offer to pay for her meal. However, that might offend Bill since he had invited her here specifically. Instead, she chose the least expensive entrée on the menu—the chicken and penne pasta.

During the meal, they discussed their favorite authors and good books they had read. Bill preferred biographies and historical works. Maggie liked the classics, especially those set in England, and an occasional good mystery.

They ordered their second glass of wine and clinked their glasses to great writers. They were soon discussing more routine matters. No dessert tonight, but they both ordered coffee.

The waiter brought two lovely china cups along with a carafe of steaming coffee. After pouring a cup for each of them, he set the carafe on a warmer on the table, along with cream and cubes of sugar in matching china. Maggie was enjoying the elegance of dining tonight and told Bill so. He seemed pleased. Bill took a sip of his black coffee and slowly set the cup back in its delicate saucer. He reached across the table and once again laid his hand on hers.

"I have an offer, Maggie, and please think about it before you say no. Rose and I have . . . I guess now I have . . . a cottage at Corolla on the Outer Banks. We didn't use it often in the last few years, so I have a rental agency that rents it out during the season. When I saw your painting tonight, I realized how much you love the beach, and it would be my great pleasure for you to have the cottage for a week this summer. You can paint, read, sleep, whatever you enjoy. I just need to contact the agency and find available times. What do you say?"

Maggie withdraw her hand even though she was certain he was

merely emphasizing the sincerity of his offer. "How generous and thoughtful, Bill. Give me a few days to think about it," she said. There were nuances attached to such an offer, and she had to be sure all the ramifications were clear in her mind.

"Okay, but Maggie, I want so much for you to go and enjoy it. It's off the beaten path and many of the people on the beach will be people who live there year-round. They're a very friendly lot. You won't be surrounded by the usual throng of tourists at this time of the year. Please don't say no unless you can give me a reason that defies argument." If he noticed she had purposefully removed her hand, he gave no sign. He simply picked up his coffee spoon and traced the pattern in the tablecloth while they finished the entire carafe. Even after three cups of coffee, Maggie still felt a bit hazy, and then she remembered she had read caffeine doesn't really erase the effects of alcohol. Maybe the evening air would.

Driving home, there were lulls in the conversation. But Maggie didn't feel a need to fill the space and apparently neither did Bill. She liked that. It had been the same with Carson over the years. Bill didn't mention the painting again.

He walked her to the door, asked for her key, and soon they were walking back into the room she had spent the better part of the afternoon rearranging. The daisies were still perky, she noted. She began to feel awkward again. Should she ask him to be seated or just thank him and send him on his way? Maggie's sense of the "proper" took hold as she turned to him.

Holding out her hand, she graciously said, "I had such a lovely evening. The dinner was great. Thank you so much. And I will think about your kind offer."

She thought she detected a slight disappointment in Bill's voice as he bowed slightly and said, "It was my pleasure. I'm so glad you enjoyed it."

He started for the door, but turned back and said softly, "I always enjoy being with you, Maggie." His eyes held hers for a moment while her heart accelerated. But just as quickly, his tone changed again. With efficiency he said, "I will call the rental agency tomorrow to check about a time for the beach. Please think positively about my offer. It's the perfect place for you to gather more ideas for beach scenes—not crowded, quaint, almost pristine in the early mornings. Okay?"

She smiled and nodded. "Again, it's a lovely offer. I will wait until I hear what dates are available." This bought her more time. She moved toward the door. He took her cue and followed. As he put his hand on the curved handle, he turned slightly and quickly kissed her forehead. "Thanks for being my friend, Maggie," and with that he was gone.

She stood behind the newly bolted door for several moments, leaning against its coolness. Slowly, she moved away and walked to the back porch. She flipped on a small lamp. The glow cast a soft light on her painting, and she walked closer to examine it. "Yes," she thought, as her heart rate accelerated for the second time in ten minutes. "I would love a week at the beach—love it, love it, love it!"

Later that night, as she watched the ceiling fan make its endless circles, she realized they had not once mentioned Carson. But, worse yet, she had not thought of him at all.

CHAPTER 12

Maggie awoke to newborn sunshine filling the room, causing the shutters to make pretty patterns on the opposite wall. She gently shook herself awake and began her mental checklist for the day. Suddenly, she remembered she hadn't seen Carson at all yesterday, and a new wave of guilt swept over her. She kicked back the sheet and thin blanket and stepped out of bed with determination. She would eat a bowl of cereal, dress, and give him an early morning visit.

After a quick shower, Maggie found her old khaki shorts and a pink cotton blouse and slipped into them just as quickly. She arranged her wet hair, hoping it would dry on her drive over. She tucked her brush into her purse, slid her feet into backless sandals, and grabbed her keys. She glanced at the clock by the bedside and saw it was only 7:42 a.m. It would be Carson's breakfast time, but she headed to see him, no matter what.

Maggie knew the caregivers fed Carson his pureed food. When she had been there at mealtimes, the sight of liquid scrambled eggs, liquid salad, or liquid meatloaf—whatever he was served—had produced mental images that stayed with her the rest of the day. Ugh! Guess that was why she avoided those times.

When Maggie arrived, a caregiver was wheeling Carson down the hall from the dining room. "Hey, there," Maggie called out.

The caregiver acknowledged her with a smile. "We're just leaving breakfast. I'm taking Dr. Bales to the sun porch. Is that okay?"

"Certainly," Maggie replied with relief. She wouldn't have to look at a yellow puddle on his plate after all.

She fell into step with his wheelchair and took his left hand, squeezing lightly. He returned the squeeze. A wonderful surprise! She patted his silver hair as they headed for the doorway.

The caregiver placed the wheelchair just out of the sun. Other residents were sitting in their chairs, too. It was a lovely, large space with lots of wicker. Cushions with bright, tropical flowers gave the room a resort appearance. Maggie pulled a chair close to Carson and sat down. Again, she took his hand in hers. This time he didn't respond.

"I painted a picture this week. I wish you could see it because you were always my best fan. It's the beach with sand, water, sea oats, clouds, and people. The colors are bright. Do you remember how we used to walk on the beach and watch the people, especially the children with kites?" She checked for any recognition in his eyes. She had once understood those warm, brown eyes as if they had the ability to speak. But today, she could tell memories of those days at the beach, once so precious to both of them, had now been erased.

Maggie prattled on. "Isn't the weather wonderful? I just love these early summer days before the humidity stifles us. This is when I like to work in our yard." Still no flicker of recognition that would indicate Carson was connecting to anything she said.

She stayed until ten o'clock when a staff member brought juice to everyone on the porch. By that time, Maggie had totally exhausted her repertoire of subjects. These days, it was so hard to think of things to say to Carson, and she often left with a sense of failure Today, she rose, kissed him on the forehead, and told him she would return that evening. He continued to gaze ahead, not even acknowledging her departure.

As she walked to the car, she knew he was sinking deeper into Alzheimer's wasteland. She saw it with other residents, too, whose eyes were vacant, holding no clues to the past. She wondered if it really mattered to him whether she visited or not. She had to hope it did. That hope was what kept her going back day after day.

Later that afternoon, the phone rang. When Maggie picked it up, she was surprised to hear Bill's baritone voice.

"Hi, I just called the rental agency and have some news about vacancies. Do you mind if I come over so I can discuss this proposal again? I want to make it hard for you to refuse, and I think I would have more success in person," he laughed.

"Well . . . sure," Maggie replied, and immediately realized she now had to make a decision. After they hung up, she began to think about the offer. She had to admit the thought of being at the beach for a whole week by herself was wonderfully appealing.

She decided to change her shorts for slacks. These days, her sixty-year-old knees didn't often get a public viewing. Maggie and her friend, Marty, had recently decided the world didn't need to see more elephant knees or varicose veins, and even though Maggie had neither, she was becoming self-conscious about baring her legs. Unfortunately, her haste to visit Carson this morning had overridden her personal fashion edicts, at least for the moment.

Bill apparently had no such reluctance about his knees. When she answered the door, he was standing there in white tennis shorts and a blue and white striped knit shirt. She wondered if he had played tennis earlier or was going to play later. All at once those questions made her curious about his life other than Friday nights and the hospital. None of your business, she quickly told herself.

"Hi," she said as she moved aside for him to step in.

"Hi, yourself. Thanks for seeing me on such short notice. I really think I have an offer you can't refuse, Maggie Bales," he exclaimed with confidence.

"Well, you certainly act fast. I didn't expect to hear anymore about this for a long time." She hoped this sounded like she wasn't too eager to go. She motioned for him to sit on the sofa while she chose one of the chairs.

Plunging ahead, he said, "This is an urgent matter right now, actually. The people who rented the cottage next week had a family emergency and had to cancel. This looks like the only vacant week this summer until late August. Maggie, I really want you to experience that part of the Outer Banks. I know you'll love it. And you can paint to your heart's content."

Maggie was surprised by his sense of urgency. He was actually flushed as he spoke. He paused and looked at her with a glint of expectation in his eyes.

She realized she had to speak. "Wow. I had no idea my answer would be required so soon," she offered, hesitating. He leaned closer, said nothing, and waited intently.

Maggie knew she had to ask some questions. "Okay, I can see this needs a response." Taking a deep breath, she plunged into uncharted waters.

"Bill, it's a gracious offer, and I truly appreciate it. Yes, I would love to spend a week at the beach. That's my greatest wish each summer, and I haven't been since Carson could no longer go with me. However, I can't think of a way to repay you, and I'm not sure I want to feel obligated. Well, maybe *obligated* isn't the right word . . .," and she started searching for a better choice.

Bill quickly began to speak before her vocabulary kicked in. "Can you explain why you think you would be obligated?"

"It's just . . . well, I wonder . . . I'm not even certain that I know why, I suppose. But I believe social etiquette requires me to reciprocate your very generous offer . . .," and her voice trailed off.

"Maggie, you owe me absolutely nothing. You are my friend, and my offer is a testimony to that. I worry about you because you invest so much time in your role as a caregiver. Remember, you need a break sometimes. Otherwise, it is very difficult to sustain day-after-day visits to see a loved one when you get so little in return. But no obligations, no social reciprocity—none."

Maggie sat silently for a moment and looked down. What he said made sense. She had read all the books about the caregiver's needs. She knew she needed to stay strong for Carson. And somehow, that idea seemed to erase some of her doubts. Quickly, her thoughts began dashing about in her head, as she sought reasons to justify the luxury of a week alone. Maybe Carson would not even miss her. Maybe she would have new enthusiasm for her visits with him. Maybe she could show him her paintings, and he would remember the beach. It was working—Maggie was finding reasons to vindicate her week away.

Laughing, she said, "Does this mean I only have one day to pack?" Bill reached for her hand and kissed it with exuberance, then seemed to realize what he was doing and immediately dropped it.

"I'm sorry, Maggie. I didn't mean to overstep any boundaries. I'm just so pleased you've agreed. Yes, you can have possession anytime after noon on Monday and stay until next Sunday. Can I take you to get a coffee or maybe lemonade to celebrate my victory?" he teased.

"No, indeed, I will need all my time to get everything ready to leave for a week. That's not such an easy task for us women, you know," she teased back.

He looked a little crestfallen but accepted her verdict. "Okay. I'll come back tomorrow afternoon and give you directions and the key. I'll let the rental agency know the cottage is off the market next week." He rose and took her hand to help her from the chair.

On the porch, Bill paused. "Maggie, I miss you already," he said quietly. Then he hurried down the walk.

As she closed the door behind him, tears sprang to her eyes. It had been so long since Carson had been able to tell her that she mattered, that she was important, that she was thought of, that she was missed.

Shaking herself back to the task ahead, she walked into her bedroom and opened the closet door. What clothes should she take? In the summers, Maggie thought even less about her wardrobe than during the school year. She searched for a pair of capri pants she remembered owning at one time. When she did locate them, she saw the dark stain she had acquired when she was refinishing a chair. The more Maggie took inventory of her choices, the more she realized she really didn't have an adequate wardrobe for a week at the seashore. Forget a swimsuit, she thought, but she would like to walk on the beach in something other than slacks since she was eschewing shorts now. Finally, she decided to make a quick trip to the mall and buy some "cropped" pants, or whatever the fashionable term was this year.

Two hours later, Maggie returned with her purchases. She had certainly thrown caution to the wind, she decided, as she pulled the contents from each bag. Three pairs of crops, several knit shirts, a pair of navy sneakers, and her favorite—a flowing, white, tiered cotton skirt. She loved the way it fluttered around her ankles and reminded her of the frothy edges of the ocean. She had a turquoise blouse that tied at the waist and would be a perfect companion to the skirt. Her last year's sandals would have to do.

Maggie walked into the kitchen and noticed the sun sending fingers of pink and gold into the sky as it sank beneath the horizon. Suddenly, she remembered she had promised to visit Carson again this evening. For the second time today, guilt began to grow inside her, but she stuffed it as far back in the recesses of her being as she could. Didn't she deserve this trip? After all, she had spent endless time with a man—no, her husband!—who hardly knew she was there. "So what if I finally get a vacation!" she yelled out loud as she grabbed her purse and headed for the car.

Carson was asleep when Maggie arrived. Dinner was over, he was back in bed, and she realized her decision to come at this time had not been well thought-out. She pulled the small chair to his bed. She sat for almost an hour, watching him sleep. She wanted him to wake and see her there. She wanted to will him to recognize her—to know she had come twice today—to know she was a faithful wife who loved him—to know she made sure he was well taken care of. But Carson never stirred. She could hear the small clock beside his bed ticking softly as the evening sky grew dark. She thought of all the evenings she had sat here with no assurance that it mattered at all to this wonderful man—this man who didn't seem to be here anymore. She thought of the nights to come, and a sadness covered her like the blankets on Carson's bed. Finally, she lifted his hand to her lips and kissed it softly. "I love you. Sleep tight," she murmured with an ache in her heart as she placed his hand across his chest and then quietly walked from the room.

Back home, Maggie returned to the task of laying out the clothes she would need, hand washing a few items, and finally lugging the suitcase from the back of the guest room closet.

"That's enough for tonight," she said to the empty room. Yawning, she slipped out of her clothes and into her favorite ratty pajamas. She had forgotten about buying any nightwear, but it really didn't matter since no one ever saw her at bedtime anyway.

That night, Maggie dreamed of the picture she had painted. She thought it was real, and she was walking along the sand behind the young lovers, hoping to capture some of their youthfulness and enthusiasm for the future. The young man stopped to pick up a wayward Frisbee, and she realized it was Bill. She kept trying to walk faster so she could get in front of them to see who the woman was, but they kept outpacing her. Finally, she began to run, but they ran, too. She started to gasp for air as she tried to catch them. She awoke with a start.

She was perspiring and felt clammy. She sat up and shook herself fully awake. "What was that about?" she asked the night air.

She lay down and tried to push the dream away. All at once, she remembered Bill's offer to buy that picture. Aha, a small payback for his kindness. She would take the picture and leave it somewhere in his cottage. A beach house was the perfect place for it, and maybe it would leave her dreams alone if it wasn't in her house. She fell asleep and awoke to sunshine.

Sunday was a blur. Church, then a hasty exit, quickly eating a sandwich at a drive-thru, visiting Carson on the sun porch, neatly packing her suitcase, mentally making lists of things to do before she left, and calling Marty to ask her to look in on Carson a few times during the week. She had told the nurse at Carolina Manor she would be gone and asked her to call Marty if there were any problems. She would ask Bill for a phone number at the cottage so she could give it to Marty. She had to be certain Carson was okay while she was away!

At a little past four, Bill called to tell her he was bringing the key over. Twenty minutes later, he was sitting in her living room. He had a neatly typed list of things to be done upon arrival and departure. She learned where the hot water heater turn-on was located as well as the icemaker button and the electrical panel in case she blew a fuse. She also learned about the storage shed's idiosyncrasies, the stubborn lock on the back door, and the list went on. Finally, Bill handed her a set of keys. As he placed them in her hand, he cupped his hand over hers. "I'm counting on your having a wonderful time. And that's doctor's orders." He waited for her response.

She blushed and regretted it. "Again, I can't say enough how much I appreciate this. I promise to be a very good tenant," she said.

"I have no worries about that," Bill responded, squeezing her hand before he released it. "By the way, I want to give you my cell phone number just in case you should have any problems. The rental agency's number is at the bottom of the list you have, but I would rather you called me if anything goes wrong."

Maggie said, "I've become pretty efficient at fixing things since Carson left, so I don't anticipate any problems at the cottage I can't handle." She liked her assertive tone.

She thought the look in Bill's eyes bordered on amusement. She didn't like being patronized. "Well, I *am* pretty efficient, Dr. Holton," she said defiantly.

"Maggie, of that I have no doubt," but she noticed he was smiling with every word.

"Okay, Mr. Smarty Pants. By the way, I need a phone number at your cottage so Carolina Manor can reach me if anything happens to Carson," she said.

"Oh, Maggie, I almost forgot. Would you like me to look in on Carson for you? I would be happy to—no trouble at all."

Maggie hesitated. "Well, I called Marty, and she will be checking on him. I'll call her every day to see if things are okay. If she has any concerns, I might call you and ask you to glance at him. Would that be okay?"

"I would truly be happy to do it," he replied. Bill handed her the paper with his number.

"Okay," she said as she stood up, "I have a lot to do before tomorrow morning." She hoped this signaled she, indeed, could be self-reliant, because she still felt a little peeved by his amusement.

Bill followed her to the door without hesitation but stopped before he opened it.

"Maggie, I think I just shot myself in the foot. Here I am sending you off to the beach, and you won't be here Friday night for our dinner. Do you think you can make it back in time for dinner Sunday night? I would love to hear how your week went, and maybe you will have some new paintings to show me. Also, while you're there, please promise you will decide on a price for the one you have on the porch."

"Agreed," she said smugly. "Dinner Sunday night will be fine. Shall I call you when I get back to town?"

"By all means. Goodbye for now and have loads of fun," he said as he lightly squeezed her arm. She watched him walk to his car and pull out of the driveway. They both waved as he turned the car to head south. She almost jogged down the hallway to her bedroom in anticipation of the week ahead.

CHAPTER 13

Maggie was dreaming of being on a ship when the alarm sounded the next morning. At first, she thought it was the foghorn, but as she left her dream behind, she automatically reached to turn off the offending sound. Excitement brought her upright. "Oh, glorious day," she sang out. She scooted off the bed in a hurry to get the trip started.

Soon she was on the road headed east on Route 64. Growing up in Ahoskie, she had vague recollections of parts of eastern North Carolina. Her high school debate team had competed in the regional finals in Greenville on the East Carolina University campus. She thought of how excited she had been the day they all piled on the bus headed for the competition. The campus was huge in her eyes. She remembered cherry trees in bloom everywhere, mounds of fluffy pink blossoms that caused her to think of cotton candy.

Her team had come in second, but she never forgot that day because it was a world she didn't know existed. If she hadn't gotten the scholarship to North Carolina State University, she would love to have studied at ECU. How different might her life have been, she wondered. There would have been no Carson, and that thought made her shudder.

She passed Tarboro and Williamston and headed for Plymouth. There were blue skies as far as she could see with not a cloud anywhere. The land was very flat in that part of the state, but long rows of towering pines hugged the roadsides and obscured her view of what lay beyond. Carson once called them "tree tunnels." Occasionally, she passed land that had been clear-cut—a laborious effort to take all the trees off the land so it could be put into production. It always made Maggie wonder how the early settlers with their primitive tools had ever managed to remove enough of the forest to have a homestead and enough cleared land for a few crops. She would not have made a good pioneer, she decided.

After Maggie passed Manteo and crossed Bonner Bridge to the Outer Banks, she pulled over and studied Bill's directions again. She would turn left and follow Route 158 past Kitty Hawk until she came to Route 12. She decided to stop at the first grocery she saw and buy some supplies. The pretty, young blonde at the check-out counter made cheerful small talk and then asked where Maggie lived. It was obvious she was used to waiting on tourists. Mandy was the name on her badge.

Maggie loaded three big bags into her car, wondering if she would eat all of this food, but the salty air always made her hungry. She had bought fresh shrimp, scallops, and Atlantic salmon, along with two bags of salad greens, some home grown tomatoes, and her favorite vinaigrette salad dressing. Breakfast would be bagels, coffee, and juice.

She judged she would arrive at the cottage around noon. If she could unload and get settled quickly, the whole afternoon was hers to explore the area. Checking her directions again, she decided she was perhaps ten miles from Corolla. She caught glimpses of the ocean as she drove. The houses were much larger than the ones when she first turned onto Route 12, some even looking like small hotels. But Bill had called his place a cottage, so she assumed the houses would change again.

She had driven the ten miles, and the houses were still large. Again, she pulled to the side of the road and checked the address. Turn right on Sand Piper Lane, Bill had written in a doctor-like scrawl. She decided to drive on for another mile or so and then backtrack if she didn't find it. But the second street she came to was Sand Piper.

"My entry into a week of paradise," she said joyfully. Nothing looked like a cottage to her. She made the third turn onto Inlet Road—the address was 310. She drove slowly. The houses were large and beautiful. Lawns were manicured, with flowers everywhere. Obviously, medical doctors made lots more money than doctors of philosophy. Somehow, thinking about Bill's economic status made Maggie feel a bit shabby.

Pulling into the driveway, she was almost dizzy with anticipation. The large, two story, white house had windows everywhere. Black shutters sat like bookends for each window. She tried to see if they were only ornamental or if they really did protect the glass in times of hurricanes. She noticed the widow's walk on top of the house. She wondered if she could get to it and walk outside for a better view of the ocean.

As she opened the car door, she could hear the waves in their relentless surges. The warm breeze played with her hair. She loved the fact there was always a breeze at the ocean, no matter how hot it was. The front door unlocked with no glitches. She was in.

She stared at the interior. Maggie had expected something rustic. The décor was lovely and auspicious. Old, wide-planked, cherry floors were polished to the point of gleaming. The furniture was upholstered in sunny yellows and blues. Oriental rugs were abundant. High ceilings with windows to the eaves almost made the rooms seem like part of the outdoors. She wondered how they ever rented it and kept it so immaculate. She decided it was definitely rented to people who put down a hefty deposit. But for the time being, it was all hers!

Maggie unloaded the groceries into the fridge and cabinets. The kitchen was as large as her kitchen and living room combined. She was certainly going to rattle around in all this space. Off to her left, she spied a smaller room that was raised one step above the kitchen floor. On closer inspection, she saw an overstuffed sofa and chair, several small tables and lamps, a bookcase filled with books, a rug that covered almost the entire floor, and a gas fireplace. "My room," she cried. She felt like Goldilocks who had found the space in the house that was "just right" for her.

There was a huge master bedroom on the first floor, a smaller bedroom down the hall with its own bath, and three bedrooms upstairs. She chose the smaller bedroom on the first floor. Somehow, it didn't seem right to sleep in the bed she supposed Bill and Rose had slept in, no matter how many other people had slept in it, too.

She decided to set up her easel on the sun porch upstairs. It offered the best view and the floor was tiled. She didn't find a stairway to the widow's walk, unfortunately. She would ask Bill about that later.

The last thing Maggie unloaded was the painting she had brought as her thank-you gift. She wasn't sure where to put it. Should she just leave it somewhere or try to hang it? Would that be too presumptuous? Anyway, she had a week to make that decision.

After everything was put away, Maggie changed into her canvas shoes and headed for the beach. She was happy to feel the tug of deep sand on her shoes just a few steps off the back veranda. She walked as far as a fishing pier to the north. Looking west, she could see the top of a lighthouse. She would have to explore that later as a possible subject for her canvas. Although paintings of lighthouses in North Carolina seemed almost as numerous as the seashells on the beach, she still wanted to try her hand at it.

In the other direction, she found interesting drift wood in gnarly shapes. No, she wouldn't collect it, she thought. Let the lamp makers, the flower arrangers, or the yard art folks take it home. She did, however, stop to admire the undulating lines, the contrasts of grays, browns, and blacks, and the weatherworn nubs of limbs long gone.

Bill had been right. Although there were people on the beach, some who nodded to her as she passed, it certainly wasn't the usual tourist-crowded, umbrella-dotted scene she and Carson had experienced before. She walked for what seemed like hours, but she could tell by the sun it was only midafternoon. Suddenly, she felt hungry. She headed back, luxuriating in the warm sun on her back. She took off her shoes and walked at the edge of the waves where it always looked like someone had added detergent to get the delicate foam that crept over her toes.

Back in the kitchen, she boiled shrimp and made a small salad. She cut a large slice from the round loaf of Italian bread. Maggie carried it out on the veranda and sat at the wicker table with a glass top. She made a vow to eat breakfast out here every day. How glorious!

She slept well that night. Before she went to bed, she had worried about unfamiliar creaks and groans in the house, but all she heard was the unending lapping of the waves on the sand. The walk had been wonderful exercise and served as a good sleeping pill, she surmised the next morning as she awoke to find the sun already high in the sky.

During breakfast, she watched several children playing in the sand in the distance while parents spread beach towels and prepared for a day in the sun. Mothers lathered their youngsters with lotions and admonished them to stay close to the edge of the water and not venture out. Books were retrieved from beach bags as adults settled in for reading and watching.

What would she do today? Go upstairs to the sun porch and check out the lighting for painting? Look at the choices of books in "her" room? Go for another walk? What a luxury to be in no hurry to make that decision. Maggie's thoughts drifted to times she and Carson had spent on the beach together. He always insisted on walking on the water-hardened sand so she could enjoy the froth on her toes. They held hands and laughed as the sea gulls swooped in playful circles over their heads. She could still see his sun streaked hair and his old plaid swim trunks he insisted were too good to toss. She closed her eyes and let the loneliness wash over her like the nearby waves. Tears crept from the corners of her eyes and made their way to her jaw where they dropped onto her thin robe and moistened her skin underneath. Maggie slowly brought herself back to the present, dried her eyes on her napkin, and made a determined promise not to spoil another minute of this day with sad thoughts.

Each day that week brought its own pleasures. She painted on the upstairs sun porch, walked endless miles on the beach, shopped in quaint stores, read every evening in her cozy room, and drank in the ocean air like a tonic. Her daily calls to Marty reassured her there was no change in Carson.

Friday, on an impulse, she took down the picture over the fireplace in the small den and hung the painting that was her gift to Bill. She certainly would change it back before she left, but she thought the colors were particularly attractive for that room, and she wanted to see it in different lights during the day. She had found a closet upstairs where she would leave her painting, and in her thank-you note to Bill for the use of the house, she would tell him to look there.

On Saturday, her last precious day, Maggie decided to drive down Route 12 all the way to Cape Hatteras Lighthouse near Buxton. She judged it would take an hour and a half, maybe longer with traffic.

As the sun was rising higher in the sky, she loaded her easel, a fresh canvas, and her painting supplies. Along with sun lotion and a wide brimmed hat she had purchased in Corolla on a whim, she headed south. Every day that week had brought radiant sunshine. However, as she drove, she noticed there were some dark clouds where the ocean met the sky. Maggie had not bothered to turn on either the television or radio that entire week, so she had no idea about weather forecasts. "Oh, well," she sighed out loud, "guess not every day can be perfect."

The drive took longer than she expected. Tourists' cars were bumper to bumper as she neared Kitty Hawk and Nags Head. Traffic crept along at the proverbial snail's pace, much to Maggie's chagrin. She didn't want to waste a minute of this final day. As she got closer to Pea Island National Wild Life Refuge, cars thinned out and she picked up speed. By the time she arrived at Buxton, it was noon.

Maggie ate a fried shrimp sandwich at a quaint sounding restaurant, Mr. Marlin's Hideaway, as she sat on a wooden picnic bench at a table covered with blue and white checked vinyl. It was obvious diners would have to share the picnic tables if the place was crowded. Not particularly interested in making small talk with strangers, Maggie ate in a hurry, hoping to finish before anyone joined her. Mission accomplished, she thought, as she picked up her paper plate and cup and headed for the trash container.

After parking at the Hatteras Island Visitor's Center, she walked around the grounds of the lighthouse until she found the perfect spot to set up the easel. It took two trips back to her car for supplies before she was ready to begin putting images on canvas.

Maggie painted until late in the afternoon. She noticed what had been a thin line of darkness on the horizon when she started out in the morning had now become a large band of color separating the ocean from the sky. There was still sunshine on the beach, but she could tell the stormy weather was creeping closer. Maybe she'd better pack up and head back.

The drive to the house was quicker than the trip down because the traffic was light. She wasn't certain what she would have for dinner but decided not to stop at the grocery. It seemed foolish to buy anything for one meal and then have to throw out the leftovers.

By the time she parked in the driveway, the sky was getting darker over the house. Maggie had seen fewer people moving about as she had driven the last miles. She decided not to carry the art supplies into the house. After all, she would be leaving in the morning. She glanced with some degree of admiration at the black and white lighthouse standing regally on her canvas as she braced it against the back seat, hoping it didn't shift and smear the fresh paint.

Swinging her purse over her shoulder, she walked to the front door and opened it. Before she entered, she removed her shoes—now grimy with sand—and left them outside. It if rained, she reasoned, so much the better. They needed a bath.

She stepped across the threshold onto one of the lovely Persian rugs and immediately water oozed between her toes. "Oh no!" she cried. The rug, the floor—the entire entrance was flooded!

CHAPTER 14

What could have gone wrong? Had she failed to notice something askew that morning? She hadn't used the clothes washer. And the dishwasher was loaded with the dishes she planned on cleaning tomorrow.

Maggie knew she had to find the source of the leak. Those lovely floors! Making her way gingerly to the back of the house, she noticed the water was everywhere. It covered the kitchen floor and seeped into the large living room. Dark patches on the rugs told her they were soaking up the water as it joined them. She walked slowly for fear of slipping. Finally, she reached the utility room and saw water dripping from the hot water heater. Apparently, the tank had already deposited its contents in the house, and only the remains dripped from underneath.

Numbers were posted beside the telephone to call in case of an emergency, including a plumber. She hurriedly dialed the number. After several rings, the answering machine picked up, telling the plumber's hours and leaving no after-hours number. Didn't all plumbers have a twenty-hour-hour emergency service? She remembered it was Saturday night. Perhaps he was just out for the evening.

She then tried calling the rental company. This time the answering machine offered a pager number. She tried that, saying a silent prayer someone would answer. No one did. Saturday night and no one wants to be bothered, she realized.

Maggie sat on a bar stool with her feet on the top rung and put her head in her hands. Why had this happened at the end of such a perfect week? She felt heartsick. After her smug declaration to Bill earlier, she now felt so incompetent. She couldn't leave until the problem was solved. She could try other plumbers, but what if she got someone who wasn't reliable? After several minutes trying to think of logical solutions, she decided she had to reach Bill and ask for the name of another person he recommended. Maggie searched for his number in her purse, wishing with all her being she didn't have to make this call.

On the third ring, Bill answered. "Hi, there, beach girl," he sang out. "I knew it was you from my caller ID. How are things going?" Even in her despair, Maggie could tell from the lilt in his voice he was glad to hear from her. That made her feel even worse.

"Oh, Bill, I'm so sorry to disturb your evening, but actually things aren't going so well just now."

His concern immediately penetrated the distance between them as he asked urgently, "What's wrong?"

"I went to Hatteras today, and when I came home this afternoon, I stepped into water when I opened the door. It appears to be the water heater. There's a lot of water on the lovely floors and even the beautiful rugs. I'm so sorry, Bill. I tried to call the plumber on the list in the kitchen, but I got the answering machine. I also tried the realty company and their pager and still got no answer. I know the sooner I get the water off the floor, the better. It's way too much to mop up with towels." She rushed on. "I'll start calling other plumbers, but I called you because I wanted to be certain I get one who's reliable. Also, I'm not certain what to do about the clean up and drying the lovely rugs." She finally stopped for a breath.

"Maggie, I'm so sorry this happened while you were there. Who knows how old that water heater is? I imagine something broke and the tank drained. I do have two names of plumbers in my office here at home that I've used in the past. I'll call them and see if I can get one out right away. I'll also have them call someone to come and clean up the water. Probably they will need large fans to dry things out. Let me get right on that, and then I'll call you back to tell you who is coming." He seemed just ready to hang up when he asked, "How's your weather? I've been a little worried about the storm."

"What storm?"

"Haven't you been listening to the weather reports?"

"No, actually, I have prided myself on not turning on either the radio or television since I arrived," she said a bit defensively.

"Maggie, there's a tropical depression just east of the Outer Banks. Our reports here tell us there probably won't be much wind damage but potentially heavy rains and lightning."

"Oh. That probably accounts for the dark clouds at the horizon today. And it's getting darker outside, but I've been too concerned about the water to pay any attention to the sky."

"Okay. Remember to stay out of the water if you hear thunder, young lady. You could get quite a shock even inside the house. And I'll call you shortly." With that, Bill was gone.

She began to explore the hallway past the bedrooms. Water in the hall carpet had seeped onto the carpet in the master. As she went farther toward her bedroom, she didn't sense the dampness in the carpet anymore. She knelt and felt of it. Dry. And her room was dry. Well, at least she could still sleep in that room, even if they did put fans in the other rooms. Amazing that her bedroom and the small, cozy room she had grown so attached to were spared the baptizing.

A loud boom caused her to turn and look out the window. She had noticed rumblings earlier when she was talking to Bill, but she had become accustomed to low-flying aircraft from the military bases close by, so she thought nothing of the roar. Now she realized she was hearing thunder. She walked to the glass door off the breakfast room and looked east. As she watched, long, jagged streaks of lightning danced above the ocean water. And sonic-type booms followed each one. She wished she could capture nature's anger on canvas, but she knew now was not the time. Besides, her supplies were in the car.

Remembering what Bill had said about lightning and being aware of all the windows around her, she decided she should go into the den and wait for his call. She wondered why the phone had not rung already. She looked at her watch. Maybe she was just anxious. Probably he was still trying to contact someone.

Maggie sat down on the sofa and realized how tired she was. Lugging the art supplies had really taken its toll. She closed her eyes and heard the rain begin to hit the windows—a staccato beat at first and then a steady hammering sound. She laid her head against the down-filled, cushioned back of the sofa. The next thing she knew, the phone was ringing.

When she answered, Bill's voice had an urgent sound. "Maggie, I couldn't find anyone to come out in this storm, so I've driven down myself. I'm less than ten minutes from you, and I don't want to frighten you by banging on the door. I didn't call you before I left because I was afraid you would feel even worse if you thought I was inconvenienced. Trust me, I'm not inconvenienced. I really don't want you there alone with the water and this storm."

She could hear the steady rhythm of his windshield wipers. Feeling a little dazed from the nap, she managed a feeble, "Thank you." Then added, "Please be careful. This storm sounds terrible," only realizing after they hung up he was almost there.

She walked carefully to the front door and unlocked it. She noticed it was nearly dark outside. She flipped the hall light switch. Nothing. Oh, no, was the electricity off? She tried switches in the kitchen and in her little haven. She tried all the switches in the bedrooms. None obliged her with light.

She walked back to the kitchen, feeling her way along the walls. Just then she saw car lights careen off a wall in the living room, and she realized Bill was there. The thought sent warm waves through her. She had to admit it would be a much better night if someone else was there, too. If anything else happened, she didn't want to be alone. She wondered where the flashlights were kept. Bill would know.

Just then, Bill burst through the door with his arms loaded. "Hey, thanks for having that unlocked," he called as he started down the hallway.

She met him halfway. "Bill, you're soaked! I'm so sorry you had to come out on such a horrible night. Goodness. I hope you have some dry clothes here." She had noticed a locked room upstairs and wondered if Bill and Rose kept personal items there.

"I think I can resurrect something," he replied. "First, though I have brought some sustenance for our bodies and perhaps our souls on such a night as this. By the way, shouldn't we turn the lights on?"

"The electricity is off," Maggie replied. Noticing the bags from a fast food restaurant up the road, she suddenly heard a rumble in her stomach.

"Well, it's a good thing you brought some food. I was letting the fridge run dry so I wouldn't have leftovers tomorrow when I leave. I don't even know what I would have eaten, much less fed to a guest. Here, let me take this while you go change. Is there a flashlight close by?"

"Should be one in the cabinet in the utility room. Let me look." He rummaged in the darkness until Maggie saw a shaft of light illuminate the doorway. "Hey, I found it! While I'm at it, I better turn off the water just to be sure that isn't part of the problem, too."

Emerging with flashlight in hand, Bill looked triumphant. "Let's find plates to put our food on and a couple of glasses. Then I will use the light to find my clothes upstairs."

"What about cleaning up the water?" she asked.

"No one is going to come out on a night like this, and there's no electricity to run the fans, anyway. We'll just leave it alone. My insurance will take care of it," he said nonchalantly. His attitude was a new one to Maggie—the Maggie who was always thinking of the most economical solution to her own home repairs.

The lightning illuminated the kitchen at times as they moved around like shadows. She was even more comforted that someone was with her as she noticed the complete darkness outside except for the intermittent, frenzied flashes.

She realized Bill was opening a bottle of wine. "Oh, my, I didn't know they were selling wine at drive-thru windows now," she joked.

"I grabbed this bottle as I was leaving home. Thought you might need a little something to ease the cares of your day, missy." And frazzled Maggie had no objection to that at all.

She told Bill the little room off the kitchen was dry. She stopped short of calling it "her" room. They carefully carried in the food and wine and sat it on the coffee table in front of the sofa. Bill found the gas key by the fireplace, fiddled with it, and suddenly bright flames erupted to erase the darkness. "There. That will give you some light while I go upstairs and change. Back in a minute. Wait on me for a toast," and he was gone.

She sat in silence watching the flames. She began feeling calmer. Perhaps she didn't need the wine for solace, but she knew in her heart she wanted its warmth anyway.

Looking far less bedraggled, Bill reappeared. "Ah, this is much more comfortable," he acknowledged. Instead of sitting, he reached for her hand and pulled her off the sofa. "Take your wine glass, ma'am," he directed. With one hand in his and one on the stem of her glass, Maggie raised her goblet for his presumed toast.

"Here's to the water heater. If it hadn't clunked out, I wouldn't be standing here with this special woman, and there is nowhere I'd rather be tonight. May the storm rage on and the electricity stay off!"

Maggie stood there in surprise. That wasn't what she had expected at all. "I honestly don't know how to respond to that," she said with a slightly nervous laugh.

"No need to," he replied. They both clicked their glasses and took a long sip. She eased her hand out of his and sat down on the sofa again, feeling a little self-conscious now.

In an attempt to put things back on a more formal path, she picked up her sandwich and asked how his trip down had been. As they began to eat, he followed with asking about her week. Her excitement while telling about her days was obvious. He ate and listened as she told him details of her walks on the beach, the inspirations for her paintings, and her cozy evenings. He finished eating before she did and leaned back with his wine, gazing at her intently. She realized she had hardly taken a bite even though she was ravenous.

"I'm sorry to be such a chatterbox," she said, with chagrin.

"Maggie, I'm loving every word. But you eat now, and I'll tell you about things in Cary."

She was so engrossed in his report of the week, the sandwich was gone before she realized it. She had sipped wine between bites, and it was beginning its magic spell. Every nerve seemed to relax as she also leaned back on her side of the sofa. She tucked her feet under her.

Without a word, Bill picked up the flashlight and went into the kitchen. He returned with the half-full wine bottle and poured more into her glass and then into his. A warning went off somewhere in the recesses of Maggie's mind, but she allowed it to linger for only a moment before kicking it into oblivion.

As Bill was shutting off the flashlight, he pointed it upward, so it threw light toward the mantel. Suddenly, the light shone on the painting over the fireplace. She had forgotten it was still there! He stood looking at the painting for what seemed like several minutes, but she was certain it was only seconds. She held her breath.

He turned to her slowly. With a husky voice, he said, "Maggie, my Maggie." He sat down close beside her while she absorbed his words. In an instant, he had put his arm around her and pulled her close to him. The firelight danced and the rain pounded, but she only felt great calm. How long had it been since she had felt so "protected?"

For a few minutes, they sat facing the fire, neither of them sure of what to say, but both of them realizing they were entering a new place.

Bill tilted her face toward his and softly kissed her—lingering kisses. She knew he was giving her time to resist, but every fiber of her body screamed for his warmth. Was it the wine? Or had the loneliness finally caught up with her? She didn't know, and just then, she didn't care. She kissed him in return. The next kiss was more urgent and lasted for what seemed like an eternity. A longed-for eternity. Finally, with her thoughts drowning in the storm outside and the storm within her, she laid her head on his chest. He held her so close she heard his heart beating in a tempo she recognized from long ago.

They sat in that warm cocoon saying nothing. He finally leaned forward and picked up their wine glasses. "Here," he said softly, handing hers to her. They sat sipping the wine with no sounds in the room except their breathing. Maggie's thoughts were numb, and she made no attempt to bring them out of their catatonic state to some level of reason.

Eventually, Bill set his glass down and gently took hers, too. He pulled her to him once again. She had a vague sense of what she should do, but somehow she didn't have the strength. Maggie, the one who was always strong, always in control, always did the right thing. And she knew—at least for the time being—*that* Maggie was somewhere else.

They shared long, lingering kisses. Maggie slowly recognized the once familiar feelings deep within her body. She shuddered slightly. Bill took his cue and began moving his hand across her shoulder to her throat. He paused for a moment at the top button on her blouse, waiting. Maggie didn't move. Slowly his hand began tugging to release it. "Maggie, Maggie," he whispered. "I have wanted you for such a long time."

As the button yielded, she felt all her restraints vanish with the ebbing rolls of thunder, and in a husky voice, she pleaded, "Oh, Carson, I want you, too."

Bill pulled away so abruptly that she fell forward and had to right herself. She wasn't certain what had happened.

In a cold voice, through gritted teeth, Bill spewed, "Maggie, I'm not Carson. And I never will be. Carson is gone, gone, gone!" His voice grew louder with each word. "You need to come to your senses and accept the fact you lost him when Alzheimer's took over. And you also need to realize . . . if you've been playing a little game where you're substituting me for him, that's very unfair."

Maggie sat stunned. She finally realized she must have used Carson's name although she didn't remember it. In a small voice, she whispered, "Bill, I never, ever thought I was substituting anyone. It must have been a slip of the tongue or the wine or whatever." Growing angry now at Bill's assumption and in a bolder voice, she added, "But indeed, I believe you have brought me back to my senses, as you said."

He reached for her again. This time, she had no trouble pulling away.

"Listen, Maggie, maybe I spoke out of turn—I don't know. But you seemed as eager for tonight as I did. You were trembling. I could feel it all through your body. Maggie, we aren't young anymore. Don't you understand? These feelings don't happen to everyone our age. We're the lucky ones, Maggie," he was punctuating each word as he forced them through clenched teeth.

"And then you called me Carson. I'm not him, Maggie. If that's who you really want, he's not here!" They both sat staring straight ahead at the dancing flames in the fireplace. Finally, Bill reached for his glass and drank a generous swallow of the wine.

His voice softened, "Maggie, I've fallen in love with you. I knew that when you were all I could think of this week—even when I was with patients. And I think you've fallen in love with me, too. But I don't think you can admit that, even to yourself.

"You're a virtuous woman, Maggie. I've known that from the

beginning. And I admire that. However, virtue needs to be ruled by common sense. Carson can give you nothing now. I can give you love and happiness again. And Maggie, there's no need for that to be years from now when Carson is gone. We can grab the brass ring now!"

Maggie flinched. Her emotions were a roller coaster of anger, sadness, and doubt. Was he right? Or was he terribly arrogant? Terribly insensitive? Would she lose him? She sat very still and looked at her lap. Bill continued.

"There should be a new clause in the wedding vows that says 'until death—or dementia—do us part.' I've been down this road, too, you know. Yes, I was faithful to Rose, also, but it was futile, Maggie. Faithful to what? To a body ravaged by a disease that will never allow it to return to us? Faithful to some long ago vows when we had hopes of a life spent *together?* Not a life with one of us at home and the other in an institution! Does your Jesus really expect you to be faithful to a shell of a man who hardly knows who you are? Answer me! Does he?"

Maggie could barely breathe. She felt sick at her stomach. Finally, when she realized he was waiting for answers, she forced her eyes to meet his.

"Bill, I've never played games with any man and certainly not with you." Her voice was barely audible. Bill leaned closer. Rather than have him come any nearer, she pushed the words harder to increase the volume. "Yes, in truth, it felt wonderful to be in your arms and to be kissed. To feel my body come alive after such a long time. I didn't know I even had such responses left. And I suppose I really don't know who those feelings were directed toward—you or Carson. I still love Carson deeply, but I realize he usually doesn't know who I am now, as you said."

She paused and gathered her thoughts again. Plunging on, she said more adamantly, "Bill, I think it is very unfair to be attacked for believing in doing the right thing, for keeping commitments, for wanting to be an honorable person. Or even for wanting to please Jesus. No, I'm not certain what He expects. I've gone to church most of my life, and I still have lots of questions. I know He represents love and forgiveness, but I also know He expects vows to be kept. For how long and under what circumstances, I don't know." She looked down at her hands. Tears began to well up in her eyes, and she didn't want him to see her cry.

In a softer, but firmer voice, Bill began. "Maggie, Rose died six months ago, but she was physically gone to me for over four years. I'm not willing to become a withered old man all alone. I've told you already I love you. Thoughts of you consume my waking hours, and they are warm and happy thoughts. I want you to love me in return. I suppose I'm saying I'm not willing to wait for you to become a widow. If you worry about your friends and perceived improprieties, we can meet at various places out of town each weekend. I'll take care of the costs, of course."

Her tears suddenly evaporated. Her face flushed as anger grew. "How dare you! How dare you! Do you really think you can buy my so-called virtue with cheap, out-of-town rendezvous? Have you really misjudged me, Bill, as badly as I apparently have misjudged you?" she screamed and bounded from the sofa.

She ran from the room, feeling her way down the hall and into her bedroom. She shut and locked the door behind her. She was suddenly so weak she barely made it to the bed. Her knees buckled as she tried to sit down. She sank to the floor. She wasn't certain how long she lay there, but in a burst of brightness, she realized the electricity had returned. She must have left the lights on when she was checking each room. She pulled herself to her feet and padded across the room to turn off the switch. She decided not to open the door to see if the hall light was on. She eased onto the bed and noticed the room had become oppressive. The air conditioning had been off, of course. Just then, she heard it click on.

She lay on the bed, still in her clothes. Bill's words played over and over in her head. Maybe she was being unreasonable to be so angry, but why did he think she would sneak around with him? Didn't the whole idea of sneaking mean they were doing something wrong? Couldn't he see that?

The ache in her heart was growing with every thought. In spite of all that happened tonight, she knew she cared deeply for him, too, but now she couldn't let him know that. Bill would only chide her again about her beliefs and letting them stand in her way. That wasn't fair, she fumed. She tried to think of everything that had been said that evening, but her thoughts kept returning to his offer to *pay* for her company and her integrity. That had hurt the most.

Maggie's emotions ran the gamut during the early morning hours. She never slept and was fully awake when the gray light of dawn made its entrance.

Maggie rose and walked with jerky movements into the bathroom. Her body felt like it had been pummeled. She looked into the mirror. Her face was pale and her mascara streaked down one cheek. Her hair was matted. "I look like a gargoyle," she exclaimed out loud.

On instinct, she turned the faucet handle. The faint hissing sound reminded her there was no water—no shower, no brushing her teeth. "Drat!" she raged at the mirror. Was she going to face Bill looking like this? She needed to use the bathroom, too. She quickly threw her clothes in the suitcase. She was glad she had left all the art stuff in the car.

She quietly opened the hall door, hoping to scoot down the hall without waking Bill. She would call him later in the day after she got home. She carried her shoes in her free hand knowing she would still have to walk through water. She didn't close her door.

But as she passed the door to the master bedroom, it was open, and she saw the bed was empty and appeared un-rumpled. Was he upstairs? The answer came when she opened the front door and saw his car was gone. When had he left?

She decided to go back inside to see if there was a note. She looked in the kitchen. She and Carson always left notes to each other on the kitchen counter closest to the back door. No, there was no note anywhere.

And he hadn't straightened up the house from their dinner last night. The plates still sat on the coffee table, along with the wine glasses. Maggie noticed Bill's glass was empty as was the wine bottle. But he had turned off the gas logs.

She picked up the plates and glasses and carried them into the kitchen. No water for rinsing, so she just opened the dishwasher and placed them on the bottom rack. The wine bottle went into garbage for recycling.

She padded across the water-soaked floor to the veranda and opened the door. She just needed one last look at the ocean beyond. Maybe she could corral that happy feeling she had experienced all week as she watched the waves roll in and out with rhythmic splendor. She stood for several minutes, but no peace came. The sand looked dull after the storm. The sea oats were soggy and lay limp against each other. Only one lonely soul walked the beach—looking for shells, she supposed. A soul who looked as solitary as Maggie felt.

Slowly, she turned and walked back to the front door. She lifted her suitcase. It felt as heavy as her spirits. She went out, locking the door behind her, and got into her car. How she dreaded the drive home. Mile after miserable mile of it.

Before she headed out of town, she stopped by a convenience store and used the restroom. She tried to wash her face and repair her make-up, but the effort yielded little reward. She hurried out of the store and kept her eyes down as she got into her car.

"Okay, Maggie. Now you have not one heartache, but two," she said with despair accompanying every word as she turned the car west toward the mainland.

CHAPTER 15

The drive home seemed endless. At times, Maggie's tears caused the two-lane road ahead to blur into a single strip of molten gray. Her heart rested on her lap like a bowling ball.

Bill's words played over and over on some endless loop she had no power to shut off. Round and round, like a recorder gone bad. And with each phrase now seared into her mind, she ranted her objections out loud, yelling to the stretches of marsh on each side of the road. Murky and dark they lay—like the pain in her heart.

Gradually, Maggie's thoughts extricated themselves from the angry cycle and began to focus on how this all began. It had been so innocent in the beginning. Of that, Maggie was certain. But somewhere along the way of dinners together and sharing life's stories, they had found more than just common ground. She realized it had ceased being about Carson and Rose a long time ago, although the pretense stayed intact.

Slowly, Maggie began to face her participation in the emotional snare that had grabbed both of them. She thought of the new clothes she had bought, the extra attention to her appearance, Bill's touches she didn't brush off. By the time she reached Rocky Mount, she finally admitted out loud Bill had some justification for his behavior.

"Maggie, you can't have it both ways," she said, gravely. An image kept trying to emerge, but Maggie's mind kept shoving it back. It was an image of Granny—disappointed.

Before she reached Raleigh, she decided to tell Bill she was equally at fault in this misunderstanding. No, they could not continue the dinners, but she would still like to be friends. Maybe they could wait to see what their futures held. She could not say, "Wait until I'm a widow," even to herself.

Maggie unpacked the car in some robotic fashion. She placed her picture of the Hatteras lighthouse on its easel on the screened porch and remembered the one she left at the cottage. She regretted giving it to Bill now, but it was too late.

She debated calling him. She could use the ruse of thanking him for the cottage, which she intended to do, anyway. Maggie Bales knew her manners. However, a hot shower and shampoo were first on the list. Then perhaps she would call. Or maybe just wait for his call.

Having showered and dressed and feeling fresh again, she headed off to see Carson. After all, Bill might not be home from the beach yet. He would have to oversee the water heater installation and drying the floors. Surely, there were emergency services available even on Sunday. He must have left in search of help before she got up this morning.

She entered the parking lot with a sense of dread. Had Carson missed her? Would he ignore her? As she reached the front porch, the sense of dread turned into an overwhelming sense of guilt. She felt an urgency to see him right away.

She hurried first to the sun porch. It was late in the afternoon by now so the sun wasn't so fierce. But there was only one resident there, with a visitor.

She almost ran down the hallway to Carson's room. He was asleep. However, he opened his eyes as she laid her purse on the dresser.

"Hi, there," she said, trying to use her most cheerful voice.

Carson gazed at her for a moment. She prayed for any spark of recognition. He turned his face away, but then looked back at her and held her eyes for several seconds.

"It's me . . . Maggie," she sang out characteristically. He dipped his head slightly, and she saw that crooked tilt to his mouth she always assumed was a smile. She wanted to hug him as hard as possible. Instead, she sat down on the bed beside him and took his left hand. To her surprise, she found herself telling him about the entire week except for last night. Her words tumbled over each other like water over stones in a stream. She couldn't tell him fast enough.

When her stream ran dry, she paused and watched him. There was no sign he understood anything she had said, but she could feel a warm pressure from his hand. How badly she wanted him to take her in his arms and tell her it was okay. Instead, he began to nod and was soon sound asleep again.

She tiptoed from the room with the same heavy heart. Maybe Bill had been right. Maybe she was just living with an illusion that Carson still deserved her loyalty. But as she hurried to the parking lot, her fierce allegiance took control once again.

"Bill Holton, I am *not* wrong to be faithful to my husband!" she shouted aloud. She slammed the car door shut and sent gravel flying as she drove from the parking lot. She was more determined than ever to tell Bill that Carson was her first obligation . . . no, her first love! Nothing he could say would change her mind, she thought, as she pummeled the steering wheel with her fist.

She stopped by the grocery to pick up a few items. As she passed a small hamburger place, she realized how hungry she was. She got two grilled cheese sandwiches to go—one for now and the other one later. The delicious smell could not be denied, so she unwrapped one while she drove and had finished half by the time she turned into her driveway. She hoped Bill had called. She hurried inside and checked her message machine first thing.

There was only a call from Marty, asking if she was home. Maggie returned her call. After an exchange of the week's events and Maggie's reiteration of her gratitude for Marty's checking in on Carson, they hung up. Maggie finished the first sandwich *and* the second. Her eating habits were usually restrained, but she needed something to fill the empty space inside. Unfortunately, the second sandwich wasn't the answer, and it lay heavy on her stomach as a reminder her emptiness was not located in her abdomen.

The rest of the evening was filled with mundane chores around the house. She listened for the phone, but it never rang. Maybe Bill felt she should be the one to apologize. After all, she was the one who ran out of the room. Maybe he was still in Corolla. But wouldn't he need to be at the office early in the morning? Finally, she went to bed. Tomorrow, she thought. Just like Scarlett O'Hara—tomorrow, she would deal with it.

She was exhausted. Sleep came quickly. However, her dreams were confusing and disturbing. She was walking on the beach, but the dark waters of the marshes she had seen that morning kept coming closer from the direction of the dunes, shoving her toward the ocean. When she awoke in the darkness, she tried to shake off the feelings of dread. The rest of the night was spent in half sleep, half wakefulness. When the tepid sunshine made its way into her bedroom, she decided not to linger in bed.

The morning passed. When the phone rang and she raced to get it, it had been a neighbor asking to borrow the extension ladder. She made her trip to see Carson. He slept most of the time she was there. The day was over, and there had been no call from Bill. She was certain now he was waiting for her to call. She went to bed rehearsing what she would say. First, she would thank him again for the lovely week. That would be the easy part.

The next day, Maggie found Bill's number she had called when the water heater broke. She almost hoped he would not answer, except she often got tangled up in her words when someone's voice prompted her to leave a message. She decided to write down what she would say in case she needed it. She wrote and rewrote until she had something that sounded pleasant, light, and not accusing. She even practiced saying it.

"Hi, Bill. It's Maggie. First, please accept my thanks for the use of your lovely beach house last week. Every day was wonderful and different, and the memories will carry me through the summer. I hope all the damage has been repaired. Second, I have thought about our argument and realize my part in contributing to the misunderstanding. Please accept my apology."

Finally, she picked up the receiver. Four rings and then the machine. Thank goodness she had the notes before her. After the annoying beep, she gave her spiel. As an afterthought, she added, "Look forward to hearing from you."

Each day that week she waited for Bill's call. When she had not heard from him by the weekend, she began to wonder if she should call again. Maybe by some fluke he didn't get her message. Was he okay? Should she locate his office number and ask about him? After all, he would never know she called. Did he hold grudges? Not a trait she admired, incidentally. Finally, she decided to do nothing.

After two weeks, the unspoken fear she might never hear from Bill again found a permanent spot to settle in her mind. Her heart ached. Day after day, she replayed the scenario of their last evening together. He obviously read her anger as the door slamming on their relationship. But would he not even be courteous enough to return her phone call? She had to conclude she really didn't know Bill at all.

The summer passed slowly. Maggie's days were filled with chores around the house and time spent with Carson. She had lunch twice with Marty, attended two cookouts with faculty friends, and read five truly vapid books. Carson's sister came for a weekend visit in August. On the sun porch, a new canvas sat bare on her easel, her brushes untouched.

Finally, school began. She felt some relief at having a purpose but an overwhelming sense of time lost. A summer she could never recapture. The dream of happy dinners with Bill erased early on.

It was a beautiful fall. Maggie always hoped the cooler days and colorful palettes of the trees would go on forever. Some years an early frost would turn the leaves brown too quickly. However, this year, every leaf seemed to be inviting closer scrutiny by the passing world. Unfortunately, this year, for the first time, even the glorious maple in her back yard failed to raise her spirits as she surveyed it each morning. Her thirty-seventh wedding anniversary was circled on the calendar.

Maggie moved through the days, willing herself to think about her classes during the day, focusing on Carson each afternoon, grading papers and preparing for classes in the evenings, and going to bed early. She always knew having a routine was her salvation when her emotions were ragged.

Her friends at school often asked her to go out for drinks on Fridays, but she always declined, saying she had to go see Carson. She and Carson had never been "TGIF-ers"—as he called them. Even if she ordered a soft drink, she still felt ill at ease in a smoky bar commiserating with colleagues about the week's events.

At last, Marty and two other friends prevailed on her to go to a movie based on a true story of a teacher who defied all odds by taking children from an inner city ghetto to the national geography finals and winning. Maggie liked the feel-good stories.

They decided to meet at the movie on a Saturday night in mid-October. It was still warm, so Maggie had dressed in slacks and a light sweater. She arrived early and walked leisurely across the parking lot toward the theater. She was looking at the posters of current movies on the outside wall when she heard a voice behind her that instinctively caused her to whirl around.

Walking toward her, unaware of her presence, were Bill and a blonde woman much younger than Maggie. She was laughing as Bill held her hand while regaling her with his story. Maggie suddenly felt so weak she reached for the brick wall behind her. At that moment, Bill saw her. He seemed to stop in mid-stride, but quickly regained his composure. He released the blonde's hand and placed his arm around her waist to steer her in the other direction. She was oblivious, but as they turned, Bill looked back at Maggie and nodded slightly.

The whole parking lot seemed to be spinning as she braced herself against the wall. She felt nauseated. Her trembling hands were ice cold. She had to get out of there. She gulped for air and began moving in a trance toward her car. People, cars, noises were all a blur as she focused totally on propelling her jelly-like legs. Once there, she managed finally to get the door unlocked and sink into the seat. She closed the door and leaned her head against the steering wheel. She could not think. It was as if her brain froze the moment she saw them. Her dazed senses were finally brought into focus when her new cell phone rang.

"Where are you?" asked Marty. "We've been waiting at the ticket counter for ten minutes and the movie is starting." Mild-mannered Marty sounded irritated.

Maggie struggled to find her voice. Feebly, she said, "I'm so sorry."

Marty sounded more concerned now. "Are you okay?"

Again, Maggie struggled. "Yes . . . no . . . I think I ate something bad at dinner. I feel sick."

Marty probed further. "Do you need us to come over? Can we help?" It was obvious they had not spotted her car.

"No, no, please go on to the movie. I'll be okay soon. I'm so sorry," she said again.

"Okay. I'll call when the movie is over to check on you."

Maggie could not even protest. She closed her phone with a dull thud and sat staring out into the night. The erratic patterns of bugs drawn to the tall security light close to her car mesmerized her. Her thoughts were equally chaotic. Finally, a chill seemed to bring her back to some form of reality. She put the key into the ignition and slowly began the process of backing out of the parking spot. Everything around her was in slow motion.

Without being aware of the places she passed or even the streets she traveled, she finally arrived at her driveway. She pulled the car into the garage and stared blankly at the smudges on the wall ahead of her.

She opened her door, fumbled for her purse, got out of the car, and walked with great hesitation into her familiar house. A house that had seen all her emotions, but never pain this raw.

What had she expected? What kind of idiot was she? Why did seeing him hurt so badly? Bill had told her this. She had just been unwilling to accept it. He said he needed someone to love. Or was it that he needed someone to love him? It didn't matter. All Maggie could think of was how Bill told her he loved her and then so easily walked away from that emotion. She could only conclude he had not really cared for her after all. Was he just going to pursue her until he had accomplished some nefarious goal and then walk out of her life?

Chiding herself with every step she took, Maggie admitted she had thought he would wait for her. How terribly naïve! She had even convinced herself his failure to return her call was part of his respect for her married state. Wrong, wrong, wrong! She chastised herself for her stupidity. Bill Holton was not a man of integrity like Carson Bales. That was "plain and simple"—Granny's words.

She began yelling at the walls as she paced from room to room. "I hate you! You're a liar! You never loved me!" Over and over, she screamed epithets to the air as if it would carry the words all the way to Bill.

Finally, exhausted, she lay face down on the bed and began to cry. She sobbed until tears would not fall any longer. She listened to her own convulsive breathing subside.

The ringing of the phone pulled her from the bed. It was Marty asking if she was okay. She assured her she was feeling much better, and, no, there was no need to come over. She could tell Marty wasn't convinced, but she didn't press Maggie.

Afterwards, she went into the bathroom and washed her face. She looked into the mirror and hated what she saw—the red blotches on her skin, the puffy eyes, the limp hair. She was no match for the younger, blonde woman. Time had taken a toll on Maggie that had not yet occurred for Miss Blondie. Why *shouldn't* Bill be more interested in a younger woman, for Pete's sake? Maggie was over sixty. Why would Bill find *her* attractive? She scoffed at believing he had meant any of those words at the beach. How could she have allowed herself to be so easily deceived? "You're an idiot, Maggie Bales!" she said to the mirror as she shut off the water with one mighty thrust of the handle.

The next day, she slept late and skipped church. She wandered around the house in her pajamas until two o'clock that afternoon. Finally, she summoned the energy to step into the shower. She spent the rest of the day with Carson. Being in the same room with him gave her a sense of belonging to someone. She talked to him while he slept. She told him what a good man he had always been, how she admired his integrity, and how she was so glad they had gotten married.

From that point on, she spent more time with Carson each day. She rubbed lotion on his arms, stroked his hair, smoothed his covers, patted his knee, and told him she loved him over and over. She needed to believe she made a difference in his day—that she still mattered to someone.

Thanksgiving came, and she ate in the dining room with Carson while the nurse's assistant fed him a tan, liquid mass that had once been turkey and dressing. She could barely look at his plate, but he ate a small portion with little hesitation, almost robotic. Could he really taste it, she wondered.

She felt a great sorrow that day. They had always had faculty and graduate students, who had no family nearby, to their house for Thanksgiving dinner. She would cook for days in advance. Carson took great pride in roasting the turkey. He got up early to get the bird in the oven while she slept a little later. Guests gathered at two o'clock bringing flowers and wine. Conversation and laughter flowed around the table. At the end of the day after everyone had gone, she and Carson would sit on the sofa with their feet on the coffee table and bask in the warm feelings of thankfulness for just being able to share with others. The memory left a pain in her heart she could not dislodge all day.

Christmas vacation came. The weather had been uncharacteristically cold for that part of North Carolina, and a light snow had fallen the week before. Snow or no snow, she could not muster the energy to haul out the Christmas decorations. The thought of putting up the artificial tree they had used for years left her weak. In the end, she put a wreath on the door, shut it behind her, and avoided looking in that direction as she drove in and out of the driveway.

She bought two pairs of pajamas for Carson and had them wrapped separately in bright paper, tied with elaborate bows. She also bought the cologne he had worn since they first met. She added a box of his favorite chocolates. There was so little he needed now.

She hoped the packages would represent a special event to him. However, if they did, he gave little indication as she unwrapped each one for him on Christmas Day and held the contents up for his approval. He nodded slightly at each offering as she exclaimed how handsome he would look in the pajamas, how wonderful he would smell with the cologne, how delicious the chocolates would taste. She should have been a saleslady, she decided. That brief thought was her only amusement during Christmas.

She spent the day in his room except when she accompanied him to the Christmas dinner. The tables were festive, and Christmas carols played through the speakers. Other families came and went as they made the obligatory visits to their loved ones. Maggie could tell those who were eager to hurry on to things that held far more excitement. And, she supposed, who could blame them?

Carson's eyes now seemed so vacant she doubted if anything flowed through them into his unraveled brain. He looked smaller each time she visited him. His right side became more drawn and misshapen. She had to work hard now to conjure up the image of him as the strong, vital man she had married.

When he fell asleep that evening, Maggie gathered up the wrapping paper and bows and pressed them into the waste basket under his sink, put the pajamas in a drawer, the cologne on the dresser, the chocolates on his bedside table, and collected her purse. She tiptoed out the door, but paused on an impulse. She turned and went back to Carson's bed, laid her hand on his forehead and whispered, "Merry Christmas, darling, and sleep tight."

Three days after Christmas, she was awakened by the ringing phone. She was vaguely aware it was still dark outside. The voice on the other end told her the news. Carson had died in his sleep. She looked at the clock—4:13 a.m. She lay back on the pillow and tried to absorb the impact of the news, but she felt nothing. Her mind kept telling her, her husband had died, but her emotions were not in synch. Finally, she began to think of the next steps she would have to take. Notifying people. Planning the funeral. What else? She and Carson had bought three plots earlier. Beth was buried in one of them. How would she handle having a grave dug? Her mind bird walked like the sand pipers at the beach from one thought to the next, in erratic paths, without resolving anything.

She padded into the kitchen without a robe. The pre-dawn chill sent a shiver through her. As the coffee brewed, she stared vacantly at the blackness outside.

Finally, as the coffee warmed her throat, the enormity of the news began to work its way to her consciousness. It came in small, merciful pieces. Her beloved husband was gone. Yes, he had been gone in many ways for a long time, but she could still hold his hand, touch his hair, kiss his forehead. Now, that was gone, too. Slowly, tears seeped from her eyes. She didn't try to stop them. She laid her head on the table and released them all. Later, she sat upright, blew her nose, and looked at the clock. Twelve minutes past six o'clock. Maggie poured another cup of coffee and knew there was work to be done.

She rose with a clear purpose. A pinkish glow was pushing aside some of the darkness outside. The tasks ahead pushed aside some of the darkness in her heart.

She called the funeral home, then waited until seven o'clock to call Carson's sister. His sister was surprised, but she, too, had lost Carson a long time ago. She would be coming tomorrow with her family. Maggie had just enough room to let them stay with her.

This called for a decision about telling her own sister. Through the years, they had seen each other at their parents' funerals, exchanged Christmas cards with brief notes, and Maggie had sent graduation gifts for the nieces and nephews when the announcements had reached Carson and her. She thought Betty had married the fourth husband now. No, Maggie decided, the stress of trying to find common ground with her sister was simply beyond her ability at this time.

She called Marty and a neighbor and asked them to notify others who knew Carson. Soon phone calls were coming, and Maggie barely had time to dress before the doorbell was ringing. Friends came with food, with offers to help, and with flowers. Poinsettias now adorned all the noticeably bare places in her living room where Christmas decorations would normally have been.

She picked out a suit for Carson. That was not hard because he owned only three. She chose his favorite, even though it was the oldest. She took the suit, a white shirt, and a somber tie to the funeral home later that day where she picked out his casket. Nothing elaborate, but not too frugal either. Maggie wanted it to represent what Carson had been in his life—strong, solid, and not ostentatious.

She had gone to the funeral home alone, even though friends had offered to go along. Maggie liked solitude when she was under stress. She could think better. She knew she was not going to fall apart, either in the room with the caskets or with the director planning the final rites. Today, she would honor Carson in a dignified manner by making plans she knew would be acceptable to him. Today, it was a matter of placing one foot in front of the other, as she always told herself when daunting tasks lay ahead. She knew she would cry again—but later.

At the funeral, Maggie sat on the first pew beside Carson's sister and listened to the choir sing Carson's favorite hymn, "It Is Well With My Soul." She thought of all the Sundays they had sat in this church and worshipped together. They had occasionally written notes on the bulletins to each other about something funny they noticed—Mr. Vester's snoring during the sermon, Mrs. Boschetti's enthusiastic, off-key rendering of hymns, little Suzanne Bailey pulling her ruffled tights off during the recessional and revealing more than her parents would have liked.

Reverend Adams, who had remained at First United Methodist

Church as other ministers came and went, had wonderful things to say about Carson during his eulogy. Carson had been a pillar of the church. Maggie took comfort knowing that Carson had "run the good race and kept the faith." Just as Reverend Adams was commending Carson's soul back to God, the December sun sent a sudden stream of light through the high windows in the arched ceiling. For a moment, it took Maggie's breath. She imagined it might be Carson smiling at her. Did he recognize her now? Oh, how she hoped so!

At the graveside service, the sun was no match for the cold wind that whipped through the mourners, and Maggie sat, chilled, in the folding chairs under the tent. After the last prayer, people filed by to speak to her. Finally, she shook the last hand and prepared to leave. The heated, so-called limousine was waiting for her, and she hurried to get inside. Just as she reached the door, she noticed a movement ahead. She saw the back of a tall, stately man in a black topcoat moving away from her. She did not remember speaking to him. He disappeared behind some people who had stopped to talk. The chauffeur was impatiently waiting for her to get in. As she settled into the seat, she was startled to realize the figure looked like Bill! Could it have been? She shook off the thought and somehow felt guilty for even letting his name cross her mind—today, of all days.

Carson's sister and her family stayed with her for the weekend. Friends dropped by with offers of help. They continued to bring food in the time-honored, Southern tradition. She enjoyed having people in the house, but she often retreated to her room to just lie on the bed and try to blot out all the noise. She wanted to feel the pain, but the noise kept it at bay. She wanted to cry but not with all the people around. So she just lay there and squinched her eyes tightly in hopes of finding strength to face them all again.

Finally, her guests were gone. She wandered from room to room. She wept over silly remembrances. Once, the kitchen sink had stopped up when she had put coleslaw in the disposal after a cookout with friends. Carson's efforts to unstop it with a plumber's snake had been so forceful, coleslaw spewed out the vent on top of the roof. She had laughed until tears came as he grumpily lugged the ladder around the side of the house for the clean-up job. However, Carson had failed to see the humor until much later. Then there was the time he had wanted to surprise her with a romantic dinner in front of the fireplace in the living room when she returned from a February art conference. He had set the table with a white cloth, candles, and their best dinnerware and lit the fire. When she arrived, the door was open, the windows were up, and the acrid smell of smoke greeted her on the doorstep. Carson had forgotten to open the damper. They both spent the rest of the evening cleaning soot from the furniture and carpet. Then they had to sleep under a mountain of blankets with the windows still flung open. So much for the romantic dinner.

A week after the funeral, a lovely bouquet of yellow roses, white lilies, and blue ageratum arrived. She took the flowers from the delivery boy and put them on the kitchen table. The best florist in town, she noted. Taking the card from its envelope, she trembled as she read, *"I'm so sorry. Bill."* She sank down in the chair and began to sob again. Now she felt even more loss and loneliness.

She picked up the beautiful flowers, carried them to the screened porch, and sat them on a table beside her idle easel. For one brief moment, she considered picking up her brushes and transferring the image to the waiting canvas, but quickly dismissed that idea. She wanted absolutely no more memories of the benefactor—ever!

CHAPTER 16

Maggie was relieved when school began in January. Her students gave her purpose each day, and during the time she was in the classroom, she escaped the emptiness at home. She was surprised she felt such a void in her heart in the evenings. After all, Carson hadn't lived there for nearly three years. And his mostly unresponsive reaction to her visits had not been especially rewarding. But apparently she had failed to recognize how going to see Carson every day had provided a connection to life as a married woman. Now there was no denying she was a widow and alone. Completely alone.

She hated the nighttime after papers were graded, and she had laid out what she would wear the next day. She hurried to get into bed, but sleep was intermittent, at best. And the weekends seemed endless. She had more time to fill now.

Friends invited her for dinner, and she accepted their invitations so as not to appear ungrateful. However, she had no enthusiasm for the requisite conversation regarding how she was getting along or their offers to help. Because she knew their intentions were honest and kind, she murmured the same benign responses. She was doing well, thank you, and, yes, she would call if she needed them. She understood those evenings were as difficult for her hosts as they were for her, and she suspected they were as happy as she was when the evenings ended.

January gave way to February, and finally March arrived when the moderate climate in North Carolina prompted jonquils to send out leaves and buds to test for sun and warmth. Maggie had six varieties of jonquils planted in four different beds. They were her favorite flower. She looked forward to seeing their bright, yellow faces each spring.

It was on such a day in March that she stopped the car in the driveway after school to inspect the sunny bed surrounding the lamp pole in the front yard. Her heart felt lighter as she looked at the blooms that resembled tiny trumpets calling out that spring was on its way. The thought sent warmth through her bones that had felt cold for months. She smiled toward the blue sky overhead with thankfulness.

She had just gotten behind the wheel to put the car into the garage when she heard a sound. She looked in the rearview mirror to see a car pulling in behind her. The sunshine on its windshield blurred the image of the driver. She watched as the door opened, and a man stepped out. Her heart nearly stopped. Bill!

For an instant, Maggie wanted to throw her car into drive and crash through the hedge in front of her—into the neighbor's back yard. Instead, she collected herself, got out of the car, and held onto the door handle for dear life.

"Hello," she said, trying desperately to keep her voice steady.

Bill stopped a respectful distance from her. His posture told her if he was wearing a hat, it would be in his hand.

"Hi," he mumbled and paused.

Maggie decided she would offer no more conversation. He had made the trip to see her. He could carry the ball.

For the first time since she had known him, Bill seemed ill at ease and at a loss for words.

"You . . . look good," he stammered.

Maggie stood very still and kept her gaze level with where his eyes should have been, though he kept looking at his feet or over her head.

"Aw . . . could we go inside? I mean . . . I came because I really need to talk to you, and I don't think we want to stand out here that long." He did not move until she did. Slowly she released the door handle and started down the brick walk to her front door. She had to rummage in her purse to find the house key. Bill remained several steps behind her. When she finally produced it, he did not jump to take it from her as he had in the past.

She unlocked the door and walked in. She did not turn to watch him enter, but instead carefully placed her purse and book bag on one end of the sofa so she could be certain of having a chair for herself. Her heart was hammering so loudly she thought he surely must hear it, but she was determined to keep her dignity, so she sat down and pulled herself erect, crossed her ankles, and waited.

Bill shut the door behind them and walked to the sofa opposite her. "Do you mind if I get some water?" he asked.

"Help yourself," she replied cordially. She did not move an inch. After all, he knew where the glasses were.

She could tell he was even more uncomfortable than she was. He was taking an unusual amount of time to fill one glass with ice and water. Finally, he walked back to the sofa and set the glass on a coaster on the coffee table between them.

With hands clasped and his elbows on his knees, he looked at her.

"Maggie, this is the . . . almost the hardest thing I've ever done. I just ask that you hear me out until I finish, and then you can say anything you wish." He paused, waiting for her to speak.

She simply looked at him, her hands in her lap, her legs still crossed at the ankles.

When he realized she was not going to respond, he began.

"Oh Maggie, I've been such a fool. A self-centered idiot!" He discharged the words as if they were poison in his mouth. "Nothing I say here today in any way justifies my behavior toward you, but I have to say it anyway because it has taken me so long to come to understand myself. Maybe it will help you understand my recent actions. Anyway, I hope so. What you think of me after my revelation is entirely up to you.

"I loved Rose, but our worlds were different. When we married, I was a red-blooded young man, as they say, whose thoughts focused on the physical side of our marriage much more often than Rose felt they should. She had been raised by very strict parents whose basic sex education to their three daughters was 'Nice girls don't.' The problem with that philosophy was they forgot to tell the daughters that idea doesn't apply to marriage. Maybe if one of Rose's sisters had married first, she would have given Rose different information. I don't know. I just know from the beginning, I felt my desires were a burden for her.

The sad part was that Rose never said no. I just knew she was eager for me to get the deed over so she could go back to her prim little world.

"I threw myself into my studies and often stayed late at the library so as not to 'bother' Rose. Certainly with all the classes, labs, cramming for tests, and all that went with medical school at Duke, I didn't have a hard time finding things to keep me occupied."

Maggie's thoughts immediately went to Carson and Clara, but she said nothing.

"As you know, we had a son. Rose adored him, but she didn't want another child. Her enthusiasm for me diminished even further. My birthday, our anniversary, New Year's Eve, and maybe half a dozen random times each year. That was Rose's idea of a satisfying sex life.

"My world became medicine, except for the weekends when I spent lots of time with William. Rose seemed to admire me for playing with him. I kept thinking if I could just get her to admire me enough, she would thaw in her attitude toward other areas of our life. I believed I must lack some sort of physical attractiveness that would make Rose, or any woman, desire me.

"To be fair to Rose, she was a wonderful wife in every other way. She kept an immaculate house and never wanted outside help, in contrast to her mother who had a service person for every mundane task one could think of. Rose was a wonderful cook. She kept herself trim and beautifully dressed.

"She would meet me at the front door each evening with a glass of wine, no matter how late I got home. She would give me a feather kiss on the cheek and place the glass in my hand. She listened to my recounting of the day as if every word was precious to her. When I finished, she would tell me dinner was ready, and we would go into the breakfast room. The food was always piping hot, although I know many times she had reheated it or even prepared new dishes because of my late hours. There were always fresh flowers on the table. In the warm months, Rose grew her own. In the winter, she bought them at the local market.

"I think those efforts kept me faithful to her. There were always possibilities for affairs with staff members. Some women seem attracted to a white coat without any real concern for who wears it. I saw fellow doctors use some bad judgment and ruin their marriages. I didn't want that to happen. My faithfulness was driven more by a desire to keep the status quo than any penchant for morality. I claim no saintly qualities—unlike you, Maggie."

Maggie had a queasy feeling. She felt like an eavesdropper. Surely, such personal matters belonged only to him—and to Rose. She really didn't care to hear about their life together. Where was he going with this intrusion on her day, anyway?

He took another sip of water and settled against the sofa, laying one arm across the back as she had seen him do before. As much as she didn't want to, Maggie could not help but notice how handsome he was.

"When I met you, Maggie, I sensed what a special lady you are. Each time after we had dinner, I found myself full of anticipation of seeing you again. In the beginning, I knew I wouldn't do anything that smacked of unfaithfulness, not because of me, but because of you. By that time, Rose had been in Carolina Manor for three years, and I saw her as my responsibility, not my wife.

"After she died, I was free of the obligation of fidelity. But I failed miserably when I projected my freedom onto you. I had fallen in love with you, and I wanted you to love me in return more than anything in the world. Even at this age, I wanted you to want all of me. The hunger I had felt for years wanted satiety. Before I grow too old, I wanted to know that someone would find me physically attractive, that someone would jump into bed with me at a moment's notice. And I wanted it to be you, Maggie.

"The night at the beach house, I was the happiest I have been in years. When I could feel you yielding in my arms, I fought so hard to keep from ravishing every ounce of you. However, I wanted to respect your body and wait for it to respond. When I thought you wanted me as much as I wanted you, I felt overwhelming happiness—not just in my body, but in my heart. It was as if the longing inside of me for the last forty years was finally going to be satisfied.

"When you spoke Carson's name, all of that wonderful feeling instantly drained from my body. The rejection I felt was like the bitterest gall I could imagine. I tried to plead my case, which was obviously a miserable failure—mainly because I didn't have a case, Maggie. When you became angry and left the room, I felt so rejected that every instinct within told me to get away from you. I didn't bother with the cleanup of the house until a week later. Nothing mattered. By the way, I put the beach house on the market and sold it within two weeks. Rose had inherited it from her parents. I never felt it was mine, anyway."

Maggie couldn't stop the sad feeling that came over her. Even with the terrible ending to the week, she still thought about that house with such happiness—the veranda where she ate breakfast, the sun porch upstairs where she painted, and even the small den where, for the most part, she spent cozy evenings reading. However, she continued to sit in silence, though she had shifted her position several times.

"This is the hardest part, Maggie. I sit here in utter shame before you—shame at my lack of judgment and at my lack of character." He picked up the sofa pillow beside him and began to twist the fringe. Maggie could tell he was searching for the right words.

"After I left you that night, I remembered a young woman on the hospital staff who, more than once, had gone out of her way to speak to me. Later that same week, I walked by her desk on purpose, stopped, and started a conversation. She was more than receptive, and before I left, we had a dinner date for that weekend.

"I want to spare you . . . and me . . . the details, but in the beginning she made me feel like I was twenty-five all over again. At first, I was very flattered by that. But I soon learned that it takes so much more than sex to have a good relationship."

Every word Bill uttered about this affair acted like a tiny steel drill boring deeper and deeper into Maggie's heart.

"The night I saw you at the theater brought back all the feelings I had been trying to disown. I thought of you all through the movie and for days afterwards.

"Anyway, Maggie, I realized I could run away from you, but I could never forget you. I went to Carson's funeral just so I could see you again, even if from afar. I never took my eyes off you during the entire service. I hadn't planned to go to the cemetery, but I felt drawn like a magnet to be where you were. I yearned to hold you in my arms and let you sob all the sorrow away. I didn't want sex, Maggie. I wanted you for the person you are, and I wanted to comfort you."

Bill paused again, collecting his thoughts, she assumed. He glanced at her to see her response. Now, she was the one having a difficult time looking at him. His reasons for going to Carson's funeral had caused a rush of warmth through her body that made her weak.

"No!" she screamed inside. "You can't let him into your heart ever again. Not ever!" She didn't realize she was pounding the arm of the chair until she saw his astonished look.

"Maggie, you look so angry," he said sadly.

She felt forced to speak. "I wish anger was the full extent of it, Bill."

He looked puzzled and waited for her to continue. When she said no more, he took another sip of water, coughed unconvincingly, and tugged at his tie.

"I ended the affair—I hate even saying that word to you—the day after Carson's funeral. At the time, I only knew I could no longer be involved with someone else when you were on my mind throughout each day. During the past three months, I have thought of a thousand things I wanted to say to you. How sorry I am for behaving as I did that night in Corolla. For walking out on you. For not returning your phone call. For being an idiot. And I've had to come to terms with what a selfish person I am . . . was, I hope.

"Maggie, I just know that you made me a better man. Thinking about you has forced me to think about me, and I don't measure up. There is lots more I could say, but I guess the bottom line is I am . . . so . . . very . . . sorry." He punctuated each of the last words with dramatic pauses.

She shifted. She had to get him out of her house. His sad eyes were melting the iciness of her earlier resolve. "Bill, I have no idea what you want from me. If you came here to say you're sorry, I think you've said it." Why did the words catch in her throat? Was the pain in her heart echoed in her eyes?

"Yes, Maggie—that—but I also came to say something else." He slowly stood up and walked to the window. Looking out, he pronounced each word softly. "Maggie, in spite of all the reasons you will deny this, I do love you, and I want you to know I will do anything in this world to be with you again." He turned and looked at her. "Whatever price

I must pay, I will. If it is today you can forgive me or ten years from now—just tell me it will happen sometime."

She dropped her head. She was trembling. Every muscle wanted to jump and propel her into his arms. "No, no, no!" she told herself. "Selfish, egotistical! How dare he even consider I would take him back," she yelled inside. She tried to control her voice as she searched for words.

"Well, that just isn't possible. I hope you have said all here you came to say," and she stood up. She moved rapidly toward the door and opened it. A cool breeze met her as she waited for him. She needed to shut the door on both him and her escalating emotions.

He seemed a little startled, and she could see he was struggling to comply with her obvious demand that he leave. He moved toward her in a wooden cadence. "I do understand, Maggie. I knew I had little chance of winning you back, but please know I had to tell you all of this so we could start with a clean slate if starting again was possible. Now I know I've lost you. As I said at the beginning, I've been a fool. And I know I don't deserve a second chance, but I had to try." His eyes were hollow in his pale face. Maggie had to look away.

He walked past her, trying not to pass too closely, fully respecting her space, she could tell.

As his car backed out of the drive, she sank down on the sofa. She could feel his warmth. She pounded the pillow he had held. She was both furious with him and drawn to him. "Why did you have to come back into my life? Why? Why? Why?" she screamed toward the ceiling.

Later, Maggie sat in the kitchen, staring out the window as the light faded. "He isn't the man I thought he was. To have an affair with some flighty, trashy girl!" She hurled the last two words into the air with as much vitriol as existed in Maggie Bales. The thoughts of Bill with her made Maggie furious. She yelled until she was hoarse—all the names she could think of that she allowed herself to utter out loud. Finally, she laid her head on her arms. She awoke sometime later in a dark room.

She noticed it was past dinnertime, but she wasn't hungry. She made her way to the bedroom and crawled into bed without changing her clothes. When she left for school the next day, she realized she never put the car into the garage.

Maggie barely made it through the rest of the week. No matter how hard she tried to concentrate on the lessons, her mind kept going back to Bill and the other woman. She could never get past that picture in her mind.

"He simply isn't trustworthy," she said over and over. Nothing like her Carson. She had misjudged Bill to be someone he wasn't. Now all she had to do was erase his visit from her memory and move on. So, why couldn't she?

Two weeks went by. Maggie tried to keep busier than usual. She went to two movies with friends. She bought plants at a local nursery and spent one Saturday in the yard, furiously ripping out long-dead flowers from last summer. She put fresh pine bark in the beds, pruned shrubs—even those that shouldn't be—used the tiller to make a new bed that she didn't even want—anything to keep busy. Never mind she probably wouldn't be able to get out of bed the next day. And she wasn't. She barely made it to class on Monday, hobbling like some elderly woman. Quite a sight, she knew.

The third week brought the stormy spring weather she had always liked, even when the skies turned eerily dark and winds blew shingles off her roof. Somehow, she thought it signaled April's desire to put a final end to winter, kicking it to smithereens. Carson could never understand her pleasure when those days came each year. "Mother nature's pruning job," she would declare as they picked up the limbs and leaves blown all over the yard.

Sunday, she went to church as usual. She always looked to see the title of the sermon in the bulletin. Reverend Adams had provocative titles. "Stoned," she read. Another sermon on the evils of drugs in our culture, Maggie surmised.

But she was wrong. The text he read was about the woman caught in adultery and brought to Jesus. When Jesus was told the custom was to stone such women to death, he only asked that the person without sin cast the first stone. Of course, she had heard this story many times before, but something was different this time. This time, the woman was Bill, and Jesus was challenging Maggie to cast that stone—*if* she were sinless.

She didn't even hear the conclusion to the sermon or the closing hymn. At the last note of the recessional, she eased past the people waiting to shake the reverend's hand and hurried to her car. She sat in the warm front seat and searched for answers. She had spent a lifetime trying not to make Jesus angry. But what about her self-righteousness? Was that getting Him pretty steamed? Why was Jesus frowning? And why *shouldn't* she throw that rock?

She sat there and argued with Jesus for quite a while. "I've certainly never had an affair! I've always been a good girl! Granny's words didn't fall on deaf ears, Jesus!"

She pled her case. She tried to think of convincing arguments to justify her right to hurl that stone. But deep inside, she knew who was winning the argument, and no matter how long she defended herself, it wasn't going to change Jesus's command. In the end, she pulled out of the parking lot and headed the car down the street. She didn't even stop for lunch.

Once home, she placed a call. Bill's answering service came on. She left a simple message. "I'm free for dinner Friday night."

Truthfully, she wasn't surprised when the doorbell rang an hour later. About thirty minutes earlier, she had glanced in the mirror for a quick check. She had repeatedly told herself he wouldn't come, but somehow she knew he would if he had really meant what he said.

He stood at her door with a huge bouquet of jonquils. "I believe you like these," he said simply.

She smiled, took the vase, and moved so he could step inside. "Yes, they have always meant the end of a bleak winter to me," she said and hoped the symbolism wasn't lost on him.

"Maybe they will mean the same for me," he replied, and then as if needing something to do, he quickly took the vase from her. "You say where you want these, ma'am," he said with a slight bow.

"Let's put them on the coffee table," she said with far more lilt in her voice than she intended.

Bill set the vase down while Maggie moved to sit in the chair next to the sofa, but before she could leave a standing position, Bill had his arm around her waist, drawing her toward him. His touch had the same magic it always had despite her earlier vow to take it slowly.

His voice was husky now, and she saw moisture forming in the corner of one eye. "Maggie, when I got your message, I had to sit down. My knees were water. I just kept saying over and over, 'You don't deserve this, Bill Holton.' Don't get me wrong here. I'm not assuming anything by your willingness to have dinner, but I am so grateful for even that gesture."

She wasn't sure if he was going to kiss her—or if she wanted him to—so she stood very still. Gently, he pulled her closer and held her tightly. "Maggie, you tell me what the parameters are."

She found her voice finally, but she didn't step back. "Let's just see where it goes. Only please, not too fast," she said into his lapel.

They stood like that for some time, holding on and swaying slightly. She could hear Bill's heart beating. The rhythm was steady, but the beat was fast. As much as she didn't want to, she finally began pulling away.

They both sat on the sofa, his arm around her. Somehow words just didn't seem appropriate. There wasn't much to say, actually. She had made it clear she was willing to see him again, and he had responded with haste. The rest was in the hands of the future. She laid her head on his shoulder, and all the heartache of the previous months receded like a child's balloon suddenly caught up by the wind and carried into the sky.

CHAPTER 17

They didn't wait until Friday night to have dinner. Bill brought huge salads on Monday night after work, and they sat in Maggie's kitchen, talking for hours. There was a new importance in talking about their lives now. Maggie even shared the story of her family.

"So, now I know why you're so stalwart in your beliefs. I think I would have liked your grandmother enormously—maybe except that part about Jesus being mad at you. Granny sure got her point across." He was smiling.

Later, they stood at the door, arms around each other. He kept kissing her gently on the forehead, the cheek, the lips. She only drew back when she felt the kisses overpowering both of them.

"We'll have to talk about this at another time," she said weakly.

"Maggie, it's your call. I'll do anything for you—anything that makes you comfortable—and keeps Granny happy." She knew he couldn't resist, and she also knew that wouldn't be the last time he mentioned Granny.

They saw each other four times that week. On Saturday night, he took her to the historic, old Legacy Inn in Elm City for a lovely, candlelight dinner. Maggie knew if she said the word, Bill would have gotten a room. But she had made a decision that week. A decision she had to explain to him.

On the way home, she said, "Bill, we have to talk about something that will be difficult for me. I guess difficult because I'm not accustomed to talking about it. Nevertheless, maybe we could take a drive somewhere tomorrow, and I'll give it a try."

"Sure," he responded, "but can't you tell me now."

"I don't want to spoil this lovely evening."

He immediately tensed. "Maggie, is it something bad—about us?"

"Oh, no. Well, yes and no. I mean, I don't know how you'll take it." Then she blurted out, "It's about sex," and she was thankful for the dark because she turned crimson.

He reached for her hand and squeezed it tightly. "Granny's been at it again, eh?"

She began to laugh and couldn't stop. Suddenly she felt happier than she had since Carson was diagnosed with Alzheimer's disease. Life was good once again—that much she knew. And yes, Carson's funeral had been little more than three months ago, but she knew—even if others didn't—that Carson would approve of her happiness.

Bill kissed her lightly as they stood just inside her doorway. She could tell he was trying hard to give her space for whatever her feelings were.

"What time can I pick you up tomorrow?" he asked.

"Anytime after church," she replied. Somehow, she knew he wasn't going to church, but she decided against asking him to go with her.

"How about I pick up some sandwiches and drinks and be here by one o'clock?"

"Sounds good. That gives me time to change from my Sunday best."

Maggie leaned against the door after Bill left. She dreaded tomorrow, but it had to be done.

As always, Bill was punctuality, itself. They were on the road and headed east in a flat ten minutes. Maggie had chosen a drive because she was too embarrassed to talk to Bill face to face.

"I thought we'd drive down to Wrightsville Beach. Is that far enough?" he asked with a grin, knowing it would take more than two hours to get there.

"Yes. That's fine, but I'm starved. Where had you planned to eat?" True, she was hungry, but anything she could do to delay the conversation was good, too.

"Okay. I think there's a small park just outside Newton Grove. It's a little chilly today. Are you game for sitting outside?"

"Maybe . . . if we find a table in the sun," she ventured.

The park was deserted. They ate quickly because clouds played peek-a-boo with the sun, and the cool April breezes fanned their bodies. Maggie shivered a couple of times, so Bill took off his windbreaker and draped it over her shoulders.

Afterwards, the car felt warm and cocoon-like when they headed east again. Bill was quiet, just waiting. Maggie knew the dread in the pit of her stomach wasn't going to go away, so she plunged in.

"Bill, I've thought of all you told me a few weeks ago. And I know it's important to you that the woman you date is . . . well . . . willing." She was searching for the words she had rehearsed, but her well-planned thoughts seemed elusive now.

She cast a sideways glance at him. He seemed intent on driving, so she began again.

"Carson and I had a wonderful marriage—a mutual marriage. I mean . . . I never felt *obligated* to do anything." She was searching again. "Naturally, part of our marriage ended long before Carson died. I missed it, but that was the way it was. But I realized the night you came to the beach I could still have those same feelings . . . that they hadn't disappeared . . . forever."

Bill just watched the road ahead. Whatever he was thinking wasn't showing in his face.

"Okay, let me try this again. I remember what you said about Rose, though I try not to, actually. I don't think I'm a frigid woman—in fact, I know I'm not. When you kiss me, I want more—okay? However, and this is a big *however*, I . . . I won't have sex with you, Bill." There, she had said it!

She paused, waiting to see if he responded. When he said nothing, her stomach felt ever more uneasy, but she had to continue.

"That was the one thing I held onto after you left—that I knew you had no memories of a night of passion *with me*. That helped me keep a small amount of my dignity. And because I have no idea where this relationship will go, I still intend to cling to that part of me." She was feeling stronger now. "If that means you want to stop seeing me, so be it!" She ended on a triumphant note—at least to her ears.

She glanced at him again. She could see the muscle in his jaw moving slightly. Was he going to head back to Cary?

Slowly he turned toward her and said, "Could I wait to respond until we get to the beach where I can take you in my arms and hold you forever?"

Her insides felt like liquid. She had expected, at best, he'd give her some argument about her old-fashioned ideas, and at worst, he would leave her at her front door and she'd never see him again. After all, wasn't sex the reason he left her in Corolla?

She slid down in the seat and laid her head against the doorframe, totally spent. This monologue had taken much more emotional energy than she had imagined. And now he wanted to take her in his arms! Wow. Warmth enclosed her as if she had just snuggled under her favorite wooly afghan. She shut her eyes and sank into it. Bill reached for her hand, and they drove the rest of the distance without a word. Maggie dozed off and on.

The breeze was even cooler at the beach, but Bill found an old jacket in the trunk and wrapped it around her. Besides the jacket, his arm around her shoulder protected her from the chilly gusts. She kept her arm around his waist as they walked in tandem. They watched the sea gulls overhead who were returning from their winter foray into more populous regions of the state where food was easier to find than here on the deserted beach. She stooped to pick up a seashell. The tide was low, but beginning to surge. They had to keep stepping up the beach toward the dunes.

They reached a pier where the sturdy wooden columns shielded them from the wind. Bill locked her in his arms and kissed her ever so gently, but for what seemed an eternity.

In a voice laden with emotion, he told her, "Maggie, I love you. I love you. I love you. Yes, I want you in every way possible, but if this goes in the direction I want it to, I'll have the rest of my life to make love to you. Right now, I promise to respect your wishes completely. Your honor and goodness are part of why I love you. Why would I ever want to compromise those? I'm overcome with happiness every moment I remember you have given me a second chance—one I didn't—and never will—deserve. I won't jeopardize that for anything."

She nestled into his shoulder. "Bill, I love you, too," she said, for the first time—even to herself.

Later, they ordered seafood dinners in a weathered, gray-shingled restaurant overlooking the waves. The tide was bringing in seaweed and froth. They ate and watched its endless motion. They talked about routine things—when her school would end, his patients, movies they wanted to see. It was that same familiar, easy conversation they had shared when this all began. However, now, there was an unspoken bond between them.

Spring always unfolds lavishly in North Carolina. Tulip trees, quince, Bradford pears, pussy willows all show off their new colors so as not to be outdone by azaleas, dogwood trees, forsythia, iris, and a myriad of nameless blooms that turn the brown landscape into a canvas of color each year.

Maggie and Bill were a part of that rebirth. They saw each other almost every day. One weekend, they went to Grove Park Inn at Asheville so they could see the redbud and dogwood trees in bloom along the mountain roadsides, but they stayed in separate rooms. In spite of Bill's protest, Maggie insisted on paying for hers. They toured the Biltmore Estate and drank wine from the local vineyards. They drove for miles on the Blue Ridge Parkway, soaking in the views. They lingered over dinner as they watched the sun go down over the mountains. In all of this, there was the quiet understanding they were sorting out their future.

Late May brought an end to Maggie's school. As always, she felt the thrill of the last day—the easy days of summer ahead of her. However, this time, the elation was even higher. More time to relax with Bill without grading papers while he sat and watched television beside her. More time to take trips to the ocean even though the wonderful house was gone.

The last day of school was on a Friday. Bill had invited her out for a nice dinner to celebrate. This time, she was in no particular hurry as she exchanged heartfelt waves with the departing students before she pulled away from the school parking lot. She had plenty of time to get a shower and change. She watched the few puffy clouds drift overhead. She drove slowly, luxuriating in her newfound freedom and in anticipation of dinner. The little chills that accompanied her first sight of Bill each time still amazed her. Would seeing him ever become routine? She hoped not.

She was paying more attention to her wardrobe now. She had gone shopping twice at an upscale boutique in Cary, something she had rarely done before. She was pretty sure Bill took notice, but then he always complimented her, so it was hard to tell. She had added some color and a few highlights to her hair, nothing drastic, but it brightened her face—so the stylist said—and she agreed. She had gotten her makeup done at a local department store when she received a coupon in the mail for a discount. She liked the effect. The salesperson had convinced her to buy several bottles, tubes, and brushes she had never owned before, along with two of the latest shades of lipstick. "It's a new Maggie Bales!" she had exclaimed when she laid her purchases on her bathroom countertop.

This evening, Maggie spent extra time with her makeup. She dressed in a new silk wrap dress—a style she had seen in a current fashion magazine at the beauty shop. It was a soft turquoise and clung to curves she hadn't exposed in the past. New dangle earrings finished the updated look. Maggie even admired herself in the mirror—something she once considered a testimony to vanity.

When she opened the front door, Bill stood there in a splendid new sport coat and navy trousers. Light bounced off his black loafers. He was the most handsome man she had ever seen. She felt a moment of disloyalty even thinking such, but truth was truth.

"Wowee, lady. You look stunning!" And she believed him. She blushed at her own vanity.

"Either I rush you to the car and whisk you to the restaurant, or I'll mess up all that lovely makeup and hair," he said with a wolfish grin.

"Hey, this took a lot of work, and I want to look nice at dinner, so I'll race you to the car," and she laughed as she started off at top speed.

He caught her just in time to open the door. Before she could slide in, he planted a kiss on the top of her head. "Not too much damage," he said as he squeezed her arm.

They drove out of the city and Maggie started to ask where they were going, but thought better of it. Soon they were traveling down a rural highway, passing farm homes and red barns. Bill turned on his signal light indicating a left turn. As they drove through an imposing stone entrance between white fences, he could see her quizzical look. "I thought you might like this place. It has a great reputation, and besides it's away from all the noise of Friday night in the Triangle." A sign said Fearrington Village, a familiar name, but a place she had never visited.

They approached a stately old farm home with an inviting porch. The furniture looked freshly painted. Ferns sat on tall pedestals by the front door. Maggie briefly wondered what it would have been like to sit on this porch a hundred or more years ago, perhaps sipping lemonade.

Inside, there were several dining rooms. Everywhere, there was wainscoting with brightly flowered wallpaper above. Each dining room had its own theme, she noticed. They were led to one with magnolia blossoms in graceful patterns meandering up the walls. The tablecloths were pale green with dark green charger plates and snow-white napkins folded in a tulip design on the plates. The host took them to a table by the window. It looked out on a peaceful, bucolic scene with black and white, belted cows in the meadow beyond. Bill had a wonderful way of making events special, she thought. All of this for a celebration of her summer vacation.

The meal was wonderful. He had the prime rib, and she had salmon with a light dill sauce. They ordered a dessert from the display tray the server presented. He called it cherry blossom. It had a meringue base filled with almond-flavored, silky ganache and topped with fresh, sweet cherries. She noticed the plate was garnished with several pairs of cherries linked together by the stems. A dessert for lovers, she mused.

Bill excused himself just after the dessert was served. She noticed, from the corner of her eye, he said something to the server. She hoped there was no complaint about his food. Hers had been delicious. Bill ignored her questioning expression when he returned. They enjoyed the dessert and talked about the possibility of a trip to the beach soon.

The sun was almost at the horizon when they finished. Bill stood up, reached for her hand, and gently pulled her from the table. "Let's walk outside and watch the sunset."

"Don't you need to pay first?" she asked in surprise.

"It's okay. I'll come back later. We'll miss it if I pay now."

He propelled her down a hallway and out a side door that opened onto a lovely garden with a gurgling fountain and several ornate iron benches. Flowers bloomed everywhere she looked. She noticed Bill had grown silent. He motioned for her to sit. She placed her purse on the bench and was adjusting her skirt when she realized Bill was in front of her on one knee. Her hands flew to her face.

"Maggie," he began seriously, but suddenly tears were flooding down his cheeks. That only prompted the same response in her. He buried his head on her knees and wept on her new silk dress. But somehow, it didn't matter. She kept stroking his hair through her tears. Finally, she began to search for a necessary tissue in her purse. She handed him one, too, and they both started laughing.

"Well, talk about a botched proposal," he said through guffaws. "If I don't get up off these old knees, you'll have to get a forklift." They broke out in new laughter.

Once he was seated beside her and they had composed themselves, he took her hand. "Guess you know what the question is, my dear Maggie. Now, do you have an answer?"

She turned glistening eyes toward him and said with every ounce of sincerity within her, "Yes . . . yes!" Then she added, "But only if you promise to make me laugh like this for the rest of my life."

"I'll do my very best," he replied, "though I hope tears don't always have to come first."

With that, he reached into the breast pocket of his jacket and pulled out a tiny pouch gathered closed by a golden cord. When its contents were revealed, Maggie saw the most beautiful diamond ring ever. It wasn't the largest, but it was so intricate and unusual.

"I wanted something that reminded me of you, Maggie, darling. I wanted it to be fragile yet strong, simple yet complex, and beautiful yet unpretentious, all at the same time. That was a tall order, the jeweler said, but I think he captured it. More importantly, sweetheart, do you think so?"

"Oh, Bill, I love it. I've never seen another one like it. Let's see how it looks on my finger, please," and she laughed because Bill had kept it suspended in midair since pulling it from its hiding place.

He took her left hand, and slid it on easily. Perfect. Then he sealed the engagement with a kiss. By now the sun had set, and only the last pink rays of the day were left to witness the event. She shivered a little in his arms—she wasn't sure if it was the end of the day's warmth or the excitement of the last few minutes. Anyway, Bill pulled her to her feet, and they started to walk back into the building. It was then they noticed at least three people watching them from the kitchen window. As soon as they realized their engagement had been observed, they ducked beneath the window frame.

She could feel the color rise in her cheeks, but Bill said happily, "I hope they got that part about your saying yes so I'll have witnesses if you ever change your mind."

She laughed. Let them look. Nothing would ruin this evening for her.

Once inside, Bill directed her back to their table, and the server immediately brought out champagne. He tried to be discreet as he poured for them, but she knew he was secretly remembering their little drama in the garden. She looked at him with a steady gaze. "Young man, I hope when you are much, much older, you will feel as much love as we have tonight."

He blushed. "Yes, ma'am, I hope so, too," and he quickly retreated to the kitchen.

They toasted their engagement, and Maggie sat back to enjoy the wine.

Bill had still another agenda. "Maggie, for several reasons," and he paused to emphasize *several* with a knowing look in his eye, "I don't want this to be a long engagement. If you want to teach again in the fall—and you know you don't have to—then let's get married soon. I want to take you on an extended honeymoon to those faraway places you've dreamed about."

Maggie had not even thought about the wedding. This all seemed too sudden. "I'm a little overwhelmed with just getting engaged, Bill. Let's think about this for a while," she offered.

"Okay. Would three days be enough thinking time?" he asked.

She started to laugh, but she realized he was serious. "Goodness. Well . . . I'll do my best to get things organized. I guess part of it depends on what type of wedding we have. What are your thoughts on that?"

"Now you have me on the ropes. I really hadn't thought about that part. I certainly hope you don't want a flotilla of sea foam green preceding you," he said with a wink.

"Oh no, I'm thinking a pink armada!" she said, trying to keep a straight face.

As they talked, he made circles on the tablecloth with his knife, a habit she had noticed before. She could tell he was giving something very serious thought. "Do you want a church wedding?" he finally asked.

"Well . . . I would like to be married by a minister . . . by Reverend Adams . . . probably in the small chapel in my church. I certainly don't want bridesmaids, rose petals, and all of that . . . but yes . . . yes, I prefer to be married in a church. What about you?"

"I want what you want, my love."

"I promise to give it careful consideration tomorrow. Tonight, the champagne just makes me want to bask in the warmth of being engaged to the man I've fallen in love with," she said in a voice filled with emotion.

"Fair enough," he replied.

The drive home was blessed by a full moon. The sky seemed more illuminated than Maggie ever remembered it. It was the perfect night. She fell asleep holding Bill's hand.

He woke her gently when they pulled into the driveway. He turned the engine off and put his arm around her. They both looked at the moon for several minutes without saying anything. She had never felt so content. A light came on in the house next door, and that broke the spell. Maggie didn't want to be the adolescent caught necking in the driveway.

"I think we should go inside," she said.

"And leave Mr. Moon out here all by himself?" Bill kidded as he reached for his door handle.

"Oh, I imagine he has lots of company on a night like this," she answered.

Once inside, Bill shut the door behind them and pulled her to him. His kisses were soft and gentle at first, like putting a toe into the water to check its temperature, she thought. Well, her temperature was getting warmer with each kiss. He sensed her willingness and began to kiss her with more intensity. The spell of the evening was weaving its magic on

Maggie. She pressed her body as close to his as possible. She returned his kisses with her own.

"Maggie, my love," he asked in a whisper, "are you ready for this?"

She lowered her head to his chest and kept her eyes closed. Was she? How would she feel tomorrow? She had spent a lifetime trying to live a righteous life and no matter how "contemporary" some of her friends were about sex, she had to answer for what seemed right to her. Granny's lessons were buried deep.

Before she could say anything, Bill answered for her. "No, my precious Maggie, I can tell by your hesitation, this isn't the time. It would cause my heart to weep if you had any regrets, and I would hold myself responsible. Just promise me you will consider setting that wedding date very soon." The forgotten memory of Carson's similar words long ago appeared briefly.

Now, the newly engaged couple moved apart. Bill followed Maggie to the sofa where she sank down on the cushions. She felt both regret and relief. She had never expected to love again. While Carson would always be her first love, Bill was everything she could want at this time in her life. She realized how fortunate she was.

"I'm thinking we should talk to the minister," she chuckled.

"No arguments out of me," he replied.

His expression grew serious. She knew he was mentally forming the words to say something important. "Would you mind some company for church this Sunday?"

She had been keeping that concern tucked away. He never mentioned church, and she assumed he didn't attend. But she knew once they were married, she would really regret it if she had to go alone.

"Bill, I would love that. I don't want to make religion a wedge between us, but it *is* important to me. I guess you know…"

He stopped her. "Yes, I do. I'm not against religion, Maggie. I just have some issues I need to work out. But you're the best example I know of someone who makes me realize maybe there's something I'm missing. Just give me a little time."

Maggie's heart sang with the anticipation of a future she thought was snuffed out with Carson's diagnosis. She put her head on Bill's shoulder, and they sat for a long time just listening to each other breathe.

CHAPTER 18

They set the date for July 10, six weeks away. With so many decisions to be made, Maggie's head was spinning when she went to bed each night.

The decision to buy a new house and sell both of theirs was a major part of the whirlwind swirling in her mind. Bill knew a realtor whom they met with one evening. She advised looking for a new place first and then putting their homes on the market. Bill urged Maggie to work with the realtor during the day, and he would join them in the evening if Maggie found something she liked.

Money was a topic that had always made Maggie uncomfortable. "Um . . . I guess we need to talk about the price range," she said, timidly. "I'm going to do my part. I just don't know what my house will bring."

Bill had a more familiar way with her now where he would ruffle her hair or tweak her nose when he wanted to tease her.

"I believe there's a clause in those marriage vows about endowing you with all my worldly goods. And that's exactly what I plan to do," he said with a glint in his eye.

"Oh, yes, but I have to say those same words to you, Mister!" she retorted. "Given that my endowment potential is probably a lot smaller than yours, I'm just trying to fit my budget."

With a more serious tone, Bill replied, "Maggie, please find a house you love, and let me worry about the rest." Maggie didn't know how to respond and decided to drop the matter for now.

Later that week, she found a home that had just been constructed.

They both fell in love with the floor plan. Each of them would have an office, and there were two extra bedrooms in case they had guests, which might include Bill's daughter-in-law or granddaughters.

Maggie was in awe of the huge master bedroom, bath, and gigantic closet. She laughed when she thought of her cramped space where she could only hang the clothes for that season. Now she would have more hanging space than she had clothes, an island of drawers, and enough shelves to store every pair of shoes and every purse she had ever owned. Feast or famine, she thought, as they signed the contract.

The back yard showed potential for flower beds among the tall trees that stood at the back of the lot. She loved shade plants anyway—hostas were her favorite. In the front, she would plant lots of jonquils—a reminder Bill had come back to her when they bloomed. She pictured them working on their new lawn together and watching it take shape— just like their new life.

Maggie's house sold three days after the realtor listed it. A new, single faculty member who was moving to town snapped it up. When she met him, she smiled at his enthusiasm and energy. She remembered how Carson had loved his own students. How he had looked forward to each new semester. How he struggled to think of new ways to teach that would reach even the most reluctant learner. She could see the same sparkle in the eyes of this young man.

She told Bill she wanted to contribute all the proceeds from the sale of her house to their new home. He was adamant. "Use your money for all the pretty things you'll want for decorations. You know us men, we don't understand all those frills. I can easily afford to pay for the house, Maggie."

She wasn't used to that kind of money. Maggie thought of how she and Carson had scrimped to pay for the modest home they had bought.

Seeing the look of puzzlement on her face, Bill continued, "Maybe we need to discuss money, Maggie. You see, I've earned a reasonable income through the years, but when Rose's parents died, they left her more money than I knew existed. Although I've established generous trust funds for our granddaughters, I still have a healthy bank account and several good investments. I don't believe in extravagance any more than you do, but you won't have to worry about money in the future. That's why I want you to keep the money from the sale of your house."

Wow, was all Maggie could think.

They went furniture shopping and bought a lovely suede sofa and love seat in a soft buttery yellow, a round, glass-top table with accompanying chairs for the breakfast room, and a massive bedroom suite for their room. They decided they would incorporate some of their own things into the new house. Bill's dining room furniture was so elegant, made lovelier with a rich patina from years of waxing, and she would love having it in their home. She wanted her own living room furniture put in the sitting room off their bedroom. Smiling, Bill said he had spent some happy evenings on that sofa and could foresee more in the future, so he had no objections.

The builder was eager to close as soon as possible, so two weeks later, they were moving furniture in and watching the empty spaces receive life and purpose.

One afternoon, Bill called and asked her to meet him at the travel agency near his office. As Maggie drove, she recalled all the times she and Carson had talked about taking trips only to have some other financial need close the door on faraway places. Now, she was finally going to a travel agent. Life is such a puzzle, she thought.

They poured over the brochures while sipping coffee the agent had provided. She had left them in a small room so they could discuss the possibilities without interruption. Maggie felt dizzy with the choices. How uncanny now she could go anywhere she chose, all she really wanted was to be with Bill, and it didn't matter where.

They finally decided to fly to Barcelona, Spain, tour for a week, go on to Rome for a few days and end with a Mediterranean cruise. "Maggie, this trip is just the beginning," Bill told her. "I want us to travel as much as possible. If you insist on teaching, we can still plan trips on your breaks, and the summers will be dedicated to seeing the world, my dear." She felt tears sting her eyelids. If happiness could be personified, its name would be Maggie.

Maggie had told Bill she was reluctant to resign from her job now because she knew it placed a hardship on her principal to find a new teacher at that late date—especially one with experience teaching art. The art program had been her contribution to her school, and she took a fair amount of pride in its success. Her students had won many awards over the years in both regional and state competitions. At least, for the next year, she planned to be in the classroom. After all, what would she do with her time, with Bill at the office all day?

On her way home, she stopped by the post office and applied for a passport. As she filled out the forms, she had a momentary shadow of sadness when she realized Carson never got this opportunity after his one trip to London. But the myriad of things she had to do scooped that thought out of the way. She paid extra to have the passport expedited. Maggie would take no chances on missing this trip.

Two days later, Maggie went to Southpoint Mall and threw caution to the wind. She bought three pairs of black slacks, two pairs of white slacks, several tops in bright colors, a lightweight jacket in a bold black and white print, three long, flowing skirts for evening, two sundresses, two pairs of sandals, and one pair of walking shoes. She had to make three trips to the car to unload the packages. She was giddy and certain she had lost all sense of reality. But if she was going on such a grand honeymoon, she really did have to have nice clothes, didn't she? She kept telling herself that this was the time in her life to splurge.

She stopped for a very late lunch at the food court. Eating a grilled chicken sandwich, she made mental notes of her wardrobe. Heavens, she had totally forgotten lingerie! How could she forget that, she wondered in amazement. Maggie had never worn underwear that had lace anywhere. Her taste was always for the functional and comfortable. She wasn't certain she wanted to change to something more frilly, but she longed to make their honeymoon as special as possible. With dogged determination, she marched out of the food court and straight to a lingerie specialty store.

An hour later, she emerged with bags containing brightly colored, lacy bras and panties that had kept her in a perpetual blush in the dressing room. And even more embarrassing had been the choosing of five very flimsy—in Maggie's opinion—nighties. Outwardly, the twenties-something salesperson had been the soul of professionalism, but Maggie had the sneaking suspicion the young woman was having great difficulty not succumbing to hilarious laughter every time Maggie flinched when she touched the chiffon nothingness of each one. Maggie Bales in a black lace bikini under a low cut black lacy top that barely covered her thighs—well, she supposed it was living proof there was no fool like an old fool!

She tried to turn the bags so the store name was hidden, but she realized the store wasn't about to be denied—the name was on both sides. She rushed through the corridors of the mall, through the protection of clothes racks in an anchor store, and bounded to her car lest someone she knew stop to talk to her and see the telltale evidence of her purchases. Her cheeks were still flaming as she drove out of the parking lot. Each time she thought of Bill seeing her in any one of those wispy purchases, she wanted to turn around and take back the whole lot, finding something much more substantial in the pajama line. Still, she had stayed slender over the years, and while gravity had certainly taken its toll, at least she didn't have bulges anywhere. Her mind darted from justification of her purchases to mortification for her newfound boldness. Okay, she would reassess the purchases tomorrow. There was still time to make returns, she told herself.

Next week, Maggie planned to go to a shop in Wilson to look for a dress for the wedding. She had been there once with a friend who was the mother of the bride, and Maggie was impressed with their selection of bridal wear. The days were clicking by too fast, and she wondered if she could possibly get everything done in the next three weeks.

Friday, Bill called to tell her some of his friends wanted to have a pool party for them next Saturday evening, and he needed to check with her to be sure it was okay. She felt a wave of apprehension, but she could tell from the excitement in his voice, he expected her to say yes.

"Of course," she managed. "Just get some information about dress, please."

"Sure, sweetheart. Oh, and I'll pick you up tonight at six thirty. Can't wait to see you, my love. I hardly get any work done these days for thinking about you, you know. If I get nabbed for malpractice, it will be because all my brain cells are focused on my darling Maggie."

After they hung up, Maggie leaned against the kitchen sink and tried to let the warmth of Bill's voice wrap around her as insulation from the sudden anxiety she felt. Why shouldn't she meet his friends? After all, Marty had hosted a small, covered-dish dinner, so several of the teachers could meet Bill. He had seemed so comfortable, and Maggie had nearly burst with pride when she sat beside him and watched his easy manner as he talked with her friends. He was gracious and humble. He later sent Marty a lovely bouquet of summer flowers to thank her for the evening.

So why couldn't she just behave the same way with Bill's friends? She could and she would, she declared to herself. However, that didn't squash the uneasy feelings somewhere deep inside. His friends would be polished, smooth, sophisticated—all the things Maggie believed she was not. Her greatest fear was that she would let Bill down—that he wouldn't feel the same pride in her she had felt in him. A shudder of that old familiar nausea surged through her body, and she gripped the sink.

After their date that night, she lay in bed remembering Bill's words as he told her how nice these people were, how eager they were to meet her, how proud he would be to show her off. Even so, her dreams were ragged, and she awoke with no sense of being rested.

The next week was so busy she hardly had time to think. She had a million details racing around in her head. She and Bill met with Reverend Adams to discuss the wedding. He began with a few sentences about the qualities required for a successful marriage and then chuckled. "I suppose you think I'm an unlikely person to be telling you these things since we're all about the same age, and you've been down this road before. So if you won't feel cheated, we will just stick to discussing the service."

When Reverend Adams asked Bill about his church membership, he responded simply, "Episcopalian." With a smile, Reverend Adams said, "Good enough, though we hope you'll see fit to join us less formal Methodists someday."

They would be married in the chapel. It provided room for about thirty guests. Bill had already invited his former daughter-in-law and granddaughters. Together, they discussed inviting a few more people, but the guest list was not yet complete. Maggie had a feeling Bill was waiting until she met his friends before they came to a final decision.

Saturday, the day of the fateful pool party, arrived. That afternoon, Maggie treated herself to a manicure and pedicure. She had bought a new dress in periwinkle blue just for the occasion. She showered and spent much more time than usual blow drying her hair. She even added a "product," as the hair stylist called it, to give her hair more volume. She applied her new make-up carefully and kept using the magnifying side of the mirror to check for any smears or unevenness. Such bother, she thought.

She spritzed perfume from the only bottle she owned. She put on the black, high-heeled sandals that showed off her newly painted "Evening Mist" toenails. Finally, she surveyed herself in the mirror and decided she had done her best. She just hoped Bill thought so, too.

When she answered the door, Bill gave a low whistle and seemed to approve of all he saw. Then why did she feel like a "gelatinous mass" on the inside—a term Carson used in jest when she made congealed salads?

Bill was so handsome she would have whistled back if her mouth hadn't been so dry. Navy blazer, white slacks, a soft blue shirt open at the neck, and black loafers with no socks. It was evident he was used to dressing for these sorts of occasions.

"Well, hello handsome," she managed.

He started to take her in his arms, but she held out her hand. "Sorry. You can't muss the merchandise," she said weakly.

"Okay, ma'am, but only until we return. Then that lovely face of yours is going to get seriously kissed."

The farther they drove, the more Maggie's nerves took over. Her hands were cold and sweaty. Oh great! This would make a dandy impression, she thought. She tried to rub them together inconspicuously for warmth even though it was a good ninety degrees outside.

Bill was giving her some background on the host and hostess, as well as guests. She listened and tried to absorb it, but she was certain she would never remember names or who was married to who. Whom, she reminded herself.

"Barbara and Jim are our hosts. I've known them for thirty years. Jim and I were in the same medical practice for several years. Nice guy—very nice. Barbara is a lovely hostess. I think you'll really like her.

I hope so anyway. I would like to ask Jim to be my best man, if you approve after this evening.

"JoAnne is the pretty blonde who is just a peach of a person. Always upbeat. She used to visit Rose even after Rose forgot who everyone was. She was about the only friend who remained loyal, actually.

"Her husband is David. David has been our . . . uh . . . my lawyer for at least twenty years. Just a super good fella.

"Trudy and Becky are sisters and look alike. No one knows who's older. They won't tell. Their husbands are Vic and Charles, and they must be sworn to secrecy because they won't let the cat out of the bag either. Sue is a widow. Sweet woman, but always a little sad. Her husband had a roving eye, and it wasn't a well-kept secret. I think she sees her life as a disappointment in lots of ways. Her children live away and seldom visit. Hope you don't get stuck with her.

"I'm not certain who else will be there. Barbara just told me she was inviting friends who wanted to meet you."

Maggie listened with growing dread. They had driven for a while. Their destination had to be near. She silently rehearsed. "No, I never had children." "No, no close family." "Yes, I have taught fifth grade for many years." "Yes, my husband died from Alzheimer's disease." She found some people attached a stigma to dementia, but she had looked at it like any other disease, and no one shied away from saying someone had cancer, she thought defiantly.

Bill glanced over at her. "Hey, you're quiet, honey. Something wrong?"

"Nothing," she managed to croak.

"That's not true, Maggie. Now what is it?" he asked with concern.

"Guess I'm just a little nervous," she replied. What an understatement! Her hands were wringing wet, but she couldn't wipe them on her new dress, for Pete's sake. She rummaged in her purse for a tissue. Maybe if she held it, it would sop up the moisture. Never in her life had she felt so intimidated. Images of her parents kept swimming through her head. Granny's little house came into her mind's eye. Suddenly, she was a shy, uncertain child again, living in Ahoskie.

Bill abruptly turned right. He stopped in the parking lot of a car dealership. He took her clammy hand, then realized just how nervous she was and put his warm hands around both of hers. "Maggie, if this is going to upset you too much, I will simply call and say you have a terrible headache. I just wanted you to meet some of the people we will inevitably be with in the future.

"They're going to love you, Maggie. You seriously underestimate yourself. You're a charmer, Maggie Bales. Why do you think I noticed you immediately? You show such strength and integrity, and besides, you're darn pretty."

At this, Maggie's eyes started to brim, so she thrust her head back, trying to keep the tears from running down her cheeks. "Oh, I can't cry. I can't ruin this make-up job," she wailed.

Bill began to laugh. It startled her. Her anger flared. Didn't he see she was dying here?!

"Please meet my finance with the clown make-up and the red nose," he said in mirth, but with such tenderness she knew he was teasing. She had to smile in return. His support was elevating her confidence even if ever so slightly.

"Thanks. You stopped those tears just in time. Oh, Bill, I know how silly I am, but I confess to feeling out of my league. I'm not very sophisticated, you know. They will talk about all the places they've been, and I've never been anywhere. They're going to know you're marrying a very common woman."

Bill put a finger on her lips. "Stop that, Maggie," he said sternly. "Common is one of the last words I can think of to describe you. You're a woman of great character. A woman who has been through a lot of circumstances that would have rendered other people helpless. Not a woman there tonight will have done what you have—stood up to errant parents, put yourself through college for two degrees, loved and cared for a challenged stepdaughter, and watched over an invalid husband with love and compassion until the day he died. Now, if you don't want to meet them, that's okay, but don't use the excuse you aren't in their league. Maggie Bales, they are not in *your* league!"

She looked at the quivering muscle in his jaw. She knew he was angry.

In a soft voice, she said, "Bill, I'm sorry. I don't want to ruin this evening for you. In fact, all I have thought of this week is how much I want to make you proud of me tonight. I'm just so afraid I will fail, and maybe you'll have second thoughts." She dropped her head as her voice grew even softer, "And just to be very honest, I'm afraid to be compared to Rose . . . I . . ."

He stopped her. "Maggie, that may happen. I don't know. Have you ever compared a second spouse to the first? Probably so. For better or worse. But that isn't the point. The point is they know I love you, and they will accept you either now or later. My truest friends will accept you immediately. Who cares about the others!" His voice boomed louder.

In spite of his irritation with her, Maggie smiled. "Bill, I fall more in love with you every time we have a bridge to cross. You take away my insecurities, even when you're cross with me. Now, warm these icy hands so they don't think I'm a cadaver, and let's get going!"

He massaged both hands until they felt warm and tingly. "We're going to be late, but I will just tell them you were irresistible, and let them think what they please."

"Don't you dare! I don't want them to think I'm some hussy!"

Bill pulled out of the lot with urgency, still holding one hand, and laughing.

Timidly, Maggie asked, "Bill, one last question. Was . . . was Rose pretty before she became so ill?"

Bill gave her a sidewise glance with a hint of a smile. "Is that what this is about? You women are real competitors, aren't you? Okay, let's just say my wives got prettier with each one. Satisfied?" Maggie couldn't suppress a modicum of relief.

Barbara greeted them with warm hugs, and Maggie appreciated that she made no point of their lateness. Soon she was being introduced to everyone. Bill kept his arm around her waist. She could feel his strength oozing into her body. She straightened her back, held her head high, and said a silent prayer of thanks for warm hands.

Women hugged her, and the men extended hands, except for David who insisted on a hug, too. He told her he never settled for handshakes when it came to pretty women. Bill told him to make it brief. "You know my motto, Bill, never be the first one to turn loose," David retorted.

Most people already had drinks in their hands and some had settled into chairs around the pool. One by one, they returned to their spots. Maggie had decided earlier she would not have any wine this evening. She wanted to be sure nothing she said was driven by alcohol, so when Jim asked what she wanted to drink, she asked for tonic water. He didn't make an issue of it, as she had feared, but returned promptly with a pretty glass and a slice of lime floating on top. She felt the pressure of Bill's hand tighten on her back just for a moment. She knew he was telling her it was okay.

The talk was easy, some banter, lots of teasing for Bill, and condolences for Maggie. It all seemed lighthearted. However, as the evening wore on, a woman named Carolyn began to reminisce. "Bill, remember the time, you, Rose, Mel, and I went to the Outer Banks for a week?" she asked. "We had such a grand time, my dear," and she looked straight at Maggie.

Maggie kept her cool. "The beach is always fun," she returned. Bill immediately reached for Maggie's hand across the chair arms. "Yes, Carolyn, that was a nice week. Maggie and I will spend lots of time at the beach, too. Perhaps you and Mel will join us sometime."

Carolyn got the point, but she appeared to pout the rest of the evening. Maggie could have hugged Bill right there in front of everyone. Perfect. He nailed it, she thought.

The breeze that had kept the insects at bay finally died down. Barbara suggested they go into the house after she noticed Maggie swatting at a mosquito. All the women except Carolyn got up as if choreographed, so Maggie followed suit. Bill rose, too, but Jim called over, "Hey, Bill, we've survived bites before. Let the guys stay out here, and the women can talk wedding talk."

Bill looked at Maggie, and she smiled and nodded. As she walked through the patio door, she realized Carolyn was still sitting with the men.

Once inside, Barbara settled beside Maggie. She had the distinct impression Barbara would shield her from any questions that got too personal. She liked Barbara.

And there were questions, but the women accepted answers without probing deeper. Maggie was the only person there who didn't have children. She decided not to mention Beth because it involved too much explanation and then the perfunctory condolences. Two women had also been teachers, but stopped teaching years ago. Maggie knew the unsaid reason—money was no longer an issue. They all wanted to know about the new house, and Maggie couldn't prevent a surge of pride from welling up as she gave its general floor plan.

Soon the men surrendered the outside to the biting critters and joined the women in the great room. Carolyn was by Bill's side when they came through the French doors. Maggie was surprised at the instant dislike she felt for her. She would have to ask Bill more about her later.

The conversation became a hubbub with loud laughter, more teasing, and a few jokes suitable for mixed company. It was growing late, and Maggie knew it was up to them, as the honored guests, to leave first. She caught Bill's eye and gave a slight nod. He immediately stood up, walked over, and took her hand. "Barbara and Jim, this has been a wonderful evening. Thanks so much to all of you for coming to meet my darling Maggie."

Good-nights were said all around, and Barbara followed them to the door.

"Maggie, we're so happy for Bill and for you. As soon as the wedding is over and you get settled, let's have lunch one day." Maggie knew she had a friend. That felt good. She leaned over and hugged Barbara. "Thank you for tonight. It was perfect," she said.

They talked and laughed all the way home. Bill told her how gracious she had been, and she felt an uncharacteristic smugness inside. She had survived! She decided not to ask about Carolyn. In the future, she would just not include her in any of their parties.

The next afternoon, they wrote out simple invitations to Jim and Barbara, JoAnne and David, two other couples at the party, three couples from the university who were long-time friends of Carson and Maggie, Maggie's next-door neighbor, and four teachers. Marty would be Maggie's attendant and Jim would be Bill's. It felt good to have that settled. The wedding was two weeks away.

It was moving so fast, but everything was on schedule. She kept admiring the ecru, tea-length dress hanging in her closet now. It fit like a dream. The scoop-neck top was mostly lace, scattered with pearls, and fitted low over the hips. Beneath that was a chiffon skirt. She would wear a matching headband encrusted with pearls. This was the dress she dreamed of for her first marriage, but finances and practicality hadn't allowed it.

She and Bill would walk down the short aisle together and meet Marty, Jim, and Reverend Adams at the altar. There would be two tall baskets of summer flowers. No candles, nothing elaborate. The wedding would take place at eleven o'clock. Later, they would go to Bill's country club for lunch.

On Monday, she closed on her house. The young assistant professor offered to buy any furniture she didn't want. Perfect. Friends helped her move the remaining items to the new house, including her clothes. She wished she and Bill could move in at the same time, but this way, it would give her time to get the house organized before his things arrived.

Bill came over the first night she was there and brought champagne. They sat on the new sofa and toasted the house and their soon-to-be new life together in it. It was harder than ever to say good night that evening. They both wanted to spend the night in their new bedroom, but neither said the words. They lingered at the front door for a long time, both hating to say good night.

Finally, it was July 9. Bill's daughter-in-law and granddaughters arrived at the Raleigh-Durham airport at noon. Maggie went with Bill to pick them up. Betsy was a tall redhead. She made an elegant statement in an emerald green pantsuit with gold earrings and bangles at her wrist. Her long hair was caught at the nape of her neck with a gold clip. Maggie guessed none of it was costume jewelry. Betsy greeted Maggie with a handshake and warm smile. Mary Laura and Margaret Rose—Bill told her the girls used both names—were typical teenagers. They took out earplugs from iPods, smiled at her, said, "Hi," and hugged their grandfather. Then the earplugs went back in. Betsy shrugged and gave Bill a hug.

"So good to see you, Daddy Bill," she said. The greeting caught Maggie by surprise. Bill hugged her back and said, "You're looking as pretty as ever, Betsy. Time is very kind to you. And the kids have grown a ton since I saw them last year."

They ate lunch together, and Betsy wanted to know all about the wedding. She seemed genuinely interested. Maggie had been apprehensive about meeting her, but Bill had assured her Betsy and Rose had never been especially close. He was hoping it would be better for the two of them. Maggie was determined to give it her best effort, but so far it didn't look like a difficult task.

Bill drove them by the new house to drop Maggie off. She had tons of things yet to do. "Good-bye" and "See you tomorrow" was said by everyone. When Bill walked her to the door, he said he would be over that evening. He wanted to drop some things off before tomorrow.

By the time Bill arrived, Maggie's bags were packed, with her passport tucked into a safe pocket. They were going to spend tomorrow night here at their new home and leave on an early morning flight for their honeymoon. She had no intention of packing on her wedding night.

Bill brought a small duffle bag and took it back to the spacious master bathroom. She followed and showed him which side was his. She watched as he put toiletries in the drawers. She had already hung towels for him. He surveyed it as if he was quite satisfied.

He turned to leave the room and noticed her well-worn, plain, cotton robe on the hook by her sink. "Is that part of your trousseau?" he grinned.

"No, and you have no idea how wanton I have become, my love," she said as she thought of the wispy nighties she had just packed.

"Well, wanton is fine with me," he said as he ruffled her hair.

He took her hand and led her back into the bedroom. He paused and looked at the bed. "Is it comfortable?" he asked.

"Very," she answered.

"Is that a guarantee, ma'am, or do I need to try it out for myself?" he teased, nudging her closer to it.

"Sir, I'm offended. I assure you, you will have no complaints."

Bill pulled her down on the bed beside him and gathered her in his arms. After three kisses, he murmured, "I still think we should try it out." Bill's voice was low and urgent.

Maggie didn't answer. She was lost in her yearning. Tonight. Tomorrow. It didn't matter. All that mattered was this wonderful man.

By this time tomorrow night, he would be her legal husband, blessed in the house of God, and what were twenty-four hours, anyway? He sensed her willingness and gently eased her toward the center of the bed. They lay side by side, one kiss leading to another. Breathing grew louder. Hands groped. Desire escalated.

Suddenly a noise sounded somewhere in Maggie's inflamed consciousness. It sounded again. Bill heard it, too. The doorbell. The blasted doorbell!

They pulled apart and looked at each other. "I'm . . . I'm not expecting anyone," she said, trying to collect her thoughts. It rang again. She jumped from the bed and straightened her clothes and hair as best she could as she jogged down the hallway toward the door, opening it in one swift motion.

"Well . . . Reverend Adams," she stammered.

"Hope I'm not intruding, but I have a couple of questions about the ceremony tomorrow. I just got back into town from a conference and dropped off Charlie Hix who lives on this street, too, when I noticed Bill's car in the driveway. I just stopped by on the spur of the moment."

She could tell the situation was dawning on him, and he realized this impromptu visit hadn't been his best idea. However, her reputation was at stake here.

"Oh, this is just fine. Please come right on in," and she made a grand sweeping gesture. "Bill just came over to put away some of his things." She felt compelled to say emphatically, "You know, he still lives at *his* house!"

Bill appeared behind her, somehow managing not to look rumpled, and they led the way to the living room, which now had Bill's chairs added to the sofas.

Reverend Adams asked about the vows they had written, who the witnesses would be, and if they preferred he wear his clerical robe or a suit.

His stay was thirty minutes, maximum, but the spell was broken. After they bade the reverend good night, Bill asked without a lot of humor in his voice, "Do you think Granny sent him here tonight?"

"If she has that power, I'm sure of it," Maggie replied with a sigh.

Tomorrow would be a long day. They said good night with butterfly kisses and a big hug.

Maggie went to bed with visions of tomorrow permeating every thought. She had never felt so much happiness. She drifted off to sleep quickly.

Shortly after midnight, the phone beside her bed rang. Groggily, she answered. "Maggie," a trembling voice said, "Daddy Bill has been in an accident. He's at Memorial and it's bad." Before Maggie could respond, Betsy hung up.

CHAPTER 19

Maggie didn't remember dressing or driving to the hospital. Somehow she must have gotten across the parking lot. Only the guard stopping her at the entrance to the emergency room lobby caught her attention, and then only for the moment she had to open her purse to show its contents. He motioned her on. At the desk, a sleepy, older woman looked up from her magazine and asked what Maggie needed in a tone that reflected too many years at the job.

"My husband . . . my fiancé was in an accident!" she screamed.

"Oo-kay. Oo-kay, honey. Calm down. What's his name?" she said in a slow drawl that gave Maggie a sudden urge to slap her.

"Bill Holton. Dr. Bill Holton!" she said through gritted teeth.

Just then, Jim, Bill's best man, appeared. He laid his arm around Maggie's shoulders and took charge.

"I'll take you back," he said in a soothing tone. When the sleepy woman started to protest about the regulations, Jim flashed his hospital credentials, and she happily went back to her magazine. Jim guided Maggie through heavy double doors and down a hallway to a small waiting room.

Barbara came running toward them. How did everyone get there so fast, Maggie wondered. Jim must have sensed her question. "Bill and I have a mutual friend who is attending physician tonight in ER. As soon as they brought him in, John called me. I phoned Bill's house because I didn't know your number. Betsy answered, and I told her to call you. I think she's on her way, too."

Barbara had a look of agony on her face. Ashen, trembling

Maggie reached out to take her hand. "How bad is it?" she asked in a whisper.

Jim answered. "From what I know, it was a drunk driver who crossed the center line. He hit Bill head-on. The trauma team is with him, and they're trying to get him stabilized. It's bad, Maggie."

Maggie felt faint, and she sank down on the worn carpet. Jim and Barbara instinctively reached for her, lifted her off the floor, and helped her to a sofa.

"I'm so sorry, Maggie," Jim continued. "Sometimes the physician in me is too blunt. They have to get Bill's vital signs stabilized before they can assess the extent of the injuries. John only told me it was a very bad accident. And that isn't good, but that doesn't mean it's fatal either."

"Can I see him?" she asked weakly.

"I doubt it. The team will be very busy working with him. I will go back in a little while and talk to John. I know he's doing all he can right now. Believe me, he isn't leaving this one to any resident."

Barbara kept holding Maggie's hand and rubbing it. She had said little so far.

Frantically, Betsy came rushing in. Her hair was down and uncombed. She wore a jogging suit. In some dreamlike state, Maggie noticed that all three women looked alike—hair askew and no make-up to hide behind. Just raw flesh and raw emotions facing a long night ahead.

Why couldn't she go back to her bed and wake up tomorrow with all the joy she had felt three hours ago? Why couldn't this be a dream? Thoughts were scattered and made no sense. None of this made sense. She just wanted to call Bill and hear him tell her this was all a mistake. To hear his familiar, comforting voice.

As the minutes slowly turned into hours, they sat huddled in the small waiting room. Periodically, Jim would leave and return with only the news that the doctors were doing their best. Once he brought coffee for the foursome, and they all drank in silence.

Maggie silently prayed the same prayer over and over, "Please, God, just don't let him die."

The first rays of dawn penetrated the blackness of the night outside their small window. The dawn of her wedding day, Maggie thought.

And the tears finally started. Barbara held her while she sobbed. Betsy stroked her arm. Maggie felt moisture on her hand and knew Betsy was weeping, too. Jim left the room again.

When he returned, he took Maggie's hand and looked solemnly into her eyes. "John says there's a chance Bill will make it. The fact he isn't already dead . . . deceased . . . is a good sign. But John thinks he has a spinal injury, Maggie. That's something they may not be able to fix."

"I don't care about anything except that he lives," Maggie said in a pleading voice.

Later that morning, Reverend Adams came. Marty appeared. Maggie had no idea how they knew. They were hugging her. Reverend Adams offered a prayer with the group. "Amen's" were heard from everyone as he finished entreating God to spare Bill's life and mend his body.

Somehow, the wedding guests were told. Somehow, the country club was notified. None of that occurred to Maggie. Her thoughts were only of Bill and what was happening behind the doors she could not enter.

As the day wore on, Jim gave them periodic updates. John was staying over. He had called two other colleagues to come so he could discuss the case with them. He wanted fresh ideas about the procedures, minute to minute. There would be a specialist in spinal cord injury arriving later. They were still focused on the internal bleeding.

Finally, John, himself, came into their small room. As he was introduced to Maggie, his kindly eyes flickered with sadness. She stood to shake his hand. He didn't release hers as he said solemnly, "I've known Bill for many years. We go back to med school at Duke. I will do everything in my power to put him back together again. I have called in specialists who will come because they know him, too, and want to do whatever they can. Each hour gives me greater hope he will survive. What I don't know is what his condition will be later."

"Thank you," she said simply. "When can I see him?"

"He's in a coma right now, induced by us. That's better for him. I will be glad for you to go back with me for just a minute. But please be prepared. I don't think you will recognize him."

"I just want to see him," she muttered.

203

John was correct. She would never have known who the person was behind all the tubes. His face was puffy and distorted with dark, bluish marks tattooing his forehead and one cheek.

She searched for his hand under the covers and squeezed it. "It's Maggie, darling. Please know how much I love you," she whispered.

There was no response. She stood silently holding his hand until John edged toward her and moved her away from the bed. "I promise to keep you posted, Maggie. For now, it's better if we have clear access to all the monitors and to Bill. I hope you understand. Oh, and I cannot tell you how sorry I am about today. Jim told me."

Maggie returned to the waiting room. Someone had brought sandwiches and more coffee. She wasn't hungry, so she just sat, mute.

Sometime during the morning, Barbara left and returned later in fresh clothes. Then Betsy left and when she returned, her hair was neatly pulled back with the same gold clasp Maggie had seen less than twenty-four hours ago. She had on a lime green blouse over white slacks. Maggie studied every detail of the outfit. She had nothing else to do as she waited.

Both Barbara and Betsy offered to drive Maggie home for a shower and change. The thought of leaving Bill was not even comprehendible to her. "No . . . no . . . I can't go yet," she mumbled.

In the evening, John came in again. Barbara moved so he could sit beside Maggie. "We think we have him stabilized, Maggie, though his blood pressure has been erratic at times during the day. If we get him through the night, then I will feel like we've got a better chance he will make it." He patted her arm. "Why don't you go home and get some rest?"

"No. Thanks, but no. I have to be here with him tonight. It's . . . it's our wedding night," she said in a low voice.

She noticed John's face soften. "Okay, but will you promise me you will go home in the morning and sleep for a few hours? Bill would want that, you know."

Maggie did know that. "Okay, if he's stable, I'll go. But only if you will let me see him before I leave."

"Fair enough." And John was off. It occurred to Maggie later John's scruffy beard indicated he had not left the hospital either.

Later that night, Barbara and Betsy left when JoAnne and David came around ten. Maggie recognized this as some sort of shift change. She silently wished everyone would go. She didn't want to talk. Her head hurt. She knew she needed to eat, but even the thought of food brought waves of nausea.

The next morning, there was still no response from Bill when Maggie held his hand. Later, Barbara drove her home and turned back the covers on her bed. She helped Maggie into bed, still in her clothes, and closed the plantation shutters. Maggie lay there in total exhaustion. She could still sense Bill's presence on that same bed not even two days ago when they had felt such life between them. Finally, she dozed off.

After waking, she called Barbara to pick her up. Then she showered and hurriedly put on an old running suit. No makeup. When she arrived back at the hospital, Jim was waiting to tell her they had been able to get an MRI. The spinal injury was confirmed—the injury was to the C-5 cervical vertebra. The worst news was the spinal cord was completely severed at that juncture. Bill also had three cracked ribs and a broken leg. "Maggie, it's good that no vital organs were punctured. His lungs and liver seem unharmed. Except for the spinal cord, we would consider him a very lucky man."

Hours turned into days. Friends came and went. Maggie slept a few hours in her own bed. Bill was coming out of the coma, she was told. Tubes were removed periodically. She was allowed to see him for short periods of time in the morning and afternoon. She continued to hold his hand and tell him how much she loved him. There was still no response—no squeeze, no flickering of the eyelids. She prayed for that each time she went into his room, and as she left, she prayed for the next time.

She met the spinal cord specialist on the fifth day—Dr. Geissler. He was a man in his early fifties, she guessed. Short, slender, gray hair. A pleasant countenance. "I'm sorry, Mrs. Bales," he began. The name surprised her. A week ago, she had already begun to think of herself as Mrs. Holton.

"Spinal injuries of this sort are very difficult. It will take a while to determine the extent of Dr. Holton's paralysis. If the cord had only

205

been partially severed, then there would be hope of greater function ultimately. However, he was not so lucky. A totally severed C-5 means loss of function from that vertebra down, so we know he will never walk again. However, patients generally have deltoid and bicep functions in their arms, and wrist flexion can be produced with the help of special equipment. We are still doing tests to determine just how much movement he will have. I wish I could give you better news."

She met his gaze. "I just want him to live," she said in a soft, steady voice.

"I believe he will," he replied with a confident tone that made Maggie believe him. A wave of joy swept over her. It gave her more courage, and she added, "I love him so much, and I will accept anything but his death."

Dr. Geissler smiled warmly at the blatant honesty on her face, patted her arm, and was off.

Two days later, a nurse came to tell her Bill had spoken her name. They rushed together to his room. His eyes were open. Maggie could tell from his expression he knew it was her. She wanted to hug him and kiss him but sensed he was still too delicate. She took his hand, and his fingers tightened slightly around hers. He softly said "Maggie" three times as he smiled at her, and her heart nearly burst with happiness. "Thank you, God," she said silently over and over.

After that, her visits were longer. Bill was too weak to endure much conversation, and the pain medication kept him very sedated. But he would usually offer up her name, maybe a faint smile, and occasionally respond briefly to something she said. She told him over and over she loved him—she was just down the hallway if he wanted her—everything would be okay. Once, in a very hoarse voice, he said, "I love you, too." That was enough to keep her singing inside the rest of the day.

Every day brought highs and lows. As his other injuries slowly healed, the doctors reduced the pain medication so Bill was more alert when Maggie visited him. He could talk to her in short sentences, but he grew tired quickly.

Two weeks after the accident, John, Jim, and Dr.Geissler came into the waiting room. Maggie knew by the grim look on their faces the news wasn't good. She jumped from the sofa. "What is it?" she whimpered.

"Let's sit down," Dr. Geissler said. Jim sat beside Maggie and took her hand.

"Mrs. Bales, we believe Dr. Holton will be paralyzed from the mid-chest down. In other words, he will be a quadriplegic. Certainly, he will never walk again or have significant function below his injury. However, I believe he can have the use of both his arms and at least one of his hands if we can fit him with the proper equipment. His grip is very weak now, but the therapists are working on that. It remains to be seen how much strength he can recapture. Quadriplegics can live for several years, but they often need intensive care. Once he is through with his hospital stay, he will need to go to rehab where they will help him become as functional as he is capable of being. Then he will need to be transferred to a long-term care facility."

He waited for Maggie's response. She lowered her eyes and let his words sink in. When would Bill come back to their home, she wondered, even then realizing he might never live in that house at all. The pain of that uncertainty shot through her heart as if Dr. Geissler had aimed an arrow at her.

"I understand," she said weakly. "Does he know this?"

"Not yet," he said. "I'm sure he will be asking soon. I know I would if it were me. I would recognize the signs of permanent paralyses, and I believe Dr. Holton will, too. When he asks, I will tell him."

"Could you let me know when he knows?" she asked.

"Certainly. And again, Mrs. Bales, I'm so sorry for this very sad situation." The three doctors rose in unison and bade her good-bye. She sat alone on the sofa and thought of the future. Whatever lay ahead, she would handle. She wouldn't question why, she thought, fiercely. As soon as Bill knew, she would tell him whatever he faced, they faced together.

Two days later, when she went to his room, the nurse at the station just outside his door stopped her. She couldn't go in at this time, the nurse informed her. She had been stopped before when they were bathing him or going through some medical procedure, so she decided to go to the cafeteria on the main floor and get a sandwich and coffee. She had been eating very little, and her energy level was at an all-time low.

Halfway through her sandwich, David walked into the dining room. He paused and looked around. She waved. She noticed a grim countenance as he walked toward her. He carried his briefcase. Somehow, that seemed out of place for visiting someone in the hospital. Nonetheless, she greeted him pleasantly and motioned for him to sit down.

"Hi, Maggie," he said. The expression didn't change. "When you finish, I would like to talk with you." Maggie's appetite quickly vanished. She pushed the sandwich to one side.

"I'm through," she said with finality. Whatever it was, she wanted to hear it now.

"Let's take a walk outside," he said still holding onto the briefcase. He rose, stood behind her chair, and ushered her out the side door into a courtyard with wrought iron benches and tables. He maneuvered her to a table partly shaded by one of the many pear trees that surrounded the area. She sat down apprehensively. David sat opposite her and put the briefcase on the table.

"Maggie, I'm wearing the hat of Bill's lawyer today. I wish I wasn't." With that, he opened the briefcase and brought out a brown envelope. He slowly opened it. A single sheet of yellow legal paper was folded inside. He glanced at her for a moment. "Yesterday, Bill had Jim call me and ask that I come to his room. I went by after work last evening, and Bill dictated this letter. I'm very sorry, Maggie."

He opened the sheet. "For whatever reason, Bill wanted me to read this to you instead of just handing it to you." David began, not able to look at Maggie's ghost-like countenance.

"Dear Maggie, I know the extent of my injuries and the prognosis. I, better than you, understand what lies ahead. You've been down the road with an invalid husband before, and I have no intention of putting you through that again. Not because I don't love you, but because I do. That love allows me to release you from this burden, both now and in the future. You're a wonderful woman. There will be other opportunities for you to love again. Please don't make this more difficult for either of us. My mind is made up. I am requesting you go on with your life. You won't be allowed to see me again. That serves no purpose. The house is yours. Bill."

Maggie's ears heard the words, but something blocked them from reaching her brain. She looked at the intricate pattern of the wrought iron on the tabletop. She mentally traced it from every angle. The artist in her saw the curves and loops, the spaces between. She sat in a trance-like state. David watched her closely.

Finally, when she showed no response, he said, "Maggie, as Bill's friend, I advised him against this. As his lawyer, I have no choice but to carry this message to you." Still he waited.

She continued the tracing. Finally, she looked at him.

"Is it the medication?" she asked.

"I don't think so, Maggie," he returned. "Jim told me he was pretty lucid now—I asked the same question, by the way."

"So, I can't see him even once more?" she ventured.

"I'm afraid not. In all honesty, Maggie—and I know this is beyond my legal purview—I think he believes this is the kindest way. He seems resolute in his decision, but I believe he fears you will try to convince him otherwise, if you see him."

"Indeed, I would!" she said emphatically. Suddenly, anger flooded her whole body. For the second time, he was leaving her with no opportunity for her to plead her case. "Will you please tell Dr. Holton this is one *hell* of a way to treat someone he claims to love!" She jumped from the bench and ran toward the door. Once inside, she ran crying through the corridors until she reached the outside. She had become aware of stares as she raced through the hallways, so she moved as quickly as possible to her car.

She started to drive home and realized she could not bear to go inside the house that was to have been their home. Instead, she headed east. She drove through the countryside with the steady beat of every word David had read drumming in her brain. She ranted at Bill, she cursed the accident, she beat her fists on the steering wheel, and finally the tears flowed down her cheeks. When she stopped the car, she was in a parking lot at the ocean. She took her shoes off and stepped onto the hot sand. She didn't flinch. She walked with purpose to the edge of the water and let the froth cool her feet. She stood there looking at the horizon. She watched a ship in the distance until it sailed out of sight. What a metaphor, she thought.

She walked for hours on the beach, shaking her fists at the seagulls, stomping through the water, ignoring the growing watermarks on her white slacks, watching the waves erase her footprints made only moments earlier. "Just like our life together," she said into the winds that blew off the water.

Finally, as the sun was setting, with its coral colors flitting over the water, she made her way back to the car. She drove home slowly, dreading to see the outskirts of town. Dreading even more her own house.

Later, she lay in the dark in the white slacks that had dried on the way home but still reminded her of the waters that had licked her feet and ankles most of the afternoon. Did Bill have any possible conception of how much pain she was in? Would anything ever wash that pain away?

She had no idea what to do the next day. Her routine for almost three weeks had revolved around constant trips to the hospital. As much as she liked solitude, she really needed to talk to someone about this. She could call Marty, but Marty didn't know Bill that well. Instead, she called Barbara. They met for lunch. Barbara sat in disbelief as Maggie told her about the letter.

"I really have no explanation, Maggie, but I do know how much Bill loved . . . loves you. When he first told us about you, he was like some teenager who was wildly smitten with his first romance. Jim and I talked about it later. How nice it was to find that kind of love when you reach our ages. Whatever motivated this, I really believe Bill thought it was for your good."

"Well, it isn't!" Maggie said emphatically. Maggie talked about her love for Bill, all their plans, her dismal future. Barbara was the consummate listener. Finally, Maggie ran dry. They finished lunch with promises to get together soon. Maggie liked being with someone who knew Bill. That link provided a connection to him.

Slowly, the week passed. Maggie couldn't make the effort for church on Sunday. Instead, she sat on the screened porch and read the newspaper, methodically, section by section. It took hours, but what else did she have to do, she asked herself.

Somehow, she moved through the following days. Marty came often. When Maggie refused eating out or the movies, Marty stayed with her anyway. More often than not, she brought food and sometimes a movie. Marty was good at operating electronic equipment. Maggie had never really tried. Maggie liked the movies they watched, not that she really paid attention to the story, but they provided a convenient excuse for no conversation. Marty left believing she had cheered up her friend, and Maggie welcomed her departure so she could crawl back into the solace of her bed for another day.

In mid-August, David appeared at Maggie's door. "Hi," he said. "Mind if I come in."

"Okay," she said tentatively. He was carrying the briefcase again. Dread filled Maggie, but she had to be polite. They settled on the sofa, and David laid the briefcase on the coffee table. He asked the usual questions about how she was. They exchanged a few pleasant comments, and David reached for the briefcase. She heard the familiar double click—signaling yet another blow, she imagined.

David must have sensed her apprehension. "I'm sorry to always be so legalistic when I see you, Maggie, but as Bill's lawyer, I have to carry out his wishes." She nodded.

He pulled out a bulky brown envelope. Inside was the deed to the house. "Bill has signed these papers. He wants you to know the house is yours to do with as you please."

Numbness set in again. "Thank you for coming," she said as she stood and moved toward the door. David was obviously caught off guard, but he rallied, shut the briefcase, and made his way quickly behind her.

As he walked through the door, he stopped and said, "Maggie, I'm really sorry. I really am. I know I keep saying that, but I can see this has upset you. I'm certain that was not Bill's intention."

"No, perhaps not," she said with a weariness that surprised even her. "Good-bye." She shut the door and leaned against it for a long time. Would the pain ever stop, she wondered.

Barbara was her source of information about Bill. She knew Barbara visited him at times, but Jim always had a report. Maggie knew he was in rehab; he was getting therapy every day; with mechanical aids, he had movement in both hands and arms; one hand still had limited ability to grip; and he was in a special motorized wheelchair.

Barbara always gave her this information willingly. What she did not tell Maggie, because she had sworn to Bill she wouldn't, was how many times he asked about her. Barbara never told her how tears had trickled down his cheeks more than once when she told him how sad Maggie was now. Each time, he had insisted it was for the best and that Maggie would move on in time. Barbara decided he was still too fragile for her to argue the point.

Maggie had never moved the suitcases she had packed for their honeymoon. They still sat on the bedroom floor. Once it occurred to her she should return the lingerie and get a refund. But it was too much effort. She walked around the luggage each time she opened the shutters.

It was nearly the end of August and time for the new school year to begin. The day before she reported for her first workday, she called a realtor and put the house on the market. She had rattled around in the empty spaces long enough. She had no idea where she would move. But she felt certain a smaller place would feel less lonely.

September passed quickly. The leaves in October were beautiful. Once, she drove by her old house just to see her beloved maple, but even then, all she could think about was the cold winter ahead. Her present house hadn't sold. In fact, there had only been three showings. It was expensive and in a new, untested area, she reasoned.

Barbara told her in early November they had moved Bill to Carolina Manor. That seemed surreal. Maggie asked how he was doing. Barbara told her that, although he was still getting therapy each day, the doctors believed he had reached his potential. He spent most of his days in his motorized wheelchair that he was learning to propel. He went to the dining room and fed himself with assistance. He watched television. He practiced typing on his laptop every day, but the progress was slow. He read books Barbara picked up for him. He sometimes wept. Still, Barbara never told her about Bill's inquiries.

Barbara told Bill that Maggie had the house for sale. She mentioned how thin Maggie was, and she could see a deep pain in Bill's expression. He suggested Barbara set Maggie up on a date with a widower who was a doctor he and Jim both knew. Nice man, he told Barbara. Barbara mentioned it to Jim, and he agreed Bob was someone Maggie might like.

However, when Barbara casually told Maggie she was planning a Friday night get-together at their house and indicated there was someone she and Jim wanted Maggie to meet, Maggie turned the invitation down flat. When Barbara reported all this to Bill, she saw both pain and relief in his eyes.

Maggie dreaded the holidays. She spent Thanksgiving at Barbara and Jim's house, along with six other couples. It was a buffet, and everyone brought a dish. Maggie took her baked pineapple casserole. It had always been a crowd pleaser, and this dinner was no exception. She promised the recipe to four of the women there.

She declined everyone's invitation for Christmas dinner. She believed Christmas was a family affair, and she didn't want to horn in. She would go to Christmas Eve services at church and home to bed immediately afterward. That would be Christmas for her.

Bill asked Barbara about Maggie again in late December. Barbara told him she had spent Christmas alone, she had lost even more weight, had hollow cheeks, and permanent ashen circles under her eyes. Maggie was always pleasant when they got together for lunch, Barbara said, but there was a flatness in her tone that worried both Jim and her.

"To be honest, Jim worries about the state of her health, Bill. You know, that mind-body thing."

Bill seemed lost in thought. Barbara had stopped pleading for him to see Maggie. He usually dismissed her quickly once that conversation started.

In January, Bill asked Barbara if he could trouble her for a favor. "Of course," she said.

"Maggie's birthday is February 5. Would you please check her school schedule and find out when her spring break is? Then buy her a ticket for a cruise to the Caribbean. I know how she dislikes the winter. Take her the ticket on her birthday. Oh, and take her a bouquet of jonquils—a large bouquet."

"Bill, I will do it, but I warn you now she seems in no mood for anything fun or spontaneous."

Barbara gathered her coat and scarf, gave him a light kiss on the cheek, and told him she was off to accomplish the mission. She had no idea where this might lead, but at least it was the first attempt at communication between those two, and she was happy to be the messenger.

On Saturday, February 5, Barbara picked Maggie up for lunch, handing her the vase of jonquils at the door. Maggie flushed. "How did you know I like these?"

"Oh, a little birdie told me."

Maggie caught her breath, ignoring the card resting among the upright stems and simply set the yellow blooms on the coffee table and went to get her coat. She felt numb as they walked out the door. Barbara seemed determined to provide cheerful conversation during their salads, and Maggie tried valiantly to uphold her side of the banter, but her heart wasn't in it. After the plates were cleared, Barbara reached into her oversized purse and handed Maggie a slender gift bag tied in multicolored, curly ribbons.

"Oh, Barbara, the lunch was a lovely gift. You needn't have done more."

Barbara remained silent, watching as Maggie untied the ribbons and reached into the bag. She lost all color as she looked at the cruise ticket, glancing once at Barbara, who saw total shock written on her face. She opened the small, white envelope containing the note Bill had written and sealed, instructing Barbara to include it with the gift. Maggie read his barely decipherable message. *"Happy Birthday. Bill."*

She stared at the jacket of the ticket for a few moments and then slid everything into the bag. She looked up at Barbara and said, "Please, may we go?"

Maggie didn't speak on the drive home in spite of Barbara's efforts to fill in the empty space with chatter. In the driveway, Maggie turned to her solemnly and said, "Do you mind to come inside for a minute?"

Maggie moved to the kitchen desk and took out a pad of paper and a pen. When she finished writing, she enclosed the message in a small envelope, sealed it, and handed it to her friend.

"Would you please give this to him?" she asked.

Barbara left shortly afterwards. Her farewell wishes for a happy birthday had a hollow ring.

She was in Bill's room within thirty minutes, handing him the envelope. She admitted to herself she had great curiosity about its contents.

She watched him slowly pull the flap loose with difficulty and remove the folded paper by bracing the envelope against the arm of the wheelchair. Bill read the note and refolded it. She noticed a tear form and trickle down his cheek. "Thanks, Barb," he said solemnly. "And thanks for all your effort. You've been a good friend. Now I need some time alone."

"Darn," she muttered as she walked back to her car. She would have given anything to know what the message was!

Bill reread the note several times. Each time, Maggie's words pierced his stoic heart.

"That is not the destination I want. Maggie."

He rang for the nurse assistant. A pleasant, efficient woman with Nora written on her badge responded. "Please get me the phone number for David Oliver," he instructed.

When Maggie returned home that evening from a birthday dinner with Marty and some friends, she recognized David's car in the driveway. Oh no, she thought! Not another briefcase ordeal. Not tonight.

She parked behind him and was gathering her purse when he appeared at her car window.

"Hi there," he said as she rolled the window down. No briefcase. Good. "I'm sorry to be here so late, but I've been waiting for you since early evening. I believe this is your birthday, and my client has given me a message for you. I promised to deliver it before midnight," he chuckled.

He held out an envelope.

Maggie took it. Her stomach started churning. She worried about an unpleasant incident right there in the driveway. She needed to steer David to the house.

"Could we go in, please? I need better light. These old eyes, you know," she said, trying for a half-hearted joke. David followed her to the door and took the key she produced. Memories of Bill overtook her.

The nausea was subsiding, but she was shaking so badly, she needed to sit down. She motioned to David to sit in the chair across from her. She kept her coat on. Slowly, she opened the second communication

215

she had from Bill in one day. Her hands trembled, and she knew David was aware of that, but she couldn't stop them.

"Dear Maggie. If the destination you referred to is 120 Carolina Manor, I would like to see you immediately. If I misunderstood, I beg your forgiveness for intruding. Bill."

She looked at David. She could tell he knew the contents of the note and was waiting for her response.

"Does he really want to see me tonight?" she asked in disbelief.

"Yes, Maggie. I know it's late, but when Bill called, I was in court. I didn't get to his room until almost four o'clock. We had a long talk, and then I had to pick up some things for him at the bank. By the time I got here, you were already gone. I called him about an hour ago to ask if he preferred you come tomorrow, but he assured me he might lose his nerve if we waited. By the way, he wants me to be there. Part of this deals with legal implications. Is that okay?"

"David, I have no idea what's going on. Whatever you need to do is fine." Her voice was hollow.

"Maggie, just my two cents worth. I believe you will want to see him."

"Okay, but let me take my car. No reason for you to drive me home."

She certainly didn't need directions. She still knew the route by heart. A thousand thoughts went through her mind. Her heart leapt in anticipation of seeing Bill one moment, and dread almost suffocated her the next.

Please don't cry, she kept telling herself. Be strong, Maggie. Be strong. Whatever did he want? But a glimmer of hope appeared somewhere deep inside when she recalled the words he had written. She had to see him. She had to. She might have to pick up the pieces again tomorrow, but tonight it was worth the risk.

In the parking lot, David pulled beside her car, and they walked into the foyer together. He followed her silently down the corridor. This was a wing she hadn't been in before, but she walked with assurance.

David caught up with her and knocked on 120. A slightly hoarse voice said, "Come in."

David stood back for her to go first. She wanted to clutch his arm, but braced herself instead for whatever waited inside.

She had tried to imagine Bill over the past months. However, she

216

wasn't prepared for how much older he looked. His hair was white now. He had lost weight, and deep wrinkles lined his face. He sat very upright in his large wheelchair. Padding surrounded him. He had on a cheery, red shirt, and a plaid blanket covered him from the waist down. Metal and plastic braces flanked his arms.

She could feel her tears begin to form, and she silently begged them not to flow. As she moved closer to Bill, she saw the same mist in his eyes.

In a slow, hoarse voice, he commanded her to stop. "Before you come closer, Maggie, I have to say this. I've rehearsed all afternoon, haven't I, David?" She looked back to see David nod.

"Maggie, what I did, I did for you—or at least, that was my reasoning. I wanted you to go on with your life. I wanted you to have fun and joy—both are a part of who you are. But Barbara and David tell me you aren't moving on like I had hoped. Everyone seems worried about you. When I got your note today, all my resolve to never see you again evaporated. If this is *truly* the destination you were referring to, then my life . . . our life . . . can begin again."

She started to speak, but he shook his head.

"I've talked to David about this, Maggie, because I demand that you have authority in all aspects of my life and be legally protected. You and I both know the future. We know there are decisions that will have to be made for my care as time goes on. So, Maggie..." His voice became even lower. She had to strain to hear him. She could tell he was on the verge of tears. He paused for a moment. She heard David shift behind her.

"Maggie Bales, if you really want this destination, then you . . . you have to marry me."

She realized the gasp was hers.

He composed himself again. "If you choose not to, I fully understand. David will explain the technical points to you later, and then I want you to think about this for at least twenty-four hours. Don't give me your answer until you're certain you have made the best decision for *you*, Maggie. I've already put you through enough."

Then he paused, and with the old twinkle in his eye, he said, "No buyer's remorse, understand?"

She stood transfixed. She looked at the gray tiles. How many times in the past had she sat and counted tiles like these, looked at their blemishes, memorized the random patterns? Life has its irony, for sure.

She wasn't certain what to do next. She wanted to kneel beside him and put her head in his lap. She wanted to yell at him for his belief he knew what was best for her. She wanted to kiss him. She wanted to walk away and never look back. Yes, she did know the future. All too well. And she sensed David was watching this unfold with uncertain anticipation.

She looked at Bill. "I've missed you," she said simply.

"Maggie, oh, my Maggie," and his voice choked, but he quickly regained control. "I want you to think about this before either of us says any more. I'll bid you good night now, and David will tell you what he and I talked about this afternoon."

At this, David took her arm and moved her slowly toward the door. Her feet felt like lead, and it took all her strength to take each step. She looked back, unable to take her eyes off Bill. He held her gaze. As they moved into the hallway, a nurse came down the corridor. She was wheeling a large, bright purple machine. Maggie knew the drill. Bill would be lifted out of his chair and into the bed with this contraption. And, if necessary, he would be changed. Adult briefs, the nurses called them, in an attempt to preserve dignity. Yes, he was correct; she knew it well.

David led her to a small sitting area. She realized he was carrying the dreaded briefcase again. How had she missed it when they walked in from their cars?

"Maggie, as Bill told you, we talked at length this afternoon. He wants to be certain you have every protection possible for your financial future. As you perhaps know, Bill has considerable assets. He has already made arrangements for his daughter-in-law and grandchildren, but unfortunately, it's true that families can divide quickly when money issues arise. He wants to avoid that for you at all costs. Also, he wants you to have sole power to make decisions about his care should you decide to step back into his life."

"I wasn't the one who stepped out," she said quietly.

David nodded. "I have advised him the surest way to accomplish what he wants for you is through marriage. That provides you with all the legal protection the law affords and is generally uncontestable. Also, I will draw up two powers of attorney when you need to make decisions for Bill's health or his estate." He stopped and looked at her, waiting for some response. She glanced at the magazine on the coffee table. The cover promised ten new ways to please your husband. She almost smiled at the simplicity. In a perfect world, she thought.

David continued, "Bill sent me to get some papers out of his safe deposit box." At this, he opened the brief case and removed several official packets. "He wants you to understand you will have some significant responsibilities in handling his investments and his interest in several real estate properties. He wants you to know exactly what you're getting into."

David proceeded to explain each paper to her. She listened without really hearing. It wasn't that she couldn't comprehend what he was saying, but her mind kept wandering elsewhere.

She finally looked up at David. "Did he say when he wants this wedding?"

David was visibly taken aback. "I believe he's waiting for your answer," he stammered. "Knowing Bill, he will want only what you want. Maggie, I have one last piece of information for you. No matter what your decision, Bill wants you to have this, and he begs that you accept it."

With that he handed her another envelope. She opened it with shaky hands. She removed a tan piece of paper she recognized as official. She could only stare at the numbers neatly typed onto lines that waved before Maggie's eyes. It was a cashier's check for two million dollars!

She was aware of David's close scrutiny. She slid the check back into the envelope and placed it in her purse.

All at once, she felt limp. "I just need to think about all of this, David. My mind seems disconnected from my body right now. It's late, and I'm exhausted."

"I understand, Maggie. Go home and get some rest. It's been a long day." They rose together and David gave her a quick hug. "And, by the way, happy birthday!"

"Thanks," she smiled weakly. "Think I'll stop by the restroom on my way out." He nodded and waved as he started down the hall.

She splashed water on her face and looked into the mirror for a long time. Her weary expression stared back at her. She wondered if Bill thought she had changed. His words kept replaying in her brain. She thought of how serious he looked—and the tears just below the surface. She stood holding onto the sink for what seemed like hours while her thoughts rushed over her like a relentless tide. Finally, she picked up her purse.

She stepped out into a long corridor. The lights were dimmed in the hallways for nighttime. A large red EXIT sign glowed at the end. With the check tucked inside her purse, she could go through that door and walk toward a newfound freedom, buy a place at the beach, paint to her heart's content, see all the museums and cathedrals of the world. She would never have to sit by another bedside, wait for a doctor's dreaded news, or count the cracks in the tiles. She stared at the large EXIT sign, blinking as the letters bored into her eyes and then on to her brain.

Opening her purse, she fumbled for a pen. With her trembling hand—partly from fatigue and partly from emotion—she wrote four words on the envelope that offered her a carefree life. Then she straightened her shoulders and turned around. She walked quietly back to room 120. Her still trembling hand opened the door, and she heard Bill's gentle snoring. She tiptoed to his bed, reached into her purse, and laid the tan envelope on the nightstand. In plain view were her words, *"Let's set the date."*

Maggie moved quietly back to the door, opened it slowly, turned toward Bill once more and whispered, "My darling, Bill, sleep tight."

EPILOGUE

Maggie's new black pumps peeped out beneath her neatly crossed ankles. The smart black suit Marty had insisted she buy for this occasion felt comfortable but foreign. Her hair was still cut in a short, casual style, but it was now mostly gray.

Today, Maggie Bales Holton was seated on the elevated chancel of the newly completed chapel at Carolina Manor. On either side of her sat the Manor's director, Mr. Wesley James, and her beloved Reverend Adams. He had retired from First United Methodist Church in Cary a few years ago, but he had continued to visit Bill and Maggie. However, it was the oversized easel on the chancel, draped with a white crepe covering, that drew the attention of the congregation as they took their seats for the afternoon ceremony.

Maggie watched as Bill's daughter-in-law, Betsy, took her seat in the front pew. The still regal Betsy now had streaks of gray in her auburn hair. Her face showed that youth was slipping away. Next came Bill's granddaughters. Mary Laura and her husband, Drew, each carried a twin—born eleven months ago—along with diaper bags and plastic containers of cereal. Margaret Rose, now a physician, took the last seat on that pew. Bill had wept with pride when she graduated from medical school with highest honors and announced she would specialize in spinal cord injuries during her residency at Duke.

One by one, familiar faces—along with those that weren't—filled the pews. Maggie noticed that JoAnne was just as pretty as ever, but David seemed more slumped than he had at Bill's funeral two years ago. Jim and Barbara edged into the pew beside these longtime friends.

Seeing them brought a great sense of comfort to Maggie. They had all become her friends, too.

Mr. James rose promptly at two o'clock and walked to the podium. "I want to thank each of you for coming today. As most of you know, this lovely addition to Carolina Manor is the result of a very generous bequest from Bill and Maggie Holton. It was Bill's specific wish that this chapel serve as a place of comfort for families when they are in need of God's soothing balm. At this time, I will ask Maggie Holton to come forward and unveil the portrait that stands before you. In the dedication to follow, the chapel will be named in memory—and in honor—of this person."

Maggie rose. She walked with resolve to the easel and gently tugged the crepe covering from the portrait. Beulah Mae Larkins's gentle eyes smiled out at those gathered in this place. Maggie had made her grandmother's eyes a little bluer and her lips a little fuller, but otherwise the likeness was as clear as Granny's image had always been in Maggie's mind. Granny sat in a straight-backed chair, wearing the same flowered dress she washed and ironed each week before she and Maggie headed off to church.

As Maggie returned to her seat, Reverend Adams walked to the pulpit, a little slower now. His hands had a slight tremor as he opened his worn and faded Bible. But in his ever-soothing voice, he addressed the congregation. "To preface my remarks today as we honor Mrs. Beulah Mae Larkins, I have chosen the following scripture from the King James Version of the Bible. I am reading from Proverbs 31. "Who can find a virtuous woman? for her price is far above rubies . . . ""

Maggie smiled.

CPSIA information can be obtained at www.ICGtesting.com
Printed in the USA
LVOW121658281112

309224LV00001B/342/P